Something inside her seemed to snap. She let go of his cock, and with fumbling urgent motions unfastened the front of her dress and the chemise beneath to pop out her breasts, full and heavy in her hands as she spoke, her voice now a hoarse croak.

'There you are, you dirty beast. My breasts are bare. That's what you wanted, isn't it? To see my bare breasts, and I'm sure you want to touch them too, like the filthy little pig you are.'

Ned responded immediately, reaching out to take one plump globe in his hand and sighing as he began to explore her. Victoria swallowed hard as her nipple popped out under his thumb, and her resistance had gone completely. She leant forward, gaping for his cock and taking it in, to suck urgently on the long hard shaft as he gave a gasp of surprise. He tasted good, and to have a cock in her mouth again felt wonderful, so wonderful she could no longer resist the dirty act he'd demanded.

By the same author:

THE RAKE
PURITY
VELVET SKIN
DEMONIC CONGRESS
CONCEIT AND CONSEQUENCE
MAIDEN
CAPTIVE
INNOCENT
PRINCESS
TIGER TIGER
PLEASURE TOY
DEVON CREAM
PEACHES AND CREAM
CREAM TEASE
DEEP BLUE
SATAN'S SLUT
NATURAL DESIRE STRANGE DESIGN
CRUEL SHADOW
TEMPTING THE GODDESS
SIN'S APPRENTICE
WHIPPING GIRL
SCARLET VICE
WENCHES, WITCHES AND STRUMPETS
THE OLD PERVERSITY SHOP
STRIP GIRL

BEASTLY BEHAVIOUR

Aishling Morgan

This book is a work of fiction.
In real life, make sure you practise safe, sane and consensual sex.

First published in 2007 by
Nexus
Thames Wharf Studios
Rainville Rd
London W6 9HA

www.nexus-books.co.uk

A catalogue record for this book is available from the British Library.

Typeset by TW Typesetting, Plymouth, Devon
Printed and bound in Great Britain by Clays Ltd, Elcograf S.p.A.

ISBN 978 0 352 34095 5

Glossary

Biter – *in full, a wench whose cunt is ready to bite her arse, meaning a rampantly lascivious girl.* Biter *might be deemed complimentary in some circumstances,* bitch biter *definitely would not, much as a highly sexed modern girl might enjoy being called dirty, but not a dirty bitch.*

Churck – *an udder, or a highly insulting way of referring to a girl's breasts.*

Gallimaufry – *now used to describe any mixed up collection of things or even thoughts, but originally a dish composed of scraps from the larder, notably chicken.*

Maid – *a term now applied almost exclusively to female servants, but originally meaning any young female. In nineteenth century Devon, both terms would have been in use, depending on social class, so that to a wealthy educated man his maid would be his servant, but to any other man she would be his daughter.*

Mazed – *literally 'amazed', but meaning crazy rather than astonished.*

Peelers – *a slang name for the police derived from Sir Robert Peel and in common use during the nineteenth century, later in Ireland.*

Sulky – *a single-seater gig, generally drawn by a single horse, and so called because only one person could ride in it at a time.*

Tweenie – *the shortened form of 'between stairs maid', whose work might take her anywhere within the house, rather than, for instance, a scullery maid who would work almost exclusively below stairs, or a Lady's maid who would work almost exclusively above stairs.*

Wheal – *has no relation to the word wheel at all, but derives from an old Cornish word for a mine, most of which were either given a female name, such as Wheal Betsy, or one that reflected the hopes of the investors, such as Wheal Fortune.*

Prologue

Genevieve gave a final kick, a graceful pirouette, stuck out her bottom, flipped the full mass of her skirts onto her back and pulled her drawers[1] wide, exposing her bare cheeks to the audience.

As usual, the response of the fifty or so men drinking in the saloon was both crude and enthusiastic: cheers, calls for more, rude suggestions and several offers of money for a more private display. Genevieve merely adjusted herself, smiled and blew a kiss as she left the stage. Upstairs, she sat down at her dressing table, immediately reaching behind her back for the laces of her corset. As it came loose she let out her breath with a long sigh, and was adjusting her breasts into positions of greater comfort when she heard the door open behind her. Again she drew a sigh, but this time of exasperation rather than relief.

'There's a gentleman wants to see you, Ginny, most particular,' Nanna Bloss stated, 'and I'll have no nonsense this time, my girl.'

Genevieve turned, looking up to the towering figure of the madame, whose confection of frills, ribbons and flounces did nothing to conceal her bulk, nor to soften the purposeful expression on her face. Steeling herself, Genevieve answered back.

'I don't want to . . .'

'Do you want that arse of yours smacked?' the madame interrupted.

‘No,’ Genevieve said quickly, and sounding increasingly petulant as she went on, ‘but I don’t want to see any gentlemen, if that’s what you call them. You said I could dance, and . . .’

‘And so you do, only what’s the good of you dancing if you’re not prepared to entertain the gentlemen you dance for? Ready enough to show your bare arse on the stage, aren’t you?’

‘It’s an artistic –’ Genevieve began, only to shut up as she was interrupted for the third time.

‘Artistic indeed!’ Nanna Bloss snorted. ‘It’s to get the boys’ pricks hard, that’s what it is, and once their pricks are hard they’ll come and spend a little money upstairs, otherwise how’m I supposed to pay my rent, and how’re you supposed to pay yours? Three weeks I’ve let you go, out of the kindness of my heart, and . . . oh, to the blazes with it!’

‘What?’ Genevieve squeaked as the big woman moved suddenly forwards. ‘Nanna! No, please! Nanna! Nanna!’

The last word was a shriek as Genevieve was lifted bodily from the stool and turned expertly upside down, so that she was now lying across the madame’s knee, bottom up and already kicking in fear and consternation at the prospect of a spanking. One brawny arm folded around her waist and she was helpless. Her skirts were bundled up onto her back, her drawers split wide and she was bare. A heavy hand descended on the cheeks of her bottom and she was being spanked.

Genevieve’s pleading broke to squeals as the slaps began to land, so hard that each one jammed her entire body forwards. After just a few her breasts popped free of her bodice, but she was in no state to put them back, with her arms flailing at the air and her legs kicking wildly to show off her cunt and anus behind. Thus all the most intimate parts of her body were on display when she heard a gasp of shock from the door.

'Don't you mind me, Mr Greville,' Nanna Bloss said, not so much as slowing the powerful spanks being applied to Genevieve's bottom. 'Just you make yourself comfortable while I give this brat what she needs.'

Twisting around as her feelings flared for the gross indignity of being spanked in front of a man, Genevieve discovered that he had withdrawn, an act at once so surprising and so courteous that what little resolve she had left immediately broke. She burst into tears.

'Hush your squalling,' Nanna Bloss snapped, spanking even harder.

Genevieve barely heard, and was in no condition to obey the command, now bawling her eyes out and thrashing her body with even more vigour, so that her legs were pistoning wildly behind her with her open cunt on full show to the door. Somebody in the corridor laughed for the view she was giving, and again she twisted around, just able to make out two of the other girls through the haze of her tears. Both were giggling at her plight, without the slightest sympathy, but they proved to be her saviours. The spanking stopped, although Nanna Bloss's hand was still resting across Genevieve's now burning bottom as she spoke.

'You two mind your own affairs, unless you want a dose of the same.'

Two more hard smacks were delivered to Genevieve's cheeks and she was released, to tumble onto the floor and sit down heavily on her well-smacked bottom, where she stayed, snivelling bitterly.

'Do be quiet,' Nanna Bloss ordered, 'anybody would think you'd never been spanked before, and what a mess you've made of your face! Paint costs money, you know, and powder too, my money. Now get up and put yourself in order, you've a gentleman to entertain.'

Genevieve opened her mouth to protest, but thought better of it. All she'd get was another spanking and still have to do it, but that didn't stop her pouting furiously as she got up and smoothed down her skirts. Her bottom was hot and painful, undoubtedly bruised, while she was sticky and uncomfortable between her thighs, adding yet more shame to her battered feelings, but she had no resistance left.

'Yes, Nanna,' she said meekly.

The madame gave no sign of getting up from the stool, so Genevieve bent over the table as she began to remove the tear streaks from her face.

'Mind you,' the madame remarked conversationally, 'some gentlemen like a few tears, only they prefer to cause them themselves, but wouldn't it have been easier to do as you were told in the first place and save all that fuss?'

'Yes, Nanna,' Genevieve admitted.

'You can come in now, Mr Greville,' Nanna Bloss called out, 'no reason to be standing out there in the corridor.'

The response was a distinctly uncomfortable cough, but Mr Greville entered the room. He was a small dapper individual in a black bowler hat, quite out of keeping with Nanna Bloss' usual clientele. He carried a note case across his chest as if to protect himself, and spoke with an accent oddly reminiscent of Genevieve's own father.

'Mrs Bloss,' he intoned, with a slight bow, then turned to Genevieve. 'Miss Genevieve Stukely, I presume?

'That's me,' she answered him.

'You keep that sulky tone out of your voice,' Nanna Bloss snapped, 'or it'll be the cane you get across that dainty backside, not my hand. My apologies, sir, she's new to the trade, and don't quite know how things stand, but she'll be fine when she gets down to business, won't you, Genevieve?'

'Yes, Nanna,' Genevieve said miserably. 'I'll be good.'

'You be sure you are,' the madame answered. 'Now let's have those titties back out, for one. I'm sure you'd like to see her titties, wouldn't that be so, Mr Greville?'

'I beg your pardon?' he responded, his face colouring.

'Shy one, huh?' Nanna Bloss answered.

In terror of the cane, Genevieve had scooped her breasts free from the top of her corset, but it only caused his eyes to pop and his face to turn redder still. He didn't move either, but stood staring in apparent horror at her naked breasts, with his mouth working slowly but no sound coming out. Nanna Bloss gave a snort of contempt, her tone changing from unctuous to aggressive as she spoke again.

'Look, Mister, do you want to have her or not?'

'I . . . no, no, absolutely not . . . the very idea,' the man answered.

'So what do you want?' she asked.

'I . . . I am Mr Samuel Greville,' he announced, stammering, 'of the firm Greville, Yates and Greville, of Okehampton in the county of Devon, England, and I am here to inform Miss Stukely of a matter of the utmost importance, not to . . . ah . . . um . . .'

Words had failed him again, but it was Genevieve's turn to blush as she quickly put her breasts away and tugged a shawl around her shoulders.

'What's that then?' Nanna Bloss demanded.

'The matter concerns Miss Stukely,' Mr Greville began, but was cut off.

'What my girl can hear, I can hear,' Nanna Bloss insisted, 'elseways they gets ideas. Now spit it out.'

Mr Greville's expression hardened, only for him to start coughing, and when he spoke again he had evidently decided to make the best of the circumstances.

'So be it,' he stated. 'Might I have a glass of water?'

'Whiskey?' Genevieve offered.

'Thank you, no. I do not partake,' he answered, raising a hand. 'No matter, I shall sit, if I may?'

'Get on with it,' Nanna Bloss cut in. 'I'll have a whiskey, Ginny.'

Mr Greville sat down, still clearly uneasy as he fumbled a pair of spectacles from a case and extracted a sheaf of paper from the note case he carried. Genevieve poured out the whiskey both for the madame and herself as he began.

'The matter on which I have travelled this not inconsiderable distance is a grave one, Miss Stukely. First and foremost, may I offer you my condolences on the death of your great-uncle, Sir Robert Stukely . . .'

'Never met him,' Genevieve answered. 'Shame, all the same.'

'You never said your great-uncle was a lord?' Nanna Bloss asked, throwing Genevieve a suspicious glance.

'A baronet, to be precise,' Mr Greville went on, adjusting his spectacles.

Genevieve began to wonder if she might have been left something in her great-uncle's will, and from the expression of greedy curiosity on Nanna Bloss' face she had clearly had the same idea. If the lawyer had been prepared to travel from England to the Dakota Territory, it was hardly likely to be a small matter either.

'The ah . . . death of your great-uncle, Sir Robert Stukely,' Mr Greville repeated, frowning at his papers, 'which places you in the position of being his sole known heir.'

'I inherit?' she queried.

'You do indeed,' he responded, 'upon appending your signature . . .'

'How much?' Nanna Bloss interrupted.

'Everything, naturally,' Greville stated with a look of distaste for the madame. 'The estate, on the western flank of Dartmoor, along with five tenant farms, along with Sir Robert's investments, which come to, I believe, somewhere short of one million pounds sterling, all associated chattels and rights, shares in the Wheal Purity mining venture . . .'

Genevieve was no longer listening, but wondering how many dollars a million pounds would make. She wasn't sure, but it would quite clearly be enough to allow her to give up dancing and escape Nanna Bloss' ever more determined efforts to make her prostitute herself.

'. . . that is, of course, subject to your taking up residence at your earliest opportunity,' Mr Greville was saying. 'I do hope that meets with your approval, Miss Stukely?'

'Yep, I'm signing,' Genevieve answered, taking the pen and paper from him. 'Just give me ten minutes to pack.'

Mr Greville gave an embarrassed cluck before he continued.

'There is, however, one rather important detail which I feel it my duty to draw to your attention, Miss Stukely . . .'

One

Lucy Capleton made a face as Richard Truscott pushed a finger into the pat of butter on her tray. She knew exactly where it was going.

'Sir, that's for your brother, sir!' she protested.

'I hardly think that even Leopold would eat a half-pound of butter with his breakfast, or need to use so much either,' Richard responded, still holding her firmly in place across the banister.

Her skirt was already up, her split-seam drawers already open, leaving her bottom bare and wiggling in the taut triangle of her pad strings as she struggled. He had caught her by surprise, emerging from his bedroom with his morning erection sticking out from between the sides of his dressing gown. Before she could give more than a half-hearted protest he had bent her across the banister so that she couldn't even use her hands without letting go of the tray, which would drop three flights to the hall below.

'Not like this, sir, it's not fair to take advantage, sir,' she whined as the piece of butter he had taken was pressed between her bottom cheeks, 'and what of your parents, sir, or if Miss Victoria should come out of her room?'

Richard took no notice of her complaints. Her bottom was buttered, first with his finger inserted into her anus, then with the head of his cock rubbing on the now slippery hole, while the look of consternation on her face grew ever stronger as she was prepared for her buggering. Several times she nearly dropped the tray, but the thought of the whipping she would receive from cook if she did made her cling on, even as he forced his penis in past the tight restriction of her anal ring. Only when a good half the length of his shaft had been pushed up her did she speak again.

'You are most cruel to me, sir!'

'Nonsense,' he answered, wedging another inch or so of cock into her rectum. 'If I was cruel, I'd take your pad off, use your cunt and maybe get a child on you, wouldn't I now?'

Lucy failed to answer, unable to deny the logic of his argument but absolutely certain that cramming his cock up her bottom was not proper behaviour between the son of a wealthy house and his maid. Admittedly there was Leopold, but that was different, and old Charles Truscott liked her to pull on his cock when she brought him his morning tea, but he always asked politely. Charles Truscott was a proper gentleman.

Richard gave a sigh of immense satisfaction as he pushed the last of his cock in up Lucy's now straining ring, leaving her with her cheeks puffed out and her eyes popping for the feel of the long hard rod in her gut. It was by no means her first buggering, but the sensation never failed to overwhelm her, and she spoke again, quickly, as he began to move himself inside her.

'Sir, please, sir . . . take my tray at the least, or I shall drop it!'

'By all means,' Richard replied.

He took the tray from her and set it down beside a case of stuffed birds on a convenient table, never once stopping the now gentle motion in her bottom hole. Lucy didn't even try to resist, telling herself that as he was inside her already it was best to surrender meekly, and that her decision had nothing whatever to do with the feeling of being buggered, which was not delightful at all, but quite horrid, despite what her body was telling her.

With her hands now free, she took a grip on the banisters, bracing herself against his thrusts as they grew harder and faster. He had taken her by the hips, no longer holding her down, but simply to get the best possible grip as he sodomised her, driving his cock so deep and so hard that the slaps of his stomach on her bottom cheeks made her feel as if she was being spanked, while the feeling in her gut had quickly gone beyond the point at which she could pretend she was not enjoying herself.

She began to gasp, and to shake her head, fighting against her rising ecstasy but almost immediately losing. Her gasps turned to a dog-like panting punctuated by little pained grunts as his thrusts rose to a furious crescendo, which grew louder until she was forced to bite her lip to stop herself screaming and rousing the house to her disgrace, and stopping, to die to a soft whimpering as he jammed himself deep one last time. He had come up her bottom.

'Ah, but that's the way to start a day,' he sighed, and gave her bottom a single firm slap as he began to withdraw.

Lucy stayed as she was, feeling excited and frustrated all at once as Richard slowly extracted his penis from her rectum. It was no good denying her feelings, or what her buggering had made her want to do, but she was full of guilt for her own reaction and unable to find the words she needed to ask him for the favour of rubbing her quim until she too had reached satisfaction. Later, once Leopold was finished with her and she could take her pad off in the privacy of her tiny room on the top corridor, she would do what needed to be done, guilt or no guilt.

Richard wiped his cock on her drawers then spoke again.

'Lay out my cape, would you, when you've done with Leopold? I have a call to make and I fancy it will be a trifle brisk on the moor this morning.'

'Yes, sir,' Lucy responded, adjusting her dress, 'but, begging pardon, sir, would you be better taking the Lydford Road, sir, after what happened to poor Sir Robert and all?'

'Nonsense,' Richard responded. 'The old fool probably saw a sheep, or maybe a bullock or something.'

'But, sir, the footprints . . .'

'Perhaps he saw a dog then,' Richard cut her off, 'but you may be absolutely certain it was not Black Shuck[2]. Damn it, we've got the thing's head mounted in the library, so it's hardly going to be running around Dartmoor terrorising the Stukelys, is it?'

'Yes, but what of its ghost, sir?'

'What nonsense!' Richard laughed.

Despite his display of bravado, Richard found himself scanning the hillsides as he walked along the flank of Sourton Tors towards Stukely Hall, where he was due to make a call on the young woman who had inherited the estate. Rationally, he knew full well that the story was nonsense and that some perfectly mundane explanation for Sir Robert Stukely's death had to exist. Nevertheless, there was no denying that the baronet had been found lying dead at the end of the yew alley which led from the rear of the Hall onto the moor, or that a number of exceptionally large and undoubtedly canine footprints had been left in the soft mud beyond the gate. He had also seen the expression on the dead man's face, which suggested a terror beyond normal human experience. Possibly the explanation would prove to be that there was a very large and dangerous dog loose on the moor, which might be mundane but was far from comforting.

He dismissed the idea. No sheep had been savaged recently, and any dog that size could hardly fail to leave its mark, or be seen for that matter. There were plenty of moormen about, not to mention the peat cutters on Rattlebrook Hill[3], the hunt, and any number of gentlemen taking their exercise. Not one had seen anything unusual on the moor, let alone the vast hellhound of legend.

There was, of course, the other matter, but the footprint had clearly been stated to be that of a dog, while to the best of his knowledge there had been no excursions since he had put the spikes along the tops of the walls.

As Richard reached the ridge of land where the tors fell away to a steep valley he recognised one of the gentlemen whose opinion had been sought after the death of Sir Robert, the painter Matthew Widdery, who was easily identifiable by his thick red beard even at a distance. Widdery was a relative newcomer to the district, having recently rented a cottage from the Truscotts, and as such Richard found himself obliged to alter the course of his walk somewhat so that instead of making directly towards Stukely Hall he climbed the far side of the valley to where Widdery had set up his easel looking out across the valley of the river Lyd.

'Good morning, Mr Widdery,' he said as he reached the artist. 'A little breezy for painting today, is it not?'

'A trifle only,' Widdery replied, 'and I am prepared for all such eventualities.'

As he spoke he had indicated his easel, and Richard saw that it was securely pegged to the ground, while the sheet of fine white paper on which the artist had been working was clipped securely in place. The little stool on which a travelling case of watercolours had been placed was also secure, but if the man was particular in the care of his utensils, the same, Richard felt, could not be said of his art.

The scene in front of them was striking to say the least, with the ground falling rapidly away to the river before rising again to the long rugged flank of Dartmoor. To the left and east the high tors rose in tumbles of grey rock set sharp against the delicate blue of the sky or soft among the greens and browns of the moor. Below them, the brilliant yellow of gorse flowers showed among fresh greens and the white of fast-moving water, while to the right and west the grey-black towers of Stukely Hall rose from among the trees, with fields and woods stretching into the distance beyond. By contrast, Mr Widdery's painting of the same scene consisted largely of smudges of muted colour and clearly owed a great deal more to his imagination than to reality.

'Is this a modern style?' Richard enquired, attempting politeness. 'Something after the fashion of Mr Whistler, perhaps, or some of these French fellows?'

'I do not seek to capture a mere reproduction of what I see, Mr Truscott,' Widdery replied, 'but the impression it provokes on the human mind, the stark grandeur of the moor with all its bleakness and melancholy.'

'Bleakness and melancholy?' Richard queried. 'Do you think so? I always found it rather a jolly place, myself. Excellent hunting.'

Widdery gave him a somewhat pained look, then spoke again.

'To me, Mr Truscott, the moor provides the perfect analogy for the barrenness inherent in the human soul.'

'I see,' Richard said doubtfully and, as the artist seemed disinclined to continue the conversation, he tipped his hat and moved on.

He had barely covered another five hundred yards, and reached a patch of steep rough ground dotted with gorse bushes, when his attention was attracted by a flash of white below. It came again, and as he stopped to focus his attention he realised that there was a figure standing by the bank where the Doe Tor Brook tumbled down from almost directly below him to join the Lyd.

His hand went to his moustache by instinct as he realised it was not only a woman, but that she was clad in nothing more than her drawers and chemise.

Puzzled, amused, and not a little aroused, he moved closer, keeping carefully to the shelter of the increasingly thick gorse. She was beyond the ancient half-collapsed wall that marked the boundary between the Stukely Estate and the open moor, so presumably a servant to the new incumbent, probably a maid. In any event, she was certainly worth watching, blissfully unaware of his presence as she dangled her feet in the cool water and combed out her long dark hair.

He briefly considered introducing himself, only to abandon the idea. She would undoubtedly be startled, and he would be robbed of the pleasure of watching her, while if he was to attempt to effect a seduction at a later date then her having been partially dressed on their first meeting might very well do more good than harm. Instead he continued his approach until he had reached the wall, which he knew he was unlikely to be able to cross without attracting her attention, and settled down to admire her.

She was seated, her chemise undone but not fully open, providing tantalising glimpses of two small but well formed breasts topped by dark and notably stiff nipples. Richard found himself squeezing his cock at the sight, and again as she stood to provide a yet more enticing view. Her chemise had come fully open as she stepped into the shallow pool and she made no effort to close it, evidently considering herself quite secure as she stretched in the pale spring sunlight. Both her breasts were now bare, with her upturned nipples sticking out in a way that seemed to him taunting, or even insolent. More provocative still, while she was facing almost directly towards him, it was evident that the rear flap of her panel-back drawers was open, leaving her bare bottom on show behind her.

Richard was hoping earnestly that she would turn around and provide him with a fuller display of her charms, perhaps even bend down and treat him to a glimpse of cunt. Instead, to his rising frustration, she remained as she was, apparently content merely to feel the cool water around her toes and the fresh moorland air on her skin. He had even begun to grow bored of watching when another movement caught his eye, a woman walking up from the direction of Stukely Hall, a burly, coarse-faced woman, perhaps a cook or house-keeper, but with the most extraordinary taste in clothes. Not only was the woman's dress flounced, tucked and ribboned as if she intended to appear in amateur theatricals, but it was a stupefying mauve in colour, while on her head she wore the largest and most fanciful bonnet Richard had ever seen.

The girl had seen the woman, and responded with alarm, fumbling for the buttons of her drawers as she jumped from the water and bending to retrieve her clothes from among a cluster of rocks. Richard, having been treated to a flash of what appeared to be a pert and well-turned bottom, stayed as he was, his curiosity now fully aroused. The girl clearly did not want the woman to catch her, but it was already too late. Before the girl could so much as fasten her drawers the big woman had reached her, and immediately began to deliver a lecture, while wagging one fat finger into the hapless recipient's face.

Despite not being able to make out the big woman's words, their gist was quite evident to Richard. A sharp telling off was in progress, and he was delighted but not altogether surprised when the big woman caught the girl by the shoulder and spun her sharply around, once more exposing the neat young buttocks, but this time to have a dozen hard slaps delivered to each cheek. The young girl remained as she was, standing, her shoulder held tight in the big woman's grip as her buttocks were slapped with sharp upwards motions. Her squeals were clearly audible to Richard, and she wriggled her way through the spanking in a way that had his cock hard in his trousers before the punishment was finished.

With the girl's bottom now blushing a rich pink, the big woman completed her lecture and turned on her heel, leaving her victim stood ruefully in the stream, rubbing her smacked bottom. Richard continued to watch, both amused and aroused as the spanked girl comforted herself, adjusted her underthings and dressed. Her gown was a rich blue, gaudy for a maid, although positively plain beside the vulgar extravagance of the other, while she seemed to find her bustle[4] an irritation.

At a sharp command from the big woman, now some way off, the girl hurried towards Stukely Hall and quickly vanished from sight. There was a quiet smile on Richard's face as he continued on his way, following the line of the old wall to a convenient stile before angling across to where a gate opened into the gardens proper and the fine yew avenue at the end of which Sir Robert had met his death. Richard paused as he reached the gate. Whatever footprints there might have been, they were long gone, and the moor rose empty to the line of tors that now formed a rampart across the horizon. It was a pleasant view, and it was easy to see why Sir Robert might have come out to smoke an after-dinner cigar and watch the last of the light fade from the scenery, which was apparently what he had been doing when he met his death.

Nodding thoughtfully, Richard turned back towards the house. It seemed most likely that the baronet had simply gone out to take the air too soon after a heavy dinner and dropped dead from a failure of the heart. He had, after all, been elderly, weighed rather more than twenty stone and had a weak heart. The footprints no doubt belonged to some large dog and might well have been left well before Sir Robert came outside. Certainly there was no cause for the superstitious fever that had gripped the local villagers and servants.

Richard saw that the lawyer, Greville, was approaching, and extended a hand as he greeted him.

'Ah, Greville, no gigantic hounds at your heels then?'

'Pray do not joke about such things, Mr Truscott,' the lawyer responded.

'You don't believe it, surely?' Richard queried.

'I believe what I see,' Mr Greville answered. 'Poor Sir Robert lying dead with his face frozen in terror and the footprints close by, far too large to have been left by any ordinary hound.'

'Well, yes, his expression must be accounted for, I suppose, but the matter is closed now in any event, is it not?'

'Far from it. I am greatly concerned for Miss Stukely's safety, as is she, following a most singular incident, not to say improprietous.'

'Improprietous? Do go on.'

'Ah, hmm ... quite. Perhaps you can make something of the matter? We came across on the *Germanic*, and disembarked at Southampton, where Miss Stukely and her, ah ... companion, Mrs Bloss, made extensive purchases. Mrs Bloss is a forceful character, and not one to keep her opinions to herself, and yet you may imagine my discomfort when having retired to their suite at the Grand she roused the staff to complain of the theft of an item of, ah ... apparel, intimate apparel.'

'Her drawers?' Richard guessed.

'Her own, no,' Mr Greville responded, colouring somewhat. 'Those of Miss Stukely. Naturally the hotel maids fell under suspicion, but all deny it vehemently. The curious thing is, that while the thief might have had the pick of a dozen fine new garments, he chose to make off with a single, used pair.'

'This doesn't strike me as especially mysterious,' Richard said. 'I suspect your culprit is a valet, or perhaps the boy who blacks the boots.'

'A man?' Mr Greville queried. 'What possible use could a man have for such an article?'

'Some fellows have peculiar tastes,' Richard replied vaguely, not wishing to go into the pleasures of masturbating with the assistance of a pair of lacy drawers, which he had done regularly for some years, either folding them around his cock or, more rarely, wearing them.

Mr Greville gave him a puzzled look that turned to shock as comprehension dawned. Richard shrugged, then went on.

'So who is this Stukely woman anyway?'

'She is the late Samuel Stukely's daughter,' Greville replied, 'and between ourselves, Mr Truscott, a most unusual young lady. It would be before your time, of course, but you may be aware that Samuel Stukely left for the Americas in 'fifty, his intention being to secure a fortune in the Californian goldfields. He failed to achieve this goal, and, I fear, became a victim of drink. All this I am only aware of due to the fact that he frequently sent begging letters to his brother, including the mention of a daughter. On Sir Robert's death she therefore became heir to the estate, and with very great difficulty I managed to track her down. She was a . . . danseuse I believe is the term, in a most disreputable establishment in an area known as the Dakota Territories[5]. I think she may most politely be described as wild, although her father seems to have provided her with at least a veneer of education.'

'Remarkable,' Richard responded. 'She is quite young then?'

'No more than twenty,' Greville assured him, 'to judge by Samuel Stukely's letters that is. She, I believe, is unaware of her exact age.'

The lawyer finished with a sniff of disapproval. As they spoke they had walked around the side of the house, and had now reached the front door. Richard gave a tug on the bell, and presently the door opened, revealing the bland countenance of Capleton, the Stukelys' butler and uncle to the Truscotts' tweenie maid.

'Mr Truscott, Mr Greville,' the butler intoned. 'If you would be so kind as to wait in the drawing room, Miss Stukely will be down presently.'

Richard returned an affable nod, passed the butler his hat, gloves and stick and moved on into the drawing room. It was almost exactly as he had last seen it when Sir Robert Stukely was still alive, panelled in wood dark with age and hung around with the portraits of generation upon generation of the Stukely family. Only the presence of several vases of brightly coloured flowers suggested a change in ownership.

Another man was already present, Dr Robinson, a neighbour whose practice covered the area and who had been the one to pronounce Sir Robert dead. Having exchanged greetings, the three men talked among themselves for a while before Capleton once more appeared.

'Miss Genevieve Stukely,' he announced, 'and Mrs Bloss.'

Richard put on his brightest smile, only for the expression to falter to surprise as he recognised Miss Stukely as the girl he had seen spanked shortly before, and Mrs Bloss as the woman who had done the spanking. A somewhat sullen look still lingered in Miss Stukely's face, despite her best efforts to smile as she greeted her guests.

As they made their introductions and spent a moment in small talk, Richard took the opportunity of assessing both women. On the moor he had been rather too far away and primarily interested in buttocks and breasts, but close to there was no doubt that Miss Stukely was strikingly pretty, with glossy hair of a rich brown colour and full flexible features that lent a great deal of vivacity to her face. Her manner was equally appealing, bold and yet with an underlying shyness, while it was impossible not to be pleased by the mixture of West Country and the Americas in her accent.

Mrs Bloss was a somewhat different matter, coarse in appearance and frankly alarming in manner. Her voice was loud and thickly accented, her opinions strong and voiced with absolute certainty, while her massive body brought him unpleasant reminders of his old nurse, increasing his sympathy for Miss Stukely's fate although doing nothing to reduce his arousal.

Presently the conversation turned to business, and the Wheal Purity Mining Company, of which Miss Stukely was now the second largest shareholder behind Richard's father. Beyond the formalities of signature and witness there was little to be discussed, although the process was rendered more difficult by Mrs Bloss' constant demands to see every detail of the accounts, stifled only when Richard offered to take her on a personal tour underground. With official business concluded, the conversation inevitably turned to the circumstances of Sir Robert Stukely's death.

'Mrs Bloss and me, we've engaged a detective,' Miss Stukely was saying, 'a most famous man, from London.'

'Mr Harland Wolfe,' Mr Greville supplied, 'whose exploits are so well recorded by his associate, a Dr Manston, while you may remember him as the man who solved the Silver Star case at Sampford Spiney.'

'Ah, yes,' Richard responded, 'where the horse had been tampered with to put it out of the running. A diligent fellow, as I recall, and clever, for all the good it did anybody. I had forty guineas on the damned animal too, you know. Beg pardon, Miss Stukely.'

Miss Stukely didn't seem to have noticed his indiscretion, but went on enthusiastically.

'Everybody says he's the best there is, and how if anyone in England can find out the truth, he's the one. But Mr Truscott, they tell me your family has as much to do with the story as mine? Can you tell me, is there really a ghostly hound?'

Richard caught himself on the brink of a dismissive remark. Quite clearly Genevieve was taking the story of the hound seriously, which provided him the perfect opportunity to appear both gallant and brave while taking no real risks whatsoever. Miss Stukely, it had occurred to him, was not only exceptionally pretty and full of life, but also appeared to lack the moral scruples that made every other woman of his own social status completely unacceptable as a mate. Moreover, her thirty per cent of Wheal Purity, combined with the holdings he himself expected to inherit, would make him a very rich man indeed.

'It is a somewhat disreputable story,' he said cautiously as he tried to work out what could and could not be said, and which of the actual facts behind the legend Dr Robinson and Mr Greville might have picked up from his father, 'perhaps more suited to the smoking room of a gentlemen's club than a lady's drawing room, and somewhat complicated.'

'Do tell me,' Miss Stukely urged.

'As you please,' Richard answered her, quickly shuffling the facts in his mind. 'The hound, as you have no doubt heard, goes by the name of Black Shuck. It is a spectral creature, supposedly from hell itself, black and of impressive size, fully as big as a well-grown calf. It appears only at night, generally behind some unfortunate soul coming home through the darkness. The legend is old, and not peculiar to Devon, but the one thing on which everybody agrees is that if Black Shuck is after you, do not run. If you do, you will be pursued, and killed. If you do not, he will let you go your way.'

'Sir Robert tried to run,' Miss Stukely breathed.

'Did he?' Richard queried.

'So it seems,' Dr Robinson confirmed, 'although he

managed no more than three paces from the gate before his collapse.'

'Did he now,' Richard responded. 'Hmm . . . that is the substance of the legend, but the involvement of my family, and your own, Miss Stukely, begins with a distinctly regrettable event in the late seventeenth century. Roger Stukely, who is, I believe, that gentleman to the left of the fireplace . . .'

The company turned to admire the portrait, which was of a handsome somewhat fox-faced young man in a magnificent scarlet coat and the long curled wig typical of the period. Even in the painting it was easy to imagine a touch of contempt in his face, even evil, although it was equally easy to see a softer more feminine version of the same features in Miss Stukely.

'. . . and John Truscott.'

'Was that Devil John?' Miss Stukely asked. 'My father used to tell me such tales of his habits!'

'No, his grandfather,' Richard explained, 'although he seems to have enjoyed a similar reputation. In any event, it seems that Roger Stukely had his eye on the daughter of one of the local farmers and, being the sort of fellow he was, he got John Truscott and a few others together with the intention of making away with her. Hardly laudable behaviour, I know, but these were hard parts in those days and saints never flourished.'

He paused, once more sorting fact from accepted fiction in his mind and wondering what he could reasonably say in front of Miss Stukely, for all her lack of gentility.

'As it goes,' he said, lying, 'they may not have been quite so bold as they liked to think, because having captured her, they locked the girl in an upstairs room.'

'Here, in this house?' Miss Stukely queried in horrified fascination.

'This very house,' Richard confirmed. 'Indeed, it was in this very room that they started to drink, heavily, and while they were doing so, the girl climbed down the ivy and fled across the moor. By the time Roger decided to go upstairs to fetch her he must have been roaring drunk, because he was so angry he set the hounds on her trail, following them on horseback.'

It had in fact been a single hound, and already in the house, but that was another detail best not revealed.

'The others,' he went on, 'gave chase, although I regret to say more because they didn't want to miss the fun than with any intention of saving her, but when they caught up she wasn't the one in need of it. Roger Stukely lay on the ground, still alive, his neck in the grip of a gigantic black hound, Black Shuck himself, it is said. John Truscott discharged his pistols at the beast, which fled, but Roger Stukely was dead of fright before they came up to him.'

'And the girl?' Miss Stukely asked.

'She reached home in safety,' Richard answered, and sat back to take a sip of the Bual they had served.

It seemed unnecessary to admit that John Truscott had in fact missed the hound and shot Roger Stukely through the head, along with the other more disreputable details of the story, and he continued.

'The girl's father is said to have cursed the Stukelys, but next time Black Shuck came to haunt the moor was nearly a hundred years later, or so it's said. In practice it was merely a wild dog of exceptional size, which Devil John shot after it had killed a man named Noah Pargade. The head is mounted in our trophy room, the head of the dog, that is, not of Noah Pargade.'

'And now the hound is back,' Miss Stukely said, almost wistfully it seemed to Richard.

'So they say,' he responded casually, 'although I for one do not intend to allow that to spoil my enjoyment of our moor, and should you ever wish company on an excursion I would be delighted to offer mine.'

* * *

By the time Richard Truscott left Stukely Hall it was nearly dark. He had taken lunch and tea, all the while doing his best to ingratiate himself with Miss Stukely. His efforts, he felt, had been largely successful, leaving the future looking distinctly interesting, also rosy, despite a couple of problems.

The first was the appalling Mrs Bloss, who as Miss Stukely's companion could be expected to be present at all times, which made courtship difficult and outright seduction impossible. At least, such was the case if the two women followed the normal rules of propriety, but from what he had observed of their behaviour that seemed unlikely.

Perhaps Mrs Bloss could be bribed? Better still, perhaps she could be paid to become an ally, steering Miss Stukely in his direction, if any steering needed to be done, or even something rather more. For a moment he let his imagination run, thinking of how glorious it would be to have Mrs Bloss give Miss Stukely a good stern spanking in front of him, on her bare bottom naturally, up which he could then drive his erect cock while she was held wriggling and whimpering across the big woman's knee.

It was a delightful prospect, although obviously impractical. His aim, after all, was to win Miss Stukely's love, which was hardly the likely outcome if he forcibly sodomised her, although having said that, Lucy Capleton seemed to enjoy it. Curious creatures, women. No, he would have to restrain his lust, keeping himself satisfied with Lucy while he approached Miss Stukely in the manner appropriate to a gentleman of means, slowly, discreetly and, above all, decorously. Only that way could he expect her to accept his hand in marriage. Once she had done so, then he could spank and bugger her.

Richard gave a satisfied nod at the thought, letting his thoughts run further. It had been a very long time indeed since he had spanked a girl himself, but he remembered how it felt to have a pair of well-turned buttocks warming under his hand as their owner kicked and squealed her way through punishment. It was a highly enticing prospect, and not one in which he intended to delay indulging himself. The ideal candidate was clearly Lucy, who had all the qualifications for receiving a spanking; a well-formed bottom, a pretty face and, most importantly, a compliant nature. Yes, he would spank Lucy at the earliest opportunity.

He was now grinning as he walked, and his cock had grown uncomfortably stiff in his trousers. Pausing to adjust himself, he saw that the moon was beginning to rise against the scarp of Dartmoor, directly behind Hare Tor. The crags stood out in perfect black silhouette against the bone-white moon, and something else as well, the figure of a man. Richard stopped to watch, then cursed softly, telling himself that if Lucy had left the door open again it wouldn't be his hand he applied to her bottom, but a whalebone riding switch.

The figure vanished, leaving Richard with a chill feeling and a sense of irritation that faded only slowly as he tried to tell himself that it would only have been a moorman, or some particularly foolhardy walker. He pressed on, faster now, keen to reach Driscoll's as quickly as possible. In order to calm his nerves he turned his mind to the second of the difficulties that lay between him and a successful union with Miss Stukely: his father.

Two

'Marry a Stukely?' Charles Truscott blustered, helping himself to a kipper. 'Have you taken leave of your senses?'

'You were in business with Sir Robert,' Richard responded.

'There's a great deal of difference between business and marriage,' his father continued. 'For the sake of God, Richard, the girl's a direct descendant of Spanish Stukely . . .'

'That was in the sixteenth century,' Richard pointed out.

'Don't interrupt,' Charles snapped. 'Lewis Stukely wasn't in the sixteenth century, was he? Beastly fellow tried to skin your great-grandfather's maid, you know that, don't you? Fellow was mad as a hatter, and a murderous one to boot.'

'Genevieve is not descended from Lewis Stukely,' Richard objected.

'Near as makes no difference,' his father countered, 'and then there was that unspeakable business with the dog.'

'Which, if I remember correctly, was as much John Truscott's doing as Roger Stukely's.'

'Well, yes, but be that as it may, the fact remains that the Stukely family carries bad blood.'

'So does ours,' Richard answered, 'and speaking of which, Genevieve has hired a detective to investigate her great-uncle's death, the celebrated Harland Wolfe, no less.'

'Good God!' Charles responded. 'You don't suppose . . .'

'I suppose,' Richard interrupted, 'that he'll take a look around, conclude that it's all stuff and nonsense, pocket his fee and return to London. Nevertheless, we must exercise caution.'

'Yes, quite,' his father answered. 'I'll have the spikes sharpened, and we'll have to make sure the fellow doesn't get anywhere near Lucy.'

'I'll tell her myself,' Richard answered, and shovelled the last piece of kidney from his plate to his mouth.

Quickly dabbing his lips, he walked from the room before his father could bring the conversation back to Miss Stukely. It was more or less the attitude he'd expected, but it had still left him feeling put out, and determined to take his feelings out on Lucy Capleton's bottom without delay. She'd managed to evade him that morning, passing through to his brother's room before he was fully awake, but he knew she would be fussing around the house somewhere, and that once he'd caught her he could do as he pleased.

She'd have to be done somewhere quiet, obviously, as while the conversation between Mrs Bloss and Miss Stukely on the moor had been almost inaudible, the slaps hadn't. Lucy was sure to squeal too, but as he strode up the stairs he decided that in the circumstances it wouldn't make a great deal of difference. If anybody did hear, and brought the subject up, he would simply blame Leopold.

He passed his sister on the landing, in her riding gear and quite evidently going out, reducing the possibility of anyone noticing still further, and he was grinning as he began his search. Lucy wasn't in any of the rooms on the first floor, heightening his satisfaction as he ascended to the second. His own room was empty. So was the one next door and, while noises could be heard through the wall, they clearly weren't being made by Lucy. Moving back across the top of the stairs, he slowed down, listening. After a moment he caught the soft tone of a voice, singing a hymn. He chuckled to himself and pushed open the door.

She stood by the window, a duster in her hand, looking both pretty and vulnerable in her simple grey-blue maid's dress, white apron and mop cap. As she saw him a look of uncertainty flickered across her face, before resolving into a shy smile. Richard stepped close, extending his finger to trace a slow line from the gentle swell of her belly, up over her breasts and neck, to her chin, which he tilted upwards so that she was looking directly into his face.

'Such a pretty girl,' he said.

Lucy didn't answer, her soft brown eyes merely staring into his, her expression full of both apprehension and more yielding emotions. Richard nodded to himself, delighting in the way she responded to him, always a little shy, always a little reluctant, but ultimately always willing. He could feel her trembling slightly, and could just imagine what would be going through her mind: uncertainty as to whether she would simply be told to show off her bottom and breasts for him while he masturbated, made to take his cock in her hand or in her mouth, or sodomised. Richard waited a moment before supplying an answer he hoped would be a shock.

'Today, my little one,' he said, 'I think I shall spank you.'

'Spank me?' Lucy gasped, immediately flustered. 'But Mr Richard, sir, I had locked the door properly last night, you saw so yourself, and I always do my work as well as I'm able, and . . .'

'Hush,' Richard said softly. 'I'm not going to spank you because you're a bad girl, Lucy. I'm going to spank you for my amusement.'

'For your amusement?' Lucy queried, her expression now puzzled as well as alarmed.

'Yes, for my amusement,' Richard said, 'now come along, let's have those skirts up, shall we?'

Lucy's face had begun to work in consternation, much as it always did in the early stages of her buggerings, but she gave no resistance, standing meekly with her feather duster still in her hand as Richard lifted her dress to expose the rear of her drawers.

'Hold your skirts,' Richard instructed.

Trembling with fright, Lucy did as she was told, holding her skirts at the level of her waist. Richard's fingers went to her drawers, not to simply pull them wide as he usually did when he wanted access to her bottom, but to undo the buttons at her waist. As the third button came free the sides of her drawers fell apart, leaving her bare from her lower back to the middle of her thighs, with her bottom framed in cheap cotton lace and folds of cloth.

'Beautiful,' he whispered. 'Is there anything in God's creation quite so fine as a young woman's bottom?'

'Don't blaspheme, sir, please!' Lucy answered, more shocked by his words than by the finger he was using to tickle the crease of her bottom.

'Blaspheme?' Richard chuckled, continuing to explore. 'God created you, did he not, so how can it be deemed blasphemous to admire his creation? To the contrary, to say so is praise, to the greatest of all artists, whose work has been imitated by all others. No, my sweet, it is not blasphemy to praise your bottom, it is an act of worship.'

'If . . . if you worship my . . . my behind,' Lucy managed, 'why do you abuse it so?'

'Abuse?' Richard queried. 'Not at all. I merely put your bottom to the use God intended, and what better use than . . . to spank it.'

As he spoke he began, slapping upwards to make Lucy's cheeks bounce and sting. It hurt, but it was a great deal less hard than she was used to, while for all her misgivings there was no denying the pleasure of holding her skirts up for him while it was done. Not that she had any intention of showing her true feelings, still protesting as her cheeks were slowly but firmly slapped up to a warm stinging glow that quickly left her wanting to push them out and accept him from behind the way he liked best.

'Hmm, you don't make much of a fuss, do you?' Richard queried after a while, clearly disappointed. 'Perhaps a different style?'

Lucy managed a small confused noise in reply, followed by a squeal of alarm as Richard raised a foot onto the window seat and flipped her over his knee. She shot out her arms to stop her head striking the floor, just in time, but her feet were left kicking in the air, while her bare bottom was now the highest part of her body. Richard was laughing as he once more began to spank her, much more effectively now, to set her gasping and begging for mercy.

'That's more the way!' Richard called. 'Damn fine sport this, eh Lucy?'

As he spoke he had landed a particularly hard slap to the curve of Lucy's buttocks and the only answer he got was a pitiful squeal, but he seemed content with it, slapping away merrily as her bottom danced and her legs kicked in every direction. It was all Lucy could do to steady herself on the floor, while her mop cap had fallen away and her skirts come down over her head, leaving her view restricted to a small patch of carpet and her body completely at his mercy.

He took full advantage, spanking her without regard for her pleas and squeals, until her bottom was burning hot and she was dizzy and faint with being upside down for so long. When it finally did stop he simply removed his knee from beneath her belly, dropped her to the floor with a final squeak of surprise, still bottom high and fully expecting a cock up it at any moment.

It wasn't a cock she got, but the handle of her feather duster, eased in up the sweaty little hole between her blazing cheeks and left sticking out between. She heard Richard swear and felt something hard slap on her bottom as he sank down next to her in a squat, gripping his cock in frenzied masturbation, and jerking himself over her reddened buttocks until she felt the wet of his semen splash on her burning skin. He'd come all over her bottom without putting it up, or even in her mouth, and her lower lip pushed out in disappointment.

Genevieve Stukely lay on her bed, ruefully contemplating her situation. She was face down, her drawers unbuttoned at the back with the panel folded down to allow the cool morning air to work on her bottom, which had just been smacked up to a blazing heat by Nanna Bloss, again. It had been the latest in a long line of spankings, all part of her battle for at least some autonomy in her new life. She was losing.

It had begun in Deadwood, with Nanna Bloss making the consequences of Genevieve refusing her a post as companion very clear indeed. On the long journey across the United States to New York and across the Atlantic on the liner *Germanic* the situation had been at least tolerable, with the madame apparently content to indulge herself in the comfortable life made possible by the Stukely fortune, and seldom dishing out more than one spanking a day. Only on arrival in England had the full extent of Nanna Bloss' greed and vindictiveness become apparent.

With direct access to Genevieve's money, rather than having to rely on their own small savings and Mr Greville's credit, Nanna had begun to spend as if the end of the world was approaching, and mostly on herself. In Southampton, for every garment Genevieve had been permitted, Nanna had purchased three or four, and always in the most extravagant style. At meals, Nanna had typically consumed at least two bottles of expensive wine, and it was little consolation that she encouraged Genevieve to do the same. Nanna's other purchases had been yet more extravagant, to say nothing of the cost of having them transported to Devon, while again very few of them had been for the benefit of anybody but herself.

Only the remoteness of Stukely Hall had put a stop to Nanna's extravagance, but that had brought fresh problems. At first Genevieve had been delighted, enjoying the open moor, the fine house and the air of antiquity and importance, an echo of which she had always retained from her father's stories. Her great-uncle's death she considered an unfortunate accident, the tale of the hound a mere legend, certainly nothing to prevent her enjoying her freedom much as she had when a little girl in the Californian hills.

Unfortunately Nanna Bloss objected, to just about everything, and her objections were enforced by the application of her hand to Genevieve's bare bottom. Being told what to do was infuriating, the pain and indignity of the spankings worse, but something else was worse still. She was coming to realise that Nanna actively enjoyed punishing her and, as the spankings grew more frequent, so the caresses to Genevieve's bottom delivered before, during and after punishment had grown more intimate.

She didn't even have any allies in the house. The butler, Capleton, and his wife, who cooked and cleaned, both maintained a cool reserve, and, so Genevieve suspected, even approved, if not of Nanna Bloss as such, then of her attitude to discipline. Certainly neither of them were going to attempt to put a stop to it, and she dared not take any of the men she had met into her confidence, even Richard Truscott, for all his obvious affection for her. Yet she had to do something.

A noise from somewhere downstairs attracted her attention and she shifted position, wondering if Nanna was coming back. Her heart had begun to hammer and she quickly covered her bottom, for all that she knew she could be stripped again in a moment and that she would only succeed in amusing her tormentor. She caught a male voice and relief flooded through her, but she still gave a start when the big woman pushed in at her door without troubling to knock.

'Still not dressed?' Nanna demanded. 'Get on with you. Dr Manston is here, from that detective you had Mr Greville summon.'

'I had thought Mr Wolfe would come?' Genevieve answered, quickly rolling her legs off the bed.

'Whoever he is,' Nanna warned. 'You mind your mouth while he's here, and stick to business with the hound.'

'Yes, Nanna,' Genevieve said meekly, 'and please could you tell Dr Manston that I'll be down presently.'

Nanna Bloss answered with a grunt and slammed the door behind her. Genevieve began to dress, pulling on her stockings and struggling into her corset, bustle and dress as best she could with nobody to help. As she struggled to do the fastenings up she was cursing softly, and promising herself that the first thing she'd do once Nanna Bloss was gone would be to secure the services of a maid, one of the many things she'd been forbidden to do.

After very considerable effort a glance in the wardrobe mirror showed that she was ready to receive polite company. A few minor adjustments and she made her way downstairs, to where the visitors were waiting in the drawing room. Dr Robinson was one, and Dr Manston proved to be a somewhat thick-set man of middle age, with a grey moustache and a bulldog expression. He greeted her affably and expressed his condolences on the death of her great-uncle, then explained what Genevieve had been waiting to ask.

'... and furthermore, I must apologise for the absence of Mr Wolfe himself. Unfortunately he is involved in a case of the utmost importance, in Bavaria, where he may be obliged to remain for some time. Meanwhile, I am at your service.'

Dr Manston gave a stiff bow as he finished. Even after just a moment's acquaintance it was impossible not to be charmed by Miss Stukely, and for the first time since leaving London he found himself glad of Wolfe's seemingly bizarre decision to go to Bavaria rather than Devon. She was tall and elegant, with fine features and an abundance of rich brown hair, worn loose in a style both attractive and youthful, for all that she was clearly a woman rather than a girl.

He had heard the legend of the hound from Dr Robinson on the way from Lydford Station, although had it not been for Wolfe's insistence that the case was worth investigating he would have put the known facts down to coincidence and an overactive imagination on the part of the dead baronet. As it was, the only thing he could think of was to attempt to apply his colleague's famous methods of detection and hope that a solution presented itself.

'Dr Robinson has explained the background of the case to me, Miss Stukely,' he said as he accepted the seat he had been offered, 'but I must ask you to relate those events which drove you to seek my assistance, that is, the assistance of Mr Wolfe and myself, omitting no detail, however trivial it might seem.'

'As you please, Doctor, although some of these details are of a delicate nature,' Miss Stukely responded with a becoming blush.

'I quite understand,' Dr Manston responded, 'but in an investigation of this sort it is essential that the full facts are known.'

Miss Stukely lowered her eyes modestly but continued.

'We arrived at Southampton aboard the liner *Germanic*,' she said, 'me and Mrs Bloss, and after finding a hotel we went out to make some purchases, which were delivered to our rooms. I changed into new linen before going down to dinner, and when we came back to our rooms a garment had been taken, my drawers.'

She was blushing, rather prettily, and Dr Manston found the blood rushing to his own face in sympathy.

'And you are certain this garment had not been taken for the laundry?' he asked.

'Don't be foolish,' Mrs Bloss cut in. 'Why take just her drawers and leave the rest?'

'Quite,' Dr Manston admitted, the antipathy he had felt towards the big woman since being introduced growing instantly stronger, 'but I must be clear on these points. What then of the hotel maids?'

'What, steal a pair of old splitters?' Mrs Bloss snorted.

'Nanna, please,' Miss Stukely said gently. 'I had thought of the maids, Dr Manston, but they were quite firm in their denials and a search yielded nothing.'

'And your room was unlocked?' he asked.

'We saw no reason to lock it. The hotel seemed so very grand.'

'It is a disgrace, no doubt,' he went on, 'and, while seemingly trivial, my colleague Mr Wolfe is convinced that it is in fact significant. Have there been further developments?'

'No,' Miss Stukely answered. 'We came here without incident, and everything has been quiet since. I have been introduced to a number of my neighbours . . .'

'Which neighbours, precisely?' Dr Manston asked, sure it was just the sort of detail his colleague would have wanted to know.

'Dr Robinson, naturally,' Miss Stukely told him, 'and Mr Greville, who brought me the news of my inheritance, Mr Richard Truscott, whose family own so much of the land in these parts, and Mr Matthew Widdery, a painter. That is all.'

'I see,' Dr Manston said, and paused, feeling somewhat stuck. 'Well, my advice for the moment, Miss Stukely, is to avoid the moor at all times.'

'I've told her that myself,' Mrs Bloss snapped. 'What I want to know is, when's your famous friend coming down? If he'll be of any use.'

'As I have said,' Dr Manston responded with deliberate coldness, 'Mr Wolfe is indisposed, but you may be assured of his earliest attention.'

'Mr Wolfe is a man of extraordinary talent,' Dr Robinson put in. 'In the instance of the theft of a local racehorse, he managed to identify which of the stable boys was lying by observing the depth to which a piece of parsley had sunk into the butter on a hot day.'

'Then the sooner he comes, the better,' Mrs Bloss responded. 'A body doesn't feel safe in her own house around here.'

'Indeed not, Mrs Bloss,' Dr Robinson responded, 'and while I would not wish to trouble you any further unless it were absolutely necessary, I must reveal another reason to avoid the moor. There has been an escape from the prison at Princetown, a most violent man.'

'Sugden, the Stepney strangler,' Dr Manston explained, 'another of Mr Wolfe's triumphs, and not a man I'd care to meet again. His sentence was only commuted from death due to doubts of his sanity, so horrid were his deeds, begging your pardon, Miss Stukely.'

'There were two policeman at Lydford Station,' Dr Robinson continued, 'and they say he has no way out of the county save on foot, or a stolen horse. He'll be picked up soon enough, I imagine, unless the moor gets him first.'

'You make the moor sound such a horrid place,' Miss Stukely responded. 'I think it is rather beautiful.'

'It's beautiful enough,' Dr Robinson went on, 'in the spring with the gorse in flower and the sunlight on the tors, but it can still be treacherous. The hill a little to the south, with a conical profile to the rock, that's Hare Tor, and you won't find a prettier view from the summit in all of western England. Looking west, you can see so far into Cornwall it's as if the whole land is laid out at your feet. East, there's the heart of the moor, and not too far below what looks like as lush and green a water meadow as you'll find in England, dotted with yellow and blue flowers at this time of year. That's Tavy Head Mires[6], where a man and his horse can sink out of sight in under a minute, and if they do, that's the last you'll see of them.'

'Really, Dr Robinson,' Dr Manston protested, 'there is no call to alarm Miss Stukely unduly.'

'Not at all,' Miss Stukely responded. 'I am glad of Dr Robinson's advice, and with good fortune this convict may stumble into the mire and drown himself.'

Victoria Truscott smoothed down the skirts of her riding habit[7], waiting her moment before entering the stable. Luke Gurney, she knew, would stand no nonsense, insisting she rode out in the manner of which her parents approved, side-saddle. The stable boy, Ned Annaferd, on the other hand, could be guaranteed to do as he was told. Sure enough, he gave a little nervous bow as he saw her, and blushed crimson as she favoured him with a smile.

'Saddle Cloud,' she ordered, 'with an ordinary saddle. My mother wishes to ride with Lady Laura Russell later this morning, and both side-saddles will be needed.'

Ned opened his mouth to speak, thought better of it and hurried off to prepare her pony. She waited, hoping that whatever had taken Luke Gurney to the carriage house would keep him there long enough for her to escape. As five minutes passed and then ten she grew increasingly irritable, swishing her riding whip back and forth in short agitated jerks until finally Ned reappeared, now leading Cloud.

Inserting one elegant boot into a stirrup, she pulled herself up, sitting sideways in the saddle as she was supposed to and throwing Ned a haughty glance to dare him to comment. He didn't, merely holding open the stable doors for her as she left, and not a moment too soon. Luke Gurney had emerged from the carriage house, holding a pair of swingletrees easily in one massive hand. He gave her a casual salute, no more, which she returned more formally as she carefully urged Cloud into a trot towards the lake.

Letting herself through a gate in the high spike-topped wall that surrounded the estate, she waited until she was quite sure that neither Luke Gurney nor the stable boy could see her before throwing her leg over Cloud and sitting in the saddle properly, then tugging on the reins to steer her pony away from Burley Down and towards Dartmoor. The down was dull, a simple gallop at best, on ground she had been familiar with since she was a little girl, and where she was all too likely to meet other members of her family. The moor was exciting, vast and open, much of it still unfamiliar, and empty enough for her to risk throwing her leg across the saddle and riding the way she liked. Better still, there was now the added thrill of some wild and dangerous man loose among the craggy tors and sharp gullies, little ancient woods and quaking bogs.

Not, she told herself, that she would take any real risks, and whatever her parents and her brother said she was quite confident in her safety. The convict would be on foot, and even the oldest and frailest of mounts could have outdistanced him easily, never mind her Cloud. She gave the grey pony a rub on his neck at the thought, smiling softly to herself. Yes, she would ride out across

Dartmoor, perhaps as far as Fur Tor, or even Great Miss Tor, from which she could see all the way down to the sea, and also the gloomy grey fortress of the prison, the sight of which always provided her with the most delicious of thrills. Maybe, if she was lucky, she would even catch a glimpse of the convict, hiding among the rocks, or even running wild and unkempt across the moor with the dogs at his heels and the warders firing at him with their rifles. It was an exciting prospect, and she dug her heels into Cloud's flanks as she reached the lane that ran towards Lydford, urging him into a canter.

She slowed as she passed through Lydford, tipping her hat to a passing cousin, and speeding up once more as the ground rose towards the moor. As she passed Stukely Hall she paused briefly, wondering if she should introduce herself to Miss Genevieve Stukely, who was only a little older than her and had reputedly spent a wild childhood in the western United States. Only when she remembered that having said she was going up to Burley Down the visit might get her into trouble did she ride on, deciding to wait for a formal introduction. Besides, according to Richard the women believed the story of the hound of the Stukelys, which suggested that they were too silly to make worthwhile company.

Instead, Victoria urged Cloud to the summit of Arms Tor and paused again to look down over the long grey-green slope, the woods and the rooftops of the Hall. Only one other human being was in view, the painter Matthew Widdery, sat at his easel among the tailings of an old mine somewhat below the peak of Brat Tor, where she had seen him before. His back was to her, and he was far too distant to notice in any case. Smiling quietly to herself, she adjusted her seat, swinging one leg across her saddle to spread her thighs over the smooth firm surface, with just the gusset of her drawers between the leather and that most intimate part of her body.

Just to sit like that felt wonderful, naughty, wicked even, exactly the sort of thing she knew she should never do and for that very reason far more thrilling than the physical sensation alone. Already she could imagine the delicious shivery sensations that she knew would come, but she was determined not to hurry. Beyond Arms Tor the land fell away in a gentle slope before rising once more towards the massive stone bulk of Great Links Tor, short turf all the way, and the best possible ground for a gallop.

She set off, walking Cloud carefully through the scattered boulders below the summit of Arms Tor before urging him into a trot, a canter, and a full gallop, now bent low over his neck with the sods flying up behind her and calling out in sheer joy as she rode. A little water was lying in the dell, showering her dress and splashing Cloud's flanks, but she didn't trouble to slow, and was still urging him on up the slope beyond, stopping only when she had reached the mass of the tor itself.

He was running sweat and flecked with foam around his mouth, while Victoria was filled with a wild exhilaration, completely happy and full of mischief too. She was no longer quite alone, with peat cutters at Rattlebrook works clearly visible, but they were a quarter mile or more away, and the presence of so many rough burly labourers only served to heighten her excitement as she wriggled her bottom onto the saddle. It felt nice, her cheeks a little sore from the ride, bringing back memories of the helpless shame-filled pleasure that always came after she'd been given a spanking, and which she'd long since learnt to turn to her advantage. Her sex felt nicer still, now wet and puffy against the hard leather, making her want to spread herself to the air and stroke the wet sensitive flesh until ecstasy took over her body.

Even among the rocks it was too risky, with the railway nearby and men loading sods of peat into the trucks. Briefly she imagined what might happen if such men caught her doing what she intended – not the reality, of shock and embarrassment on both sides, but a fantasy, in which they would extract the price of their silence by making her take their members in her mouth, a thought so exquisitely improper it sent a shiver through her body not far removed from climax. She closed her eyes, remembering how she'd been taught to do it with a mixture of shame, resentment and deep arousal and, equally shameful, how she'd been taught to play with herself in return.

It had to be done, and quickly, perhaps at Arms Tor after one more gallop. To think was to act, and she wheeled Cloud once more, turning down slope and quickly urging him to speed. Again the sensation of being straddle-legged on the saddle took over, now so strong she had to cling on with all her strength to keep her seat. She let herself bounce to the rhythm of his running, her bottom slapping hard on the saddle, pain balanced by ecstasy with every smack, her sex now fully spread, deliberately hurting herself, until the dull heavy slaps of leather on flesh suddenly gave way to a sharp sting.

Victoria gasped, nearly rolled from the saddle, and as she hauled frantically on the reins she felt moisture between her legs, not the slippery slimy feel of her arousal, but a more fluid wetness that could only be blood. She made a face as she dismounted, now feeling rather sorry for herself, yet still highly aroused. Tethering Cloud to a stunted thorn bush in the lee of Arms Tor, she went in among the rocks, making a last check to be sure nobody was near before finding a cranny where she could inspect herself without fear of discovery.

She bunched up her riding habit and the petticoat beneath as she sank into a squat, slipping a hand in around the side of the panel of her drawers to find her quim. A carefully applied finger made her wince so badly she had to bite her lip and confirmed her worst fears. She had split her maidenhead, and not just a little, but all the way, opening the tight hole she was supposed to hold sacred for the insertion of her husband's penis on her wedding night. A sigh of vexation escaped her lips, then a little squeak of pain as she ill-advisedly gave in to instinct and penetrated her freshly deflowered cunt.

Standing up once more, she let her skirts drop and propped herself against a rock, ruefully considering what she'd done and the possible consequences. Briefly she considered claiming that the convict had caught her and raped her, only to dismiss the idea. Her word would be taken against his, no doubt, but her reputation would still be ruined, while if it turned out that he'd been caught or was nowhere near the moor at all she'd find herself in a very difficult situation indeed. It was much better not to tell anybody and hope that when it came to her wedding night her husband would either fail to notice or accept her explanation. Meanwhile, she needed to touch herself very urgently indeed.

For a few minutes more she tried to hold off, but the thoughts and images running through her mind wouldn't go away. She was deflowered, and while that brought a bitter shame it also brought excitement as strong as at any moment since she'd first lain on her bed with her thighs spread wide and his fingers busy between them as she sucked on his penis. Her imagination was running wild, thinking of how it might have been if instead of simply bursting her maidenhead on horseback she had been taken among the rocks by the peat cutters, or really caught by the convict and made to take him in her mouth until he was hard before being bent over a rock and had from behind, or simply indulged herself with the most convenient cock . . .

She shook herself, smiling for her own filthy naughty thoughts. Her maidenhead was gone, there was no sense in crying over her loss, but there was every sense in making it an occasion to remember. Squatting down once more, she lifted her skirts and lay back against the rock, trapping them to leave her hands free. With her eyes closed, she sought for the naughtiest and most desirable of the thoughts milling in her head as her fingers begun to twitch open the panel of her drawers. The buttons came loose, one by one, each exposing a little more flesh, until at last the panel fell away and her bottom was bare. Taking the flap in hand, she pulled it up between her thighs, just as if she had been about to pee, and with that came a fantasy so deliciously dirty she knew no other would do.

That was how it would happen. She would need to go and choose a private place among the rocks, squatting down just as she was with her thighs wide and her quim and bottom naked to the air, showing all those unmentionably rude details of her body. He would be watching, but she would be unaware of his presence, let alone that his cock was growing gradually hard over the sight of her half-naked body. She would do her piddle and he would watch, gloating over his intrusion into such an intimate act as the yellow fluid squirted from her well-spread quim, her cunt, to use the rudest possible word she knew, her about to be violated cunt . . .

At the thought, Victoria let go, sighing in pleasure as hot piddle bubbled out over her fingers and onto the grass and earth beneath her. She let it all come out, savouring the moment as she imagined lust-filled male eyes on her body and a thick hard cock being prepared for her now open hole. Only of course it wouldn't be open, as he watched her piddle she would still be virgin, but not for long.

A little wriggle of her bottom shook the last few drops away and she began to masturbate, the way she had been taught, using two fingers to spread her sex lips so that anyone watching got a good view, and a third to tease the excitable little bump between. With the first touch she knew it wouldn't be long, the sensation was simply too exquisite to hold back. She began to rub in earnest, thinking of how the watcher would wait until she'd finished her pee and come up behind her, completely unexpected, how he'd tip her forwards so she was kneeling in a puddle of her own piddle with her bare bottom stuck out towards him, how she'd squeak in alarm as his hands closed on her hips in an unbreakable grip, how she'd beg him to let her take him in her mouth instead, and how he'd ignore her and drive the full length of his monstrous cock to the hilt in her virgin cunt, splitting her maidenhead on the way.

Victoria's scream rang out across the moor, hastily cut off as she bit her lip. She was still rubbing, the thoughts raging in her head as contraction after contraction wracked her body, until her muscles finally gave way. Only as she sat down with an audible squelch in the muddy pee puddle underneath her did she stop rubbing, but she was too exhausted to care and stayed as she was, dizzy with the aftermath of her climax as the mud squeezed slowly up between the cheeks of her bottom and into her cunt.

By the time she had finished cleaning herself up with her petticoat she had already fabricated a convincing story of how she'd had to dismount awkwardly and soiled her skirts, and also made a firm resolution to keep the condition of her quim a secret. Once decent, she peered cautiously out from among the rocks, only to find that no less then three men were gathered around the gate where the gardens of Stukely Hall opened onto the moor. Despite the distance she was fairly sure one of them was Dr Robinson and another the lawyer, Greville, both of whom could be relied on to tell her mother and father where she'd been.

Fortunately, Cloud was tethered out of sight, allowing her to stay behind the ridge and make her way down to the Rattlebrook. Following the stream, she began to daydream. It was in the same sharp valley where Roger Stukely had met his end, supposedly under the teeth of Black Shuck, but in reality due to John Truscott's wild and no doubt drunken aim. Despite her vivid fantasies her sympathy was with the girl, and she found herself wondering how she would have coped, only to dismiss the idea. She was a Truscott, and nobody would have dared molest her.

It was a satisfying thought, but less so than it might have been. The busy peat works was now well behind and above her, the steep-sided valley quiet but for the rustle of the stream and the occasional cry of a skylark. Suddenly an encounter with the convict no longer seemed romantic, but frightening, terrifying even, especially with Cloud hemmed in by steep slopes to either side and the path too narrow to turn easily, so that when she caught a movement she pulled quickly on the bridle, and froze.

Some way ahead, where the valley turned before opening out to Tavy Head Mires, a man had just emerged from an old tinner's hut[8] which still supported half of its roof. Only as she took in his appearance did her fear fade. He was quite clearly no convict; his caped tweed suit both tailor-made and expensive, while his lean grave face suggested intelligence and introspection rather than the near bestial depravity she would have expected from the description of William Sugden, who had apparently strangled three men with his bare hands. The convict was also said to be short but massively built. This man was tall and somewhat spare, with quick mannerisms and a confident manner as he lit a briar pipe, hardly the behaviour of a man on the run. Only when he ducked back inside the hut did she continue, now a little faster and no longer so keen to explore.

Richard Truscott toyed irritably with the tip of his walking cane for a moment and then replaced it in the rack and selected another which, while lacking the engraved silver head, had the considerable advantage of being a sword stick. The news of the escaped convict had come as a great irritation, replacing an entirely mythical menace with a very real one and forcing him to alter his plans of displaying his bravado by walking Miss Stukely on Dartmoor. The man was by all accounts desperate and, if he had stayed on the moor, probably starving as well, definitely not the sort of person one would wish to encounter on a romantic promenade.

Not that the convict was particularly likely to be on Burley Down, where Richard intended to take a brisk walk before dinner, but there was no harm in taking precautions. Leaving the house by the rear, he ignored the direct path down to the lake and angled towards the wall instead, inspecting the spikes as he walked along it. Luke Gurney had been instructed to sharpen them, and many of the points already glistened in the sunlight, while the lock in the gate onto the down had been freshly oiled, presumably for the sake of general maintenance.

His mind turned to the problem of Genevieve Stukely as he climbed the zigzag path up the steep wooded face of the down. His problem was straightforward – convincing his father of the virtues of the match – but not easy. No doubt his mother, a romantic through and through, would support him privately, but she invariably deferred to his father's wishes. Victoria could also be counted on for support, but despite the fact that their father doted on her it would make little difference. Leopold, on the other hand, had possibilities, albeit at considerable risk.

It was at least a line of thought worth exploring, and he did so as he continued to climb. One thing at least was clear. He would have to seduce Genevieve first, and not merely into some mild dalliance but full erotic indulgence, perhaps even taking her virginity, and also introducing her to the pleasures of a good buggering. She seemed a sweet girl, and honest, so after that surely the scheme would prove practical.

He had reached the old folly at the summit of Burley Down before he stopped, and sat down on the steps to look back over Driscoll's and the hills of north Devon beyond. Off to one side a string of smoky plumes marred the otherwise verdant landscape where the mine chimneys of Wheal Purity and others belched smoke into the air. Sir Robert Stukely's wealth had allowed considerable new investment and greatly augmented the value of their holdings, but Richard would have preferred to own all of a relatively small mining company than most of the largest in the area, another excellent reason for marrying Genevieve Stukely, but one his father had already proved indifferent to. For some while he considered his options, but again and again came to the same stumbling block. It would have to be Leopold.

With his mind made up he walked into the folly, smiling at memories of childhood games with Victoria and their cousins, also other, less childish amusements in the more recent past. Purely on a whim he rose on tiptoe to peer into an urn in which he had once concealed a short birch which he had been applying to Jane Russell's delectable young buttocks when his mother made an unexpected appearance.

To his surprise the urn was not empty, but contained a small lantern, which he was sure was from the old sulky which had cracked a spoke and was still awaiting repair. There was even oil in the pan, and it had clearly been used recently, no doubt in some illicit nocturnal adventure. He wondered whose it might be, and whether there was anything to be gained from his knowledge.

Lucy was the most likely, as her pert face and fulsome curves were admired by every young man in the district, although as he indulged himself with her in every way save taking her virgin quim there was little to be gained by knowing she kept other assignations. Victoria was another possibility, as with her ardent nature she was quite likely to have found herself some unsuitable lover, but, like Lucy, there was nothing to be gained from applying pressure to her. The same was true of Luke Gurney, while Ned Annaferd was surely too young to have attracted one of the little moppets from the village into an indiscretion? It was impossible to conceive of either the butler or the cook doing anything of the sort, both being in their fifties and married to one another. That left only his mother's maid, Eliza.

Eliza had long proved resistant to his advances, taking a haughty attitude quite inappropriate for a mere maid, which did even more to arouse his passion than her tall slender figure. Several years older than him, she had never permitted so much as a fumble of her breasts, and had slapped him more than once. The most he had ever achieved was to watch her undress through the keyhole of her room, and that had provided no more than tantalising glimpses of a small well-tucked bottom and a pair of apple-sized breasts. If she was involved in some kind of assignation, which had to be illicit or there would have been no call for secrecy, then without question he could hope for rather more, which would provide another excellent diversion while engaged in the more taxing seduction of Genevieve Stukely.

Three

Staring glumly from the window of the tower room at Stukely Hall, Genevieve wondered if Dr Manston would do at all. He was full of determination, undoubtedly a brave man, but seemed entirely lacking in the skills needed in detection, to say nothing of the reputation. He'd failed to find any suspicious footprints, marks of interference around window catches or even any distinctive cigarette ash. Instead, he had wandered the moor with Dr Robinson, armed with a stout ash stick and a revolver that was apparently a relic of his time as an army surgeon. He was doing the same this morning, and was now visible as a tiny figure close to the summit of Brat Tor, where he had stopped for a conversation with the painter who seemed to have an insatiable appetite for Dartmoor scenery.

In consequence, Genevieve was alone in the house with the one thing she really feared, Nanna Bloss; completely alone, as the Capletons had taken the trap to Tavistock market to stock up with provisions. As Genevieve stared from the window her bottom cheeks were twitching in anticipation of the spanking she was sure she would get, for having tried to put her foot down about the extravagance of the grocery list made out by Nanna for the market.

She heard the big woman call out for her from somewhere downstairs, and bit her lip, wondering if she should do as she was told or hide and hope Dr Manston came back before Nanna Bloss caught her. The house was big, with odd little rooms and cupboards, several massive wardrobes and a maze of attics. To hide would be easy enough, but it would only postpone the inevitable, and when the spanking came it would be that much harder.

Nanna Bloss called again and Genevieve gave a little sob as she turned for the door. She was going to be spanked, and that was bad enough, but in addition to the pain, and the humiliation of going bare bottom across the big woman's knee, she knew full well that once it was over the punishment would bring a yet more shameful heat to her rear cheeks, and to her quim.

Her pretty face was set in a fixed pout as she made her way down to the first floor, where Nanna was calling from the large bedroom she had appropriated opposite Genevieve's own. It commanded a view of the garden and the moor beyond, where Dr Manston and the painter were still visible on Brat Tor.

'Seems like your Doctor friend will be a while,' Nanna Bloss said, nodding towards the window. 'Time enough for a good spanking, I dare say.'

Genevieve hung her head, unable to speak for the lump in her throat. Nanna Bloss had been at the window seat, but got up and moved to the bed, patting her lap as she sat down.

'Come along then, let's have that naughty bottom out of your drawers.'

Knowing that protest would only make for a yet more undignified scene and a yet harder spanking, Genevieve came forwards meekly. Nanna Bloss gave a low chuckle to see her victim so compliant, and assisted Genevieve into spanking position across her lap, bottom up with her hands and feet braced on the carpet, her glorious hair dangling around her face.

'This is to teach you to keep that tongue of yours in your head,' Nanna Bloss announced as she began to fiddle with Genevieve's skirts, 'and there's been a sight too much of that lately, so we'd better make it a hard one, don't you think?'

Genevieve didn't answer, her mouth working between a sulky pout and the urgent biting of her lips as her dress was hauled up onto her back.

'We'd better make it a hard one, don't you think?' Nanna Bloss repeated, her tone now threatening.

'Yes, Nanna,' Genevieve answered, the bubble of consternation in her head now so huge she could barely get the words out.

'That's better,' Nanna answered, tucking up Genevieve's petticoat. 'Aren't they a nuisance, these bustles, when it comes to getting a girl ready for punishment? Mark you, I say it's a conceit of you to wear one, I do, at your age.'

Genevieve bit down a new stab of humiliation at the remark but said nothing as the whalebone cage of her bustle was worked back on itself, creating a bizarre ruff of silk and lace around the small of her back where her petticoat had caught on it. Only her drawers remained, and Nanna Bloss' fingers were already on the first button. Her eyes closed tight, Genevieve was already choking back tears as she felt the button go and knew that a small triangle of bottom flesh had been exposed. A second button was tweaked open and another piece of flesh was bare, a third, the central one, and the upper part of the panel was loose, exposing the gentle V where her crease opened between her cheeks.

'Maybe it'd be good to have you in pinafores, with no drawers underneath?' Nanna Bloss joked. 'How'd you like that in front of all your gentleman friends?'

This time Genevieve was unable to restrain a sob, for all that she knew Nanna Bloss would never inflict such an obvious humiliation. She was too old to be treated like that, pure and simple, if only just.

'Don't like that, at all, do you?' Nanna Bloss chuckled as her fingers went to the second last button. 'Quite the little lady, you like to be, don't you? Don't you?'

'Yes, Nanna,' Genevieve answered miserably as the button was undone.

One button remained, holding up the outside of her drawers, and as it was flicked open the panel fell down completely, leaving the full spread of her bottom bare, and the rear lips of her sex too. She was shivering badly, with the tears squeezing slowly from beneath her eyelids as a heavy hand settled on her cheeks.

'D'you know what I'd like to do?' Nanna continued as she began to fondle Genevieve's bottom. 'I'd like to put you in that pinafore and take you over my knee with all of them watching, no drawers mind, so your little hiney's bare, and give you the walloping of a lifetime while they all watch.'

Her words stung, but nothing like so much as the heavy swat she had delivered to Genevieve's bottom with the last of them. Another followed, and a third, the spanking building in speed and force until Genevieve's bottom was bouncing to the slaps and all four of her limbs were waving wildly in the air. It hurt crazily, robbing her of any chance of keeping the least shred of dignity, with both anus and quim on show as her thighs pumped and her buttocks parted in her desperate struggles.

'That's the way, fight it!' Nanna Bloss cackled. 'Makes it all the better for me, that does. Let's see that bottom dance, girl, and maybe Nanna'll give you a treat once she's finished.'

The words barely penetrated Genevieve's mind, which was lost to a haze of pain and the helpless fury of being held down and smacked despite fighting with every ounce of her strength. She was too far gone to think of trying to take it meekly, wriggling her body in purely animal reaction and yet still acutely aware of her spread sex and flaunted bottom, keeping humiliation among her woes.

'Yes, I think I shall,' Nanna Bloss said happily, still spanking. 'I shall indeed. Who's to stop me after all? But not yet. Not 'til I've had my fill of your tail, little Ginny, and that won't be for a while, oh no . . . smack . . . smack . . . smack, little Ginny, smack . . . smack . . . smack . . .'

She'd slowed down, punctuating her words with single hard spanks to Genevieve's now burning bottom, each one producing jerks and kicks, and once, a little soft fart. Nanna Bloss merely laughed and began to spank faster again, quickly reducing Genevieve to a wriggling thrashing mess once more, now nearly blind with tears and unable to hold herself back in any way at all, and when she was finally released she sprawled on the ground with her legs akimbo.

The room swam above her, hazy areas of colour blurred by her tears, while her nose was running badly and she had wet herself a little. Her bottom was a hot throbbing ball and her quim was slippery with juice, shamefully slippery, which added to her bitter sobbing as she slowly rolled over onto all fours and tried to get up, only for a heavy foot to settle on her back.

'Not just yet, you don't,' Nanna Bloss grated, and there was a tone to her voice Genevieve had never heard before: lust. 'You've a job to do, a job best done by whores, on their knees.'

A frightened glance showed the massive woman seated as before, the leg raised on Genevieve's back revealing a mass of expensive lace petticoat trim and a great deal of coloured silk. Genevieve felt her stomach go tight as she hastily wiped her face and swallowed her mouthful of mucus to let herself speak.

'No, Nanna, not that, please?' she begged.

'Oh yes, that,' Nanna answered, 'and don't fuss. You'll learn to like it, if you know what's good for you.'

Nanna Bloss had shifted her weight, allowing her to free the great mass of her skirts from beneath her tree-trunk thighs and monstrous buttocks. Although she no longer had a leg on her back, Genevieve found herself unable to move, but stared in mute horror as the big woman exposed herself, tucking her skirts well up before splitting her vast heavily laced drawers to reveal a fat richly haired cunt among the folds of silk and lace.

'I think you know what to do,' Nanna breathed. 'You always do, you brothel girls.'

'I . . . I'm not a brothel girl . . . I'm not a whore,' Genevieve managed.

'You would've been, soon enough,' Nanna assured her. 'Now get on with you.'

'Must you make me?' Genevieve pleaded. 'Isn't it enough that you spank me, without . . . without . . .'

'How else to entertain myself?' Nanna interrupted. 'Now get your head in there and start licking, unless you want a taste of the cane first?'

Genevieve shook her head and swallowed hard, her eyes locked to the swollen reeking cunt she was expected to put her mouth to. Her bottom was still burning hot, the need in her own sex almost too strong to deny, and yet the thought of the cane still made her cheeks twitch. She had seen a girl caned, in the saloon with an audience of jeering laughing men to look on, and it was a fate she very badly wanted to avoid. She gave one last look into Nanna Bloss' eyes, but found no mercy, only lust and amusement and contempt, then she was crawling forwards on her hands and knees.

'That's my girl,' Nanna drawled. 'Now you just lick 'til I say to stop, oh, and stick out that sweet little hiney as I can see what I done to you.'

With her humiliation growing more bitter by the instant Genevieve obeyed, sticking up her bottom to show off the smacked cheeks.

'Let's see you properly,' Nanna Bloss said, reaching

out to adjust Genevieve's petticoat and bustle to improve the view. 'Now lick.'

Still Genevieve hesitated, keen to obey for fear of the cane, but it was more than she could do to bury her face in the rank hairy flesh in front of her.

'Need a little help do we?' Nanna Bloss chuckled, and took Genevieve by the hair.

She gave out a despairing squeak as she was pulled in, and another, quickly muffled by a faceful of wet cunt and pubic hair. Nanna Bloss didn't wait to give further orders, but began to use Genevieve's nose to masturbate with. Helpless, able to breath only by gasping in lungfuls of cunt-scented air, Genevieve began to wriggle and kick her feet.

'Lick me then, you silly bitch,' Nanna Bloss laughed, and Genevieve's tongue came out.

Her first taste of the big woman's quim made her gag, but with her hair gripped tight there was nothing she could do but swallow and go on licking. She was still snivelling, and there was as much of her own snot as there was of Nanna Bloss' natural juice in her mouth when she swallowed the second time, thick and salty on her tongue and in her throat, while her face was thoroughly smeared.

Nanna Bloss gave a contented sigh and relaxed back a little on the bed, but she kept her grip in Genevieve's hair, allowing no escape. Knowing for certain that she'd be kept in place until the big woman was done, Genevieve found herself with no choice but to do her best, using her tongue to lap the swollen bulb at the top of Nanna's cunt, the same place her much smaller bump gave her so much pleasure when she allowed her fingers to stray.

A nagging voice in the back of her head was telling her that was what she wanted to do now, giving in completely to her humiliation by rubbing her quim until she too had come. Yet she held back, knowing it would be the final act of surrender, and that once she'd done it, and Nanna had seen her do it, she would be nothing more than the big woman's plaything, a shapely toy to be used for sex at leisure.

The thought set her snivelling and running tears once more, but the grip in her hair was tighter still and Nanna had begun to moan, while the huge fleshy thighs were squeezing around Genevieve's head in slow powerful contractions. She began to lick harder, desperate to make the big woman come before she lost control of her own feelings, and a moment later was rewarded by a grunt of ecstasy from above her, a tug that nearly pulled her hair out by the roots and crushing pressure on her head as Nanna Bloss came to climax.

Genevieve was released and immediately sat back, panting for breath, her mouth and nose thick with the taste and scent of cunt, her make-up plastered across her face in a thickly smeared mess of her own snot and Nanna's cream. The urge to reach down and touch herself was close to overwhelming, but she held back, even as Nanna spoke.

'You'll be wanting to diddle yourself, I'll lay a bet? Go on then, do it, and I'll watch.'

Shaking her head, Genevieve tried to find an answer that would come close to expressing her emotions or, at least, the emotions she wanted to express to Nanna Bloss, but the words never came, her fear of the cane was too great. Instead she scrambled to her feet and fled, with her skirts still up, sure that Dr Manston or the Capletons would choose that moment to come back and catch her with her bare red bottom bobbing behind her but too far gone to stop herself.

In her room she flung herself on the bed, beating at the eiderdown with her balled fists in a mewling pathetic tantrum, as much for her own reaction as for what had been done to her. Her bottom was still hot, her anus a sensitive needy spot between her cheeks, her quim wet and urgent, dribbling juice into her open drawers even as she thumped the bed and the tears streamed down her face.

She heard a movement outside her door, the creak of floorboards beneath a heavy weight, and froze, knowing that if Nanna Bloss did anything else to her she would give in. Nothing happened, the footsteps passing towards the stairs, and Genevieve rolled over onto her back, drawing a long sigh of relief, followed by a sob as she realised she was going to do it anyway.

Telling herself that it was the sensible thing to do it while her tormentor was elsewhere, and that therefore it wasn't really a disgrace, she reached down between her thighs. Clutching the still loose panel of her drawers, she pulled it up, holding it over her belly as her thighs came wide to spread her naked cunt to the warm spring air. Her other hand went down, burrowing among the moist folds even as she sobbed with humiliation for what she was doing.

It didn't matter. She had to do it. One finger went lower, to touch the taut arc of skin that protected her virgin hole, and into which she knew full well she'd have had not one but several cocks thrust had it not been for her deliverance from the saloon. That at least was a mercy, but as she touched herself she couldn't help feeling regret and wondering what it was like to have her hole filled by a man.

Her finger went lower still, tickling her anus until the little hole had begun to twitch and pulse, always a delight whenever she rubbed herself. She'd stopped crying, her ecstasy taking over as she toyed with her bottom hole, her mind no longer full of thoughts of her spanking and being made to lick cunt, but of the joy of running naked in the empty woods, of easing fingers up her bottom because she dared not probe her cunt, and of rubbing herself to blinding ecstasy in the sure knowledge that however loud she screamed there would be nobody to hear.

Unfortunately that was not true in Stukely Hall, and even as her back arched in ecstasy and her gasps turned to cries she knew that Nanna Bloss could hear, burying her climax in a welter of shame before she had even come properly.

Richard Truscott strode confidently towards Stukely Hall. The day was warm and still, an ideal opportunity to suggest a stroll to Miss Stukely, and with luck the cumbersome Mrs Bloss might even be put off by the steep moorland slopes. He could then demonstrate his casual indifference to both hellhound and escaped convict while relying for safety on the non-existence of one and his sword stick for the other.

Thus he would be able to make the opening moves of his seduction, while he could then take his inevitable arousal out on Lucy that evening, or perhaps even Eliza, assuming she was the one holding moonlit trysts at the folly on Burley Down, of which he was now tolerably certain. Her room had a fine view of the down, while Lucy's didn't, and nor did Victoria's. Luke Gurney was still a possibility, though not a likely one, as to Richard's certain knowledge the big groom was happily rogering at least three of the women from the village.

All he had to do was catch Eliza in the act and make her choices very clear: the shame of exposure, or a little assistance with his cock now and again. She was certain to make the right choice, as the very fact that she needed to make a secret assignation rather than meet her lover openly made her guilt plain. Why this should be, Richard was less certain, although there were several options. The lover might be a married man, or a man of higher social status, a churchman even, or just possibly another woman, which opened up yet more interesting possibilities.

The previous night she had gone to bed early and, although he had watched from his window until gone midnight, no light had shown from the temple. This night he hoped for better things, and as he approached the door of Stukely Hall his imagination was running riot, picturing a secret orgiastic society of lesbians who he would be able to bend to his will for fear of exposure.

He rapped on the door, and was only mildly taken aback when Mrs Bloss appeared in the opening in place of Capleton.

'Good day to you, Madame,' he said, tipping his hat. 'I trust my visit is not an inconvenience, but I was passing and wished to be sure that all is well with Miss Stukely?'

Mrs Bloss' expression was none too friendly, and she cast a doubtful look back into the house before admitting him.

'She's upstairs,' the big woman stated flatly, then produced a yell that made Richard start.

There was a brief, somewhat embarrassing pause before Miss Stukely appeared. She seemed a trifle red around the eyes, and Richard immediately wondered if she'd been crying, perhaps in fear over the hound, which was all to the good.

'I was hoping you might do me the honour of accompanying me on a walk, Miss Stukely,' he offered. 'As you observed on the occasion of my previous visit, the moor is at its best at this time of year.'

'I'd be delighted,' Miss Stukely answered without hesitation, somewhat to Richard's surprise. 'Will I need a cape, do you think?'

'Not at all,' he assured her. 'The weather is remarkably clement.'

'What of this convict fellow?' Mrs Bloss demanded. 'And the hound, if such a thing exists.'

'Black Shuck only runs at night,' Richard answered casually, 'and as to the convict, I hardly think he would dare to accost an active man. If the fellow's on the moor at all he must be weak with hunger by now.'

'All the same,' Mrs Bloss answered, 'you're to go no further than the ridge, where you can be seen.'

'You won't be accompanying us then?' Richard enquired.

'I've better things to do with my time,' Mrs Bloss answered, and started up the stairs.

Leaving the house by the back, Richard waited until they were in the yew alley before offering his arm. Again Miss Stukely showed no hesitation before taking it, making him wonder if he might not attempt a somewhat bolder course of action that the one he'd decided on. She was certainly friendly, constantly smiling and her talk almost playful as they walked alongside the stream where he'd watched her bathing her feet and having her bottom smacked.

The memory made his cock start to harden and set him wishing that she was of a lower station in life or that less rested on her successful seduction. Even with her open friendly manner he was sure the most he could hope for was a chaste kiss, but what he wanted to do was roll her on her back and take her then and there in the wet grass or, better still, put her on her knees and ease his cock in from behind, either to her cunt or up her bottom.

'Mr Widdery is a most individual fellow, is he not?' she was saying. 'Always hard at work with his painting, and such an enormous beard.'

'Like a quick set hedge,' Richard joked. 'It's a wonder he can see at all.'

Miss Stukely gave a light laugh. Encouraged, Richard went on.

'And the fellow can't paint at all, nothing but wet areas of rather vague colour. We must bid him good afternoon, of course, and you can see for yourself.'

'I would enjoy that,' Miss Stukely answered, 'if, perhaps, you would provide me with a little assistance on the slope.'

‘Gladly, Miss Stukely,’ Richard responded, ‘or, if I might be so bold, gladly, Genevieve.’

Miss Stukely responded with a smile and Richard began to steer her up the steep slope towards where the painter was seated. The ground was rough, with tussocks of grass interspersed by boggy patches and granite boulders, making their progress slow and affording him ample opportunity to offer her his assistance. She didn’t seem to mind at all, even when he took the opportunity to place a supporting hand beneath her bustle to help her up onto a rock. He had not touched flesh, even through her clothes, but she had realised, and the glance she cast back at him was more than a little flirtatious.

Richard’s throat had grown dry as he remembered the sight of her well-turned bottom naked, and then jiggling to the smacks from her companion’s hand. His cock was now hard, and creating a conspicuous bulge in his trousers. Miss Stukely didn’t seem to have noticed, fortunately, for all her playfulness he was sure that the display of his erection would be much more than she could cope with, at least yet.

They had come up with the painter in any case, and to his relief Richard found his cock deflating as they went into the normal routine of greetings and comments of entirely false admiration for Widdery’s work. As before, he seemed more concerned with giving an overall impression of the colours visible to him than capturing even an approximate likeness of the scenery, so much so that Richard found himself wondering if the artist suffered from extreme short sight and could in fact only see what he had painted.

Hoping that mild sarcasm might be lost on the apparently somewhat pompous Matthew Widdery but amuse Genevieve Stukely, Richard attempted a critique.

‘Mr Widdery takes his ideas from Paris, my dear, where the French have abandoned the mere reproduction of form in favour of more abstract concepts, but we must not allow ourselves to think that this implies any lack of skill. Far from it, as Mr Widdery will no doubt make plain, such work . . .'

He stopped. A noise had risen on the light breeze, a low mournful baying so full of malevolence and distress that he felt the hairs rise on the nape of his neck. It stopped, then came again, louder than before, leaving the three of them struck silent together. Richard found his voice first.

'What in hell's name was that?'

On the flank of Hare Tor, Dr Manston echoed Richard's sentiment, only with considerably greater fear. He was alone and the sound had been uncomfortably close. His hand was shaking as he drew his revolver, but the gentle curve of the hillside stretched empty both to the rocks above and to the lip of the valley below. Nevertheless he cocked the gun, his eyes darting nervously from side to side as he tried to divine the direction of the sound and waited in mingled hope and fear for it to come again.

It was not easy, the sound seeming to have come from two directions at once, the great empty space beyond the lip of the hill and behind him. In one case that meant Tavy Head Mires, in the other, the rocks of Hare Tor, in which case his line of retreat was cut off. Cocking his revolver, he began to move slowly up slope, not towards the rocks, which would provide shelter for whatever might be among them, but somewhat to the side, where he could be sure of getting a clean shot.

Moments before he had been doubting the entire story and even wondering if Wolfe was suffering from the not inconsiderable strain imposed by his career. Now he had no doubts whatsoever in his colleague's genius. The sound had been unearthly, and of extraordinary volume, but there was no question in his mind that it had been made by a dog, ghostly or otherwise.

Harland Wolfe had instantly dismissed all possibility of the supernatural, but Dr Manston wasn't so sure, and had to remind himself forcibly of the reassuringly mundane theft of Miss Stukely's nether garment in Southampton. If the creature came at him, a well-placed bullet would be enough to put an end to it, but his throat was still tight with fear as he moved towards the ridge.

No monstrous hound leapt from among the rocks, the bloodcurdling howl was not repeated, and as he came to the ridge he saw Dr Robinson far below, moving across a strip of land beyond which smoke rose from the chimneys of a line of quarrymen's cottages. He returned his revolver to his pocket and hurried down the slope, waving his stick for attention. Dr Robinson seemed not to notice until they were only a couple of hundred yards apart, but then stopped and they had quickly come together.

'Did you hear that call?' Dr Manston asked, doing his best not to show his agitation.

'A quarter hour or so ago, from somewhere towards the mires?' Dr Robinson queried, apparently none too concerned. 'Yes I did. It was a bittern, I believe.'

'A bittern?' Dr Manston demanded.

'A species of heron,' Dr Robinson explained, '*Botaurus stellaris*, not common in these parts admittedly, but . . .'

'I known what a bittern is . . .' Dr Manston interrupted, then hastily apologised. 'I am sorry, I confess to a degree of agitation. I would have sworn it was the call of a hound, and one of unusual size at that.'

Dr Robinson gave a somewhat forced laugh.

'No, no, although it is an easy enough mistake to make and I can appreciate your concern. The moor is an odd place, and can play tricks on the mind, particularly if one is alone.'

'So I see,' Dr Manston agreed, despite being far from convinced, 'but in any event I think I will conclude my researches for the day. Are you heading towards the Hall?'

'More or less,' Dr Robinson answered. 'I was called to a case of measles at Wapsworthy Cottages and was making my way home.'

'Then I shall join you, if I may,' Dr Manston responded.

Richard Truscott swallowed the brandy in his glass and poured out another measure. Despite his best efforts to make a show of bravado in front of Genevieve Stukely the events on the moor had left him distinctly unsettled. The awful howling noise had not been repeated, but that did little to calm his nerves. He had lived on the edge of Dartmoor all his life and never heard anything like it. Even the baying of the local pack in full chase was put to shame, and that was audible on the flank of the moor from Driscoll's.

Now, as he sat by his window in the dark to wait for a light from the folly, he was having to remind himself that he was the hunter rather than the hunted. The moon was up, creating patterns in a wrack of clouds and throwing Dartmoor into black relief, also Burley Down. For all his rationality it was easy to populate such a landscape with great ghostly hounds, and to dwell on the legends of the past.

He remembered how he had laughed when told that a book of ghostly tales had been published telling how the ghost of Devil John rode out from the old estate with his hounds on moonlit nights, and his anger at the more salacious volume claiming that John's son Henry had driven a sulky around the paths at Driscoll's with his naked maids harnessed up in place of horses. His father had even considered a lawsuit, but with the original sulky and some very peculiar leather harness rotting in one of the stable stalls the idea had been abandoned.

After another swallow of brandy he tried to tell himself that he wasn't so very different from Henry, or Devil John himself for that matter, and that if he did meet their ghosts on Burley Down they would probably give him an encouraging word, or come to watch while he sodomised Eliza. The thought put a smile on his face and he lifted the brandy glass once more, only to stop with it held an inch from his mouth. High on Burley Down, a light had flashed on.

There could be no mistaking it: white and clear, suddenly extinguished and then coming again – a signal. Richard swallowed the rest of his brandy and tossed the empty glass onto his bed. Moving closer to the window pane, he peered out into the night. The signal came again, then stopped, leaving the land black once more and the night silent all around him. He stayed exactly still, his eye fixed to the gunmetal sheen of the lawns, which anyone on their way to the down would be forced to cross.

For a long while nothing happened, until he had begun to doubt even that he had seen the light, before he caught a faint click, right on the threshold of audibility. A moment later a shadow shifted by the stable yard, and a grey figure moved out onto the lawn, unmistakably female, but not nearly tall enough for Eliza, or even Victoria.

'By God, it's Lucy!' he hissed. 'The little minx!'

He moved quickly, slipping from his room and down the stairs as silently as he was able. In the hall he selected the sword stick from the rack, telling himself it was a sensible precaution in case there was trouble with her lover and had nothing to do with his night fears. Devil John, he was sure, would have gone without hesitation, but armed.

Letting himself from the back door, he scanned the lawns, but there was no sign of Lucy. He moved slowly forwards, keeping to the shadows as he made his way down past the lake. The gate was open, and he cursed quietly, telling himself that whatever else might happen, Lucy had earned herself a whipping. He locked it behind him and started up the zigzag, keeping to the verge as he began to consider his best course of action.

First, he would need to identify the lover. In the enticing but highly unlikely event that it was another woman he would wait until they were lost to their passion and then accost them together and make a thorough pig of himself at their expense. If it was an old man who had somehow managed to inveigle Lucy into selling herself he would simply accost the fellow on the spot, perhaps making him watch while Lucy was put through her paces. If it was a young man he would wait until the two of them were done, enjoying the view, and afterwards, sodomise Lucy in her own juices.

It was a tempting prospect, and he hurried forwards, sure that Lucy would have at least five minutes on him, and keen not to miss the show. Only when he reached the top of the woods did he slow, a trifle breathless, and move more cautiously forwards to where the folly stood out black against the sky. A flicker of light sprang up within and he stopped, his heart now beating fast. He caught a glimpse of Lucy's face, and something else, a parcel.

At the thought of her pilfering the house he moved forwards with greater purpose, telling himself that if it was the case he'd double her whipping. He caught her voice, barely more than a whisper, and another in reply, male, and so harsh that he faltered in his step. Lucy was now clearly visible, unwrapping her parcel, which proved to contain bread, a hunk of cheese and a bottle of beer. Somewhat puzzled, he moved closer still, to the back of the temple.

He peered cautiously inside, just in time to find himself face to face with a great squat man, wild-eyed, dirty and bearded, his massive frame clad in the torn remnants of prison garb. Richard swore, snatching at the handle of his sword stick, but too late as the man shot out one great fist. Lucy screamed as Richard staggered back under the blow, measuring his length on the grass as the man leapt over him and away into the night, still clutching his bread and cheese.

'Damn!' Richard swore. 'My eye, how that hurts!'

Lucy had come to him, babbling incoherently as she knelt by his side, words that only slowly became distinct as his head cleared.

'... do not, reveal me, please? I beg of you, sir. I know it is wrong, but he is my cousin, and such a sweet boy, when he was a lad, but drink turned his mind and he became as he is, and ...'

'What in hell's name are you gabbling about?' Richard managed, sitting up. 'That was the convict they're looking for, Sugden, wasn't it? He's your cousin?'

'Yes, sir, my cousin,' Lucy went on. 'Aunt Edith's sister Agnes' boy ...'

'Your aunt, at Stukely Hall?'

'Yes, sir. She and uncle Jan were giving him food, but with the detective there and Black Shuck abroad, they asked that he could come to me. I could not refuse, as you must surely see, though I know I have done wrong, and I beg you not to report the matter, sir ...'

'For goodness sake shut up for a moment,' Richard broke in. 'I'm hardly going to turn you into the police, am I, in the circumstances?'

'No, sir, I don't suppose you would,' Lucy admitted.

'Exactly,' Richard agreed, 'but your damn cousin can go and feed himself somewhere else from now on.'

'But, sir ...'

'I'll have no excuses, Lucy. You left the damn gate unlocked, do you realise that? I ought to whip you until you bleed!'

'No, sir, please!' Lucy begged. 'Whip me if you must,

but if I am not to help him, how will poor little Billy feed himself?'

'Poor Little Billy?' Richard snorted. 'The man's a hulking great brute, Lucy, and a maniac too, by all accounts. I dare say he can kill sheep with his bare teeth if he has a mind.'

'But sir, the carcasses would be found, and . . .'

'That was not meant as a serious suggestion, Lucy,' Richard broke in. 'Your aunt will have to look after the wretched fellow, that's all.'

'But, sir, the detective, and Black Shuck!'

'Dr Manston is no detective,' Richard pointed out. 'He's just acts as bulldog for Harland Wolfe, who's safely in Bavaria, and he has all the imagination of a granite gatepost.'

'But Black Shuck!'

'There is no Black Shuck!' Richard stormed. 'Now let's get back to the house, and you can cut me a steak for my eye.'

Four

'What in hell's name happened to you?' Charles Truscott demanded as Richard sat down at the breakfast table.

'There's no call for profanity, Charles,' his wife chided, 'but whatever has happened, dear Richard? Your poor eye is quite discoloured and looks ever so sore.'

'He's probably been fighting down at the village inn,' Victoria remarked, tilting her nose up.

'I have been doing no such thing,' Richard responded, and gave way as his father began to speak again.

'I recall a similar instance, when I was defending your mother from some blackguard of a lawyer. Great fat fellow, he was, and gave me a fine shiner, before I got him with a flattening iron.'

'I think we've heard enough, Charles,' Nell Truscott said quietly.

'The matter is in fact rather serious,' Richard went on. 'It seems this convict fellow is a cousin of Lucy's, and she's been taking food up to him. He's the one who blacked my eye, but more importantly the silly girl left the gate open on the way up.'

'Oh great heavens!' his mother exclaimed.

'No harm done, I trust?' his father queried.

'No,' Richard told him, 'but we can't have him running around the countryside. I have told her the fellow must get his victuals elsewhere in future, but she's in a fine state over it, because he was being looked after by old Edith Capleton at Stukely Hall before, and Lucy's terrified the hound will get him, although having met Billy Sugden my sympathy lies entirely with Black Shuck.'

'But what of this convict?' Nell demanded. 'He is a most dreadful man by all accounts, and surely quite desperate.'

'Desperate not to be caught, that's for certain,' Richard agreed. 'But as long as he's being fed I don't suppose he's a threat to anyone so long as they keep their distance.'

'You'll have to make it plain to her he's not to come near,' Charles Truscott insisted. 'Imagine the consequences if a lot of Peelers descended on the district? Lucy can tell her damn aunt to deal with the matter, and I dare say a few shillings would be well spent to make sure they do as they're told.'

'My thoughts exactly,' Richard agreed. 'I shall speak to her again, but there's no sense in her when it comes to Black Shuck. She swears her uncle's seen him several times, and apparently Ned claims to have been followed on one occasion.'

'I do not feel we should dismiss the legend so completely,' Nell Truscott put in. 'Can we doubt that there is a spirit world and that sometimes the ghosts of our ancestors return?'

'Stuff and nonsense!' Charles responded.

Richard addressed himself to a fried egg as the long familiar argument between his parents on spirituality began again. Victoria took the opportunity to slip from the table with no more than a mumbled request to get down, while he turned his thoughts back to Lucy. Now that his eye hurt rather less he had begun to wonder if the turn of events might not provide him with an excuse to give her a proper whipping. It would be fun, without question, and she would probably submit herself to it easily enough if he presented it as just punishment for her behaviour. If she squealed too much and aroused attention, he could always explain that he'd decided it was necessary in order to get her to remember to lock gates properly in future. His mother would disapprove, but she could hardly protest.

By the time he had dabbed his mouth with his napkin he had decided to do it, but perhaps that afternoon. For the time being the long night was catching up with him and it seemed a better idea to doze in the hammock slung between two ancient apple trees beside the front lawn. He went out and made himself comfortable, only to find Lucy herself rolling milk churns out from the stable yard. After watching her work for a few minutes he called out.

'Lucy, my dear, a minute of your time, please, when you're done with that.'

'Yes, sir,' she called, and Richard relaxed back, enjoying the idea forming in his mind.

Presently Lucy ran over, bobbing a curtsey beside his hammock.

'Last night,' Richard remarked, 'you left the gate open.'

'Yes, sir,' she answered, 'and I can't apologise enough, sir.'

'Your apologies last night were quite sufficient,' he told her. 'I am more concerned with whether you will repeat your mistake.'

'No, sir, never again, sir, I promise, sir,' Lucy stammered. 'I won't forget, sir.'

'You won't,' he assured her, 'and the reason you won't is that I intend to whip your bottom for you, hard enough to make absolutely sure you never forget again.'

Her pretty face began to work in distress, filling him with a cruel glee and he went on, savouring every word.

'I'm sorry, Lucy, but it has to be done. You understand, I'm sure, that it simply won't do, Lucy, when you're coming and going all the time, and I'm sure you appreciate that it's for your own good?'

'Yes, sir,' Lucy answered miserably.

'Splendid,' Richard answered her, 'and to make absolutely certain you don't forget I aim to make a little ritual of the matter. First, you are to fetch a pair of pruning shears and cut a quantity of birch twigs, from along here, so that I can see you're doing it properly . . . whatever is the matter, girl?'

Lucy's face had begun to work more furiously still, and there was a catch in her voice as she spoke.

'Please not here, Mr Richard, sir. Mr Gurney will see, and he'll know what I'm about, and Eliza, like as not, and cook, and Ned Annaferd, and . . .'

'Good,' Richard interrupted, 'to have your fellow servants know you're going to be beaten will do wonders for your humility. You rather like Ned Annaferd, too, unless I'm very much mistaken, and I'm sure he'd love to see you thrashed, so you should be grateful for the opportunity, I rather think.'

He was having considerable difficulty keeping his tone of voice serious, while the self-pitying look on Lucy's face and the way her breasts had begun to quiver beneath her bodice were setting his cock hard in his trousers. If he carried on tormenting her she was sure to notice, and probably to realise that he was far from sincere. She was still standing there, opening and closing her mouth as she tried to find some effective protest, which made it even harder not to laugh.

'Come on, run along with you,' he told her.

She went off back towards the stable yard, her face set in a gloriously sulky pout. Richard tucked his arms behind his head to give himself a better view of the straggling birch trees further towards the gates of the estate and settled down to enjoy himself.

Lucy was soon back, now red in the face from having to ask Luke Gurney for the pruning shears and presumably explain why she needed them. Richard allowed himself a light chuckle at the thought, but did his best to maintain a stern look as she began to cut birch twigs. She was trembling so badly she kept dropping them, while the way her bottom stirred beneath her dress every time she reached up to make a cut was making it difficult to contain himself at all. As soon as she'd got a decent handful together he called her over.

'That should suffice,' he announced. 'Now take a ribbon from your hair and bind them together to make your whip.'

Her response was a single miserable nod, and her hands were shaking badly as she undid the ribbon and used it to lash the birch twigs together. Richard gave a thoughtful nod as he surveyed the result. At his school the thing would hardly have qualified as a birch at all, but it would no doubt prove effective enough on Lucy's tender little bottom.

'I will at least spare you the shame of being whipped in public,' he remarked, although he would never have dared do it. 'Up to my room with you.'

He climbed out of the hammock and made his way indoors, Lucy following with her head hung low and the birch dangling from one hand. Richard climbed the stairs as quickly as he could, not wishing to have to answer any awkward questions, but nobody else seemed to be around. In his room he quickly locked the door behind them, and tried to keep his voice even as he addressed her.

'When I spanked you before it was for pleasure. This is a punishment. Now bend across the bed and bare your bottom.'

'Yes, sir,' Lucy answered, and her hands had gone back to her skirts.

Richard watched in rising excitement as she stripped herself with trembling fingers. She had no proper bustle, only a small horsehair pad beneath her maid's dress, and a single petticoat, so as it all came up she was left showing the seat of her cheap cotton drawers, so thin that the outline of her buttocks was clearly visible beneath. For a moment she hesitated, before putting her hands to the rear split and spreading her drawers to expose herself, her sweetly rounded bottom now bare and inviting, with the cleft promising yet more intimate secrets as she bent down over the bed.

'Stick it out,' Richard ordered, stepping close.

Lucy obeyed, pulling her back in with a little sob as her cheeks parted, revealing the pouted rear lips of her well furred cunt and the soft dimple of her anus. He took up the birch and tapped it on her bottom, making her clench her cheeks in apprehension for the coming pain.

'Four dozen strokes, I think,' he said, 'which you will count, and if you lose count, we will start again. Do you understand?'

'Yes, sir,' she answered, her voice a sob, and Richard smacked the birch down across her bottom.

She let out a squeal like a tormented pig and immediately went into a little pained dance with her legs kicking up and down and her buttocks jiggling frantically, a sight at once so ridiculous and so erotic that Richard had to steady himself against the bed post. Very sure she wasn't paying attention, he quickly adjusted the rock-hard pole of his cock in his trousers.

'One,' she gasped, when she'd finally managed to bring herself under control.

'Yes, one,' he replied, 'and if you make such a fuss with every stroke we're going to be here all morning, aren't we? Now get back in position.'

Lucy obeyed, now snivelling slightly as she stuck out her bottom to let her cheeks part and make the best possible target for the birch, which Richard raised high before bringing it down hard. Again she squealed and kicked, but this time he laid another stroke in before she could recover herself, another, and more, whipping her with firm regular strokes as she went into an agonised wriggling display and struggled to count the blows at the same time.

By six she was gasping, whimpering and shaking her head between ever louder squeals and jerks of her body, yet still trying to count and to keep her bottom stuck well out. By the dozen she'd begun to cry, snivelling out her feelings with the spit running down her chin and her nose a mess of snot. By two dozen she'd lost control altogether, writhing against the bed, so that he was forced to twist her arms behind her back to keep her bent into position. By three dozen every last bit of resistance seemed to have been beaten from her body and she lay whimpering passively over the bed as he thrashed her. By four dozen she was slumped with her legs akimbo, her cunt spread wide and wet, the red arc of her maidenhead clearly visible, all sense of modesty gone as she lay gasping and shaking in her pain.

She'd stopped counting long before, but Richard was in no mood to be pedantic. His cock felt fit to burst, and he could no longer even be bothered to keep up the pretence of giving her a punishment. Quickly pulling his fly wide, he freed his erection and sank down behind her, lapping at the thick white juice running from her cunt and teasing it up between her buttocks to lubricate her anus.

Lucy managed a choking sob as she realised she was to be buggered, but that was all. Sure he would come in his hand if he didn't get his cock up her soon, Richard spent only a short while licking her cunt and anus to get the smaller of the two holes open, then stood and pressed his cock between her flaming welted cheeks. He watched the head go in, her ring spreading, wet and slimy to the pressure, and pushed, sinking his cock up her bottom hole to the neck, and deeper, forcing himself up inch by inch until his full length was immersed in the tight warmth of her rectum.

There was no mistaking the tone of her gasps as he buggered her, not pain but pleasure, for all the criss-cross of tiny red welts covering the skin of her bottom and for all the thickness of his shaft straining out her anal ring. He chuckled, enjoying her helpless ecstasy just as he had enjoyed her humiliation and her pain. It was all too good, far too good, and with a last animal grunt he had spunked up her bottom.

No sooner had Richard Truscott extracted his cock from her rectum than Lucy Capleton ran from the room and to her own, where she quickly jammed a chair under the door handle before throwing herself onto the bed, face down. Her hands went back, pulling up her dress and opening her splitters to go bare bottom, and one hand stayed behind her to stroke the welts left by Richard Truscott's birch. It felt so good, an exquisite hot stinging that came together at the wet eager heart of her quim, better even than the aftermath of a good spanking. Her sole regret was that it hadn't been harder, and longer, because she felt she needed more, a lot more.

A sigh escaped her lips as she continued to explore her welts and the hot thick skin between. She knew it was wrong, that only a sinful dirty girl would enjoy the things men did to her, let alone do the things she did in response, but she already knew she was a sinful dirty girl and would do it anyway. There was still guilt to push down as her fingers slipped between her bottom cheeks, but that didn't stop her touching her freshly buggered anus. Richard's come was still oozing from the sore little hole, and with a last touch of regret for her lost innocence she inserted a finger deep into the hot sloppy interior as she remembered how good his cock felt in the same dirty cavity.

Her other hand went under her tummy to find her cunt and she was masturbating freely, one finger working her bottom hole while another rubbed on the tiny sensitive bump between her sex lips. She thought of her punishment, how awful it had felt to be made to pick and bind her own birch where everybody could see, how full of shame she'd been as she bared her bottom, how the pain had been unendurable at first, making her lose count, only to give way to a helpless heated ecstasy which had held as the whipping finished, as she was sodomised and spunked up, as she masturbated her dirty little bottom hole and her aching creamy cunt to a blinding dizzying orgasm that left her panting weakly on the bed with spots dancing in front of her eyes.

She stayed as she was for a long while, her finger still well up her bottom, thinking vague thoughts of how she really ought to be helping cook, but too exhausted to move. A lot of guilt had come back, as it always did when she had finished with herself, but she knew she'd be doing it again before too long, perhaps, once her bottom had healed, after another, harder birching. Not that she could possibly ask for such a degrading punishment, but if she left the gate open again, only when it was safe naturally, perhaps she would get what she needed.

Victoria Truscott reined in Cloud beside the grey bulk of Great Links Tor. She found it an amusing irony that while she had been forbidden to ride on Dartmoor the convict had all the while been lurking on Burley Down, and so had made her escape from the breakfast table before her parents could get around to banning her from riding out altogether, which seemed inevitable. It was also intensely frustrating, robbing her of her greatest pleasure in life, at least, her greatest pleasure besides toying with herself, and that at least she knew she would always be able to do.

What was more, the convict was cousin to Lucy Capleton, who was therefore clearly responsible for him being around at all, and while the thought of a wild desperate man excited Victoria, it also frightened her. To imagine herself caught and used up her recently deflowered quim was one thing; to see her brother with a black eye and think how she might so easily have been waylaid was quite another.

She had still been in the stable yard while Lucy made the birch, and had watched with considerable satisfaction, only sorry that it wouldn't be her who applied the thing to the stupid girl's rump. As she rode out she had been wondering if it might be practical to do so when, after all, Lucy was their servant and ought to do as she was told. It was a satisfying thought.

Another annoyance of being unable to ride where she pleased was that it would make the scheme she had been considering the night before a great deal more difficult, not that it was exactly simple anyway. It had always struck her as grossly unfair that even Leopold could indulge himself with apparent impunity, while she was supposed to keep herself pure until her wedding night. Now, with her maidenhead gone anyway, she could take a lover, and so enjoy the fleshy pleasures her brothers did.

Unfortunately there were problems. Her parents turned a blind eye to what Richard got up to with Lucy, and indulged Leopold because it was the only sensible course of action. That did not mean they would be so tolerant in her case. Nor could she risk somebody getting a child on her, which made her most obvious choice impractical, and indeed, most others.

She drew a heavy sigh as she turned Cloud back towards Arms Tor for the long gallop, wishing that life was less complicated and that she could get a good stiff fucking without endless consequences.

Dr Manston stood on the summit of Arms Tor, shaking his head ruefully. He had done his best to follow his colleague's methods, but had achieved nothing. Even the strange noise he had heard had proved to be of mundane origin, no more than the call of a rare bird, while Dartmoor was proving to be far less gloomy, sinister and lonely than he had been led to expect. Even now, the great sweep of moor rising up to the rocks of Great Links Tor could hardly be considered any such thing. Picturesque was a better description, especially with a young girl in a cheerful blue riding habit as the centrepiece, her grey pony kicking up the sods as she rode towards him at a joyous gallop.

Determined to further the investigation as best he could, and by no means averse to making the acquaintance of such a vivacious and apparently beautiful woman, he hailed her, raising his stick and calling out to ask if she might spare a minute of her time. She reined her pony in, casting him a single doubtful glance, then dismounted.

'Allow me to introduce myself,' he said quickly, eager not to give her cause for alarm. 'I am Doctor James Manston, the colleague of Mr Harland Wolfe, of whom you may have heard. I am currently resident at Stukely Hall, where I am investigating the unfortunate matter of Sir Robert Stukely's death.'

'Miss Victoria Truscott,' she replied boldly, and added a curtsey.

Dr Manston smiled and bowed in return. Close to, there was no doubt whatsoever that she was beautiful, with a mass of honey-blonde hair pinned up beneath her riding hat, and a bold, almost insolent face made sweet by a splash of freckles across her cheeks and nose. Her bodice, he couldn't help but notice, was pleasingly full, while the elegant lines of her riding habit promised more of the same below.

'How may I be of assistance, Dr Manston?' she enquired.

'Um ... ah ... yes, quite,' he answered, hastily jerking his thoughts back to the matter at hand. 'If I may, I would like to ask you one or two questions. I take it you are familiar with the moor?'

'This part, certainly,' she replied. 'I have ridden here since I was a little girl.'

'I see,' he replied, and on a sudden thought, changed his tack, 'but before I go on, and without wishing to seem importunate, is it wise for a young lady of your age and station to be riding alone on the moors? The convict Sugden is at large, you know.'

'I hardly think Sugden could catch my Cloud,' she laughed, patting the neck of her pony, 'and besides, with both the police and army men out looking for him, what could he possibly gain by accosting me? He would only give himself away.'

Her sheer artlessness had sent a pulse of blood to Dr Manston's cock, but he found himself too embarrassed to explain to her what the convict might like to do. Clearly she was quite unaware of the more brutal elements of human nature, and he told himself that it was not his place to destroy her innocence.

'Nevertheless,' he said, 'I would advise you to avoid the moor until the fellow is caught. However, as you are so familiar with the area, may I ask if you have noticed anything unusual over the last few months?'

'I haven't seen any spectral hounds, if that's what you mean,' she answered him, followed by a laugh at once so full of joy and contempt that it sent the blood to his cheeks. 'But there is a man living on the moor, and I do not mean Billy Sugden. He's a gentleman, or at least, he dresses like one.'

'Are you sure of this?' Dr Manston asked. 'Can you describe him at all?'

'Absolutely sure,' she answered. 'My brother Richard has seen him too, standing on the top of Hare Tor one night. He's a tall man, rather stern looking, and he's living in one of the old tinner's huts along the Rattlebrook Valley, just where it opens out to the mires.'

'I fear I am not perfectly acquainted with the country,' Dr Manston admitted. 'Could you show me this place?'

'If you wish,' she answered.

She mounted her pony once more and set off towards the heart of the moor. Dr Manston followed, attempting to watch his footing and the enticing curves of her figure at the same time, and failing, so that by the time they were picking their way down the valley he was muddy to his knees. Victoria Truscott seemed not to notice, speaking only to point out the occasional landmark or warn him of a piece of particularly treacherous ground.

At length they reach the tinner's hut, where she took her leave. Dr Manston waited until she was out of sight before approaching the hut, his revolver drawn, but it proved empty. At least, it was empty now, but there was ample evidence of occupation. The mud of the floor was covered in boot prints, while a crude bed of bracken and reeds had been made to one side. There were crumbs and tobacco ash, also the remains of a small fire.

Well pleased with himself, and thinking of the commendations he would receive from his colleague, he began to take samples and make notes, detailing each discovery and breaking off only to glance from the door in case the mysterious occupant was approaching. After the best part of an hour he was finished and decided to leave on the grounds that he lacked proof of wrongdoing and so might well destroy the case rather than solve it if he accosted whoever was living in the hut.

His mood was buoyant as he made his way back towards the Hall. Miss Stukely would no doubt be delighted with the progress he had made, and since arriving at the Hall her opinion had become increasingly important to him. Her beautiful eyes, her bright smile, the way she gave a gentle toss of her hair when she was amused, everything about her fascinated him, to the point where as he thought of her he was also chiding himself for having admired Miss Victoria Truscott's more opulent figure.

Only at the moor gate did he stop, and abruptly. By one of the ancient granite gateposts was a piece of ash, small, yet unmistakable, and around it were other speckles and a small piece of brightly coloured paper. It could only mean one thing. A man had stood there smoking, and he was convinced the ground had been clear the day before. He took a sample, then made a careful survey of the area, which quickly revealed a number of clues.

There were footprints, his own boots and Dr Robinson's, relatively dainty ones presumably belonging to either Mrs Bloss or Mrs Capleton, possibly Miss Stukely herself, and others, larger, with a smooth sole and a square toe, not at all unlike those he had observed in the tinner's hut.

'The game is afoot,' he muttered to himself.

'You can get up now,' Nanna Bloss instructed. 'Dr Manston's back.'

Genevieve pulled back from between the big woman's thighs, using the back of her hand to wipe a generous portion of cunt cream from around her mouth.

'He'll be gone again after lunch, I'll warrant,' Nanna continued. 'You can finish me off then.'

'Yes, Nanna,' Genevieve answered, hiding a sigh as she got to her feet.

Her mouth tasted of Mrs Bloss, her bottom was hot, and her quim too. She had been spanked again, held squalling over the big woman's knee and then put on her knees to lick. Nanna Bloss had been taking her time, amusing herself by rubbing Genevieve's face into her cunt, and had been nowhere near ready to come, so Dr Manston's arrival was more of an irritation than a relief. Now she would have to be polite to him over lunch and after, knowing all the while that as soon as he went back onto the moor she would be taken back upstairs, probably spanked again and made to start where she had left off.

Having restored her appearance, she went downstairs, but was surprised to find that Dr Manston was still outside. Mrs Capleton was evidently preparing lunch as the smell of boiled mutton and cabbage suffused the air, although it didn't seem to be quite ready. Genevieve went out to join Dr Manston, whom she found crouched down halfway up the yew alley, using a large magnifying glass to examine the ground. He rose as he saw her.

'Miss Stukely!' he declared. 'I have important news, of a disturbing nature I fear, and yet which with good fortune will enable me to bring the case to a successful conclusion within a short period.'

'Do go on,' Genevieve urged.

'You will no doubt note these footprints,' he stated, pointing to the ground. 'Most can be identified as belonging to members of the household or known visitors, but not all. A man has been here. He is tall, in good physical condition, and smokes cigars of a brand made in Savannah, Georgia.'

'Who is this man?' Genevieve asked, doing her best to sound alarmed. 'Do you think he is a danger to me?'

'That would seem to be the case,' Dr Manston said, 'but do not fear, Miss Stukely. I shall guard you with my own life, if necessary, while I hope to lay this fellow by the heels in quick time. While I do not yet know his identity, I have discovered his lair, an old tinner's hut out on the moors. All that remains is to ensure there will be sufficient evidence to bring a successful prosecution and call up the police to make an arrest.'

'I declare that you are a marvel, Dr Manston,' Genevieve said warmly, 'and I feel safer in your care than that of any other.'

'It is nothing,' he replied, 'a few simple deductions, that is all, but I will say now that I hold your esteem of greater value than the merely professional. Indeed, Miss Stukely, although I have known you for but a short time . . .'

He broke off, looking suddenly uncomfortable, and Genevieve turned to see that Nanna Bloss had come out through the door.

'Doctor Manston has discovered some most important facts,' she stated. 'A man has been here, tall and in the prime of life . . .'

'How can you possibly know his size and age?' Nanna demanded.

'A simple deduction, Mrs Bloss,' Dr Manston supplied. 'The size of his boots tells us that he is of considerable height, while the degree by which they have sunk into the soil in comparison with my own allows me to judge his weight at perhaps one and one half times my own. The length of his stride is also considerably greater than my own, so he is not a ponderous man. Furthermore, the position of his cigar ash indicates that he spent some considerable time standing at the gate post, smoking, while the band from his cigar tells us that he may well be a resident of Savannah, Georgia. Are you quite well, Mrs Bloss?'

The big woman's face had turned the colour of dough.

Victoria lay back on her bed with a deep sigh. It had been wonderful, more wonderful than she could possibly have imagined, and better still for being so perfectly naughty, making a secret she knew she could never divulge to anybody, even Richard. He would be horrified, she was sure, which made it all the nicer, and as she stretched out luxuriously with her eyes closed and her mouth in a smile of serene contentment she played the scene over in her head.

She remembered the shock when she'd first seen him, and the instinctive rush of fear that had left her whole body tingling even as she realised he was not what she'd thought. She remembered the sorrowful look in his eyes and her sympathy for his hollow stomach. She remembered his cock.

It had been black, and thick, immediately tempting her to take it inside herself. She had resisted, telling herself it was not what she wanted at all, but she had known that was merely the echo of all the preaching voices down the years, the voices telling her how to behave, judging her, imposing their own values on her regardless of her needs. They spoke of God, and the promise of heaven and the threat of hell, but his thick black cock had been more desirable than anything they could offer, no matter what the cost.

Had it not been safe she knew she could never have done it, but the little cluster of rocks where they'd met had been just as safe as she could imagine. With Cloud tethered by the edge of the mire she'd known she would get warning if anyone did approach, and the rocks and the three little thorn trees had them hidden completely from view, leaving her quite alone with him, and his thick black cock.

At first she had merely spoken to him, promising to bring him some food and a warm blanket, and telling herself over and over again that she wouldn't give in to her desire. He had been willing from the first, his cock stirring just from her presence, and as it grew larger, so had the temptation to touch. When she'd finally given in and reached out to take it in her hand the shock had been something close to orgasm.

She'd told herself that was all she would do, just touch, but like any man he had grown excited, quickly swelling to full glorious erection in her hand. She had told herself that she would just masturbate him and later toy with her quim over the memory, but the feel of him in her hand and the memory of how good a cock felt in her mouth had been too much for her.

She had sucked him, and just the thought of that was enough to send a shiver through her body each time she let the words run through her brain. First she had kissed him, pouting out her lips to touch them to the hard cock shaft, still not sure if she dared actually put the huge stiff member in her mouth. She had licked him, gaining courage slowly as her arousal increased and revelling in his strong male taste. Finally her lust had overcome her and she had sucked him, a moment of pure bliss as she had opened her mouth around his shaft.

She had thought he would come, and she had wanted it, however dirty it was, done right down her throat and in her face, so that she could soil herself with his mess while she rubbed her cunt, which by then she'd known she was going to do, on the spot. All she'd got was a little salty mouthful as she'd masturbated him into her open mouth, but he'd stayed hard, and with that she'd known she was going to make the final surrender and take him in her cunt.

Undressing had been truly spiritual, infinitely more so than anything she had ever experienced in a church, stripping to give herself for the first time, stripping for the one she had chosen to take her. He had watched as she did it, never once taking his eyes from her body, his cock staying rock hard. She'd gone nude, every single last stitch gone, because that was how she wanted to be, not merely with her breasts and bottom bare or her nightie tugged up around her neck as she had been for every other sexual encounter of her life, but stark naked, the way nature had made her.

Once she was nude she'd gone back on all fours again, to suck for a while, pulling back only when he'd begun to grunt and push himself into her mouth. She'd then turned around, her bottom lifted and her back arched deep, her thighs set wide to offer the open sloppy hole between, her broken yet still virgin cunt, in which she desperately needed his cock.

He'd obliged, mounting her, and as she'd felt his weight on her back and the rough hair between her open buttocks she had known there was no going back. She'd known she was going to be fucked, and there was no getting out of it. Nor had she wanted to, sobbing in ecstasy at the feel of his cock probing for her cunt, and crying out loud at the awful, delightful moment of shame as he found his target and pushed his beautiful cock deep up inside her.

She had never imagined it would feel so good, let alone the way he had fucked her, driving himself in up her hole at a furious pace, with his belly slapping on her lifted bottom and her breasts swinging back and forth with the motion. From the moment her cunt filled she'd been reduced to a panting gasping mess, her bottom stuck up for entry as if she were a bitch on heat, her fingers clutching at the rough moorland grass and her mouth wide.

He'd fucked her exactly as she'd always wanted to be fucked, on her knees from behind, fast and hard, driving her up to a peak of arousal so strong she had slumped face down in the grass, unable to support herself. Still he'd rammed his cock in and out, humping her bottom until she was dizzy with pleasure and drooling into the long grass around her face and, as she spread her thighs in an effort to take him deeper still, his great pendulous ball sack had begun to slap on her cunt.

To have her quim slapped by his big black balls had been too much. She started to come and, as her hole began to contract on his intruding cock, so did she. As she had screamed out her pleasure into the grass she's been able to feel his come squashing out from around her well-fucked hole, to dribble down her spread cunt and wet his scrotum as it slapped between her lips. Her screams had grown louder, her contractions painfully tight, and still he'd pumped himself into her, giving her an ecstasy that had taken her to edge of madness and left her slumped as his come trickled slowly from her now fully deflowered cunt.

He had withdrawn slowly and sat down on the grass, watching patiently as Victoria slowly recovered her wits. It had been some while before she'd found the strength to dress, and so wonderful had her experience been that she had experienced no great difficulty in suppressing her qualms and guilt for what she'd done. After all, if God had given them the facility to take such pleasure in each other, how could it be wrong?

Not that she was going to tell anybody, and the very fact that she had such a secret gave an added touch to her satisfaction as she stretched once more, now thinking of how she would wait until the house was quiet, or at least as quiet as it ever was with Leopold around, and then masturbate herself to a slow climax, perhaps with a candle pushed in up her cunt so that she could imagine it was his cock.

It would happen again, she told herself as she rolled over onto her face and stuck her bottom up a little, of that there was no question. She couldn't wait long, and her orgasm couldn't wait at all. Quickly pulling up her nightie to get her bottom bare, she slipped a hand between her thighs and began to rub, her mind running over all the delicious details of her virgin fucking, until at last she fixed on the thought of how she would have looked with him on her back, black on white, a picture at once so exquisite and so utterly, superbly naughty she could no longer hold back her orgasm.

Satisfied, if only briefly, her mind went to the practicalities of the situation and her promise of food and a warm blanket. It was a promise she intended to keep, even if she didn't get fucked again, but at dinner that night her parents had made it very clear indeed that she was not to ride out at all, unless it was with Richard or Luke Gurney. Her only option then was to make very sure that the police learnt the whereabouts of Billy Sugden and put him under arrest.

Five

'Did you know that Dr Robinson employs a negro cook?' Richard Truscott asked conversationally.

'Is he any good?' his father enquired, forking half a sausage into his mouth.

'Trained in Paris, apparently.'

'Ah, ha, well no doubt we will be invited to dine, once this business with the convict and the hound has died down. Do we have any news, by the way?'

'Yes, I do. Lucy assures me that Sugden will in future be feeding at his aunt's.'

'I might ride there again, please, Papa?' Victoria enquired.

'No you may not,' Charles growled.

'I wouldn't advise it,' Richard added. 'He claims he's seen the hound, apparently, and dare not go back out on the moor.'

'Where do you suppose he might be then?' Victoria asked. 'Not on our land, surely.'

'Lydford Woods, perhaps?' Richard suggested. 'There's plenty of shelter, and I understand there have been reported sightings near Bovey and at Dunsford, so the police are on entirely the wrong side of the moor.'

'He's a damn nuisance, wherever he is,' Charles put in. 'In Devil John's day he'd have set the pack on the fellow, but if you do that sort of thing nowadays you'd never hear the end of it.'

'So I should hope,' Nell Truscott remarked.

'I imagine Lucy would be rather upset,' Richard said. 'She seems extraordinarily fond of him, considering his character. Isn't it strange how the gentlest women often seem to have a partiality for maniacs.'

'Don't speak about your brother that way, Richard,' Nell chided.

Richard shrugged and went back to his breakfast, only to remember the other detail he had learnt from Genevieve when he had dined at Stukely Hall the previous evening.

'Oh, yes, and that Manston fellow has apparently found someone living rough on the moor and lurking about at the rear of Stukely Hall, an American apparently, but a gentleman all the same. Miss Stukely is taking it very calmly, but that awful Bloss woman seems terrified.'

'We must leave, Ginny!' Nanna Bloss declared. 'And the sooner the better.'

'I am not leaving, Nanna,' Genevieve responded. 'This is my home now, and I am a lady of some fortune . . .'

'You're a little backstairs brat, that's what you are, and always will be,' Mrs Bloss cut her off. 'Now will you see sense, or do I have to tan your hiney until you do?'

'Not again, please,' Genevieve pleaded. 'I am still sore from the last time, and no matter how often you spank me it will make no difference. Eventually we must face our fate, and here there is at least a good chance that Dr Manston will catch Saul Roper before he can reach us.'

'Roper would tear Dr Manston apart with his bare hands!'

'Dr Manston has served in the British Army . . .'

'As a surgeon!'

'. . . and carries his revolver at all times.'

'Do you imagine Saul Roper goes unarmed?'

'I am tired of running,' Genevieve responded. 'I have made my home here and intend to stay. If you wish to leave I will provide you with . . . with a thousand pounds.'

'Oh, you'd like that, wouldn't you?' Nanna Bloss answered. 'Well, that's not how it's going to be. You're coming with me, my girl, and you'll pay my way, or you know what happens.'

'But, Nanna,' Genevieve protested. 'It is hardly my difficulty if Saul Roper has caught up with us. I will not go, and that is my last word on the matter.'

'I'll see you disgraced,' Nanna Bloss threatened.

'Nanna, please, be sensible,' Genevieve urged. 'Leave for a while, and when Saul Roper is safely jailed you may return. Perhaps you would like to visit southern France, where I believe the climate is most agreeable?'

'They've no reason to jail Roper, not here,' Nanna Bloss pointed out, 'and if he can find us here he can find me in France. Now do as I say or it'll go the worse for you.'

'But, Nanna . . .' Genevieve began.

Nanna Bloss' response was a snort, cutting Genevieve off as she reached out. Genevieve managed a single plaintive squeak as she was hauled forwards and across the big woman's knees, one of which immediately kicked up to get her bottom in prime spanking position.

'Nanna!' Genevieve squealed. 'No! Not again!'

'Yes, again,' Nanna Bloss answered her as she began to fiddle with Genevieve's skirts. 'It's the only thing that keeps my mind from Saul Roper, this is, and I've a mind to teach you some respect and all.'

Genevieve didn't answer, but her face had set in her usual sulky pout as her bottom was prepared for spanking, skirts and bustle turned up, drawers unbuttoned and the panel folded back to show off her bare bottom. Nanna Bloss' hand settled on her cheeks and she braced herself for the pain, only to start as a low cough sounded from behind her. Twisting around, she saw that Capleton the butler was standing in the doorway and her face flamed scarlet with humiliation. She struggled to get up, but Nanna Bloss kept her firmly in place as she spoke.

'What is it, Capleton? Can't you see I'm busy about a private matter.'

'The post, Madame,' Capleton replied tonelessly, although he had allowed his eyes to stray to Genevieve's rear view.

Nanna Bloss gave another snort and picked up the letter he was holding out to her on a silver tray, still keeping Genevieve firmly in place. Capleton had obviously heard what was going on and come in deliberately, Genevieve decided, and promised herself that she would dismiss both him and his miserable wife as soon as was possible.

The spanking still did not begin, Nanna Bloss resting an elbow in Genevieve's back to hold her in place as she opened the letter, only to give a gasp of horror and let go. Taken completely by surprise, Genevieve fell off, sprawling legs akimbo on the carpet to provide Capleton with a fine view of her spread quim just as he turned back to see what the matter was.

Around her on the carpet lay five small desiccated orange pips.

Dr Manston walked briskly up the slope towards Hare Tor, his face set in grim determination, his hand clutching the butt of the revolver in his pocket. With the threat sent to Mrs Bloss the time to wait was past and the time to act upon him. The unfortunate woman was now resting in her bed, attended to by Mrs Capleton.

The sun was strong in his face and the heat had yet to begin to fade from the day, but he barely slowed until he had crossed the ridge and could look down into the Rattlebrook Valley. The stone hut stood as before, with no sign of life evident, yet he approached carefully, moving from rock to rock and doing his best to keep the folds of the land between himself and his target. Once across the stream, he moved up the slope, making certain he could not be seen from the doorway. He reached the hut, slipped his revolver free and cocked the hammer, took a last deep breath and rushed in, to find it empty.

For a moment he stood nonplussed, the pace of his heart gradually declining to a normal rate. If the man was not there, he might be anywhere, perhaps collecting victuals, perhaps about some sinister deed, perhaps even near the Hall. Yet the police had been called and Capleton was standing guard with a shotgun, while the hut was clearly still in use. He decided to stay, and sat down, grim faced, with the revolver cocked in his lap.

An hour passed, and a second, with the sun moving slowly across the sky and the shadows gradually lengthening. Now and again he would peer cautiously from the door, but saw only ravens and the sheep grazing on the opposite side of the narrow valley. His patience began to wear thin, but he clung doggedly to his resolve, pacing back and forth in the confines of the hut, until, as his watch showed that afternoon had moved on to evening, he at last stepped outside.

A man was visible, some way up the valley, and Dr Manston jerked back into the shadows of the hut, his heart hammering once more. Flattened against the wall immediately beside the door, he waited, listening. He caught the scrape of a boot on rock, a click perhaps made by a walking cane striking granite, and nearby.

'It is a lovely evening, my dear Manston,' said a well-known voice. 'I really think that you will be more comfortable outside than in.'

'Great heavens, Wolfe!' Dr Manston cried as he emerged from the hut. 'However did you get here?

However did you know I was in the hut? No, don't answer that, doubtless I left a dozen obvious clues. Come inside. There is a desperate fellow in hiding here, and . . .'

'I hope I am not entirely desperate?' Harland Wolfe replied. 'Indeed, but for a few minor particulars I think I have my case complete.'

'Complete?' Dr Manston echoed. 'Well if that is so you have the advantage of me, the more so now that my only real lead has gone, and frankly, Wolfe, I do think you might have told me.'

'To the contrary,' Harland Wolfe replied. 'You have many skills, my dear Manston, but acting is not one of them. Only by having you genuinely believe I was far away could I be sure you would not somehow reveal my presence, and to do so would have been to put our man on his guard. Besides, am I not right in thinking that had you known I was here you would have consulted me by now?'

'Today, certainly, if not before,' Dr Manston admitted. 'There has been the most extraordinary development. Not an hour ago Mrs Bloss, who is Miss Stukely's companion, received a most singular missive, an envelope, with no inclusion save for five dried orange pips, at the sight of which she fainted dead away, and is still in hysterics.'

'Singular, certainly,' Harland Wolfe replied. 'I trust you noted the postmark?'

'Certainly. It was handed in at Lydford Post Office, perhaps two miles from Stukely Hall.'

'As I might have suspected,' Harland Wolfe said.

'I know something of the villain behind this too . . .' Dr Manston began, and stopped. 'Unless . . . I confess to confusion, my dear fellow. If it is you who has been living here, then was it also you who stood at the gate to the rear of Stukely Hall smoking a Savannah cigar and wearing square-toed boots?'

Harland Wolfe gave a light laugh.

'We shall make a detective of you yet, Manston! But no, it was not me who stood at the gate to the rear of Stukely Hall smoking a Savannah cigar and wearing square-toed boots. You have read my monograph on the distinctive ashes of cigars, cigarettes and pipe tobaccos, have you not?'

'Why, yes,' Dr Manston replied.

'Then surely you can tell the difference between those of an English pipe and an American cigar, although perhaps without going into specific brands?'

'Frankly, no,' Dr Manston confessed.

Harland Wolfe gave a tolerant smile and continued.

'Nor was it me who carefully affixed a number of scuff marks around the catches of the lower windows of Stukely Hall to make it look as if there had been an attempt at forcing entry, a clue you appear to have overlooked.'

'Who then?' Dr Manston demanded. 'We must lay hands on this fellow without delay, Wolfe, before a mischief is done!'

'I hardly think that is necessary,' Harland Wolfe replied, staring down the side of the valley. 'Indeed, at present my most urgent requirement is for a hot meal followed by an equally hot bath. Even in fine spring weather the Dartmoor streams carry a chill.'

'But . . .'

'I shall explain all presently, perhaps over dinner. Meanwhile, pray indulge me. Is Mrs Capleton a competent cook?'

'Her food is a little plain, perhaps, and the house is naturally in something of a foment.'

'Ah ha, perhaps one of the local inns might prove a better choice. I wonder if lobster might be too much to ask? West Country lobster is said to be excellent, and . . .'

'I do feel you're not taking this entirely seriously, Wolfe,' Dr Manston interrupted. 'What of the murderer?'

'The murderer,' Harland Wolfe replied, 'is biding his time, and so must we.'

Genevieve smiled and bobbed a curtsey as the tall man entered the room.

'May I introduce Mr Harland Wolfe,' Dr Manston stated, his voice curiously grave in comparison to before.

'Delighted,' Genevieve responded, bobbing once more. 'Have you eaten, Mr Wolfe? Perhaps . . .'

'Dr Manston and I have dined very well, thank you,' Harland Wolfe replied, 'and over the course of dinner he has explained the situation in great detail.'

'Are you able to help us, Mr Wolfe?' Genevieve asked.

'I hope to bring the case to a conclusion, certainly,' Harland Wolfe responded, 'although in practice it has now become two cases, for one of which I have no client. Perhaps if you would be so kind as to shut the door, Dr Manston.'

Genevieve watched, now somewhat alarmed, as Dr Manston did so.

'First, Miss Stukely,' Harland Wolfe stated, 'you should have no doubt that your life is at risk. I say this not to frighten you, but as a plain statement of fact. However, so long as you on no account go out onto the moor alone, you are quite safe.'

'I am relieved to hear it, Mr Wolfe,' Genevieve replied.

'No doubt,' he agreed, 'but the situation is a serious one, and I really do feel that, whatever your motives, your attempts to frighten Mrs Bloss can only make matters unnecessarily complicated, perhaps dangerously so.'

'Mr Wolfe!' Genevieve began, but was silenced by a gesture of his hand.

'Pray do not trouble to deny it, Miss Stukely,' he stated. 'I have watched as you laid your clues, the footprints, the ash and so forth and, in any event, I think I can say without false modesty that they would not have distracted me for long.'

Genevieve burst into tears, immediately inciting the sympathy of Dr Manston, while Harland Wolfe merely shook his head.

'There is little use in theatrical display, Miss Stukely,' Harland Wolfe stated. 'However, no real harm has been done and I ask only that you do nothing further to interfere with the case.'

'Thank you,' Genevieve sobbed.

'However,' Harland Wolfe went on, 'from the strength of Mrs Bloss' reaction on receiving the five orange pips it is clear that there is a background to the situation, perhaps one that might interest me professionally. If I give you my word that the matter will go not further, perhaps you would be good enough to explain?'

Genevieve gave a miserable shake of her head.

'I cannot, Mr Wolfe,' she begged, 'and I must implore you as a gentleman to let the matter rest. In return I promise you I will do nothing further, and no doubt Mrs Bloss will recover presently. I am sorry, truly, and to you also, Dr Manston, for you have been so kind to me, and I have deceived you cruelly.'

'Please don't mention it, my dear,' Dr Manston responded, patting her hand.

Lucy Capleton made a last adjustment to her pad and pulled her drawers closed behind. Her quim now felt comfortably secure, and there was no denying the pleasure of the way the strings lifted her buttocks, making them feel fuller and keeping her conscious of her rear charms, to say nothing of the slippery open feeling of her well-buttered bottom hole.

Content with her preparations, she returned to the kitchen, where her tray was ready, with a wooden bowl full of steaming gallimaufry and a tankard of water. She picked it up and made her way upstairs, a little nervous as always despite what had become a familiar twice daily routine, and as was so often the case when she reached the second floor landing she had to remind herself that her position was absolutely secure and that she earned some three times what a maid might normally have expected.

Her tummy gave a twitch as she bumped open the door to Richard's room with her bottom, but he was downstairs, drinking a preprandial cocktail and could neither assist her nor molest her. The window was closed, the room warm with orange sunlight, making it a trifle stuffy but distinctly masculine in aroma. Lucy closed her eyes and drew the scent in, her body responding instinctively with a slight hardening of her nipples and a warm flush between her thighs.

Setting the tray down, she opened the inner door, moved the tray after her and locked the door once more, a routine now so familiar she barely had to think about it. The masculine odour had become notably stronger, and grew almost rank as she pushed the second door open and peered cautiously within. Unlike Richard's room, the shutters were closed, plunging everything into a hot reeking gloom.

'Mr Leopold?' she queried.

There was no response. She drew a heavy sigh and quickly put the tray down once more.

'Up to your little tricks again, I suppose?' she said.

She was grabbed, powerful arms closing on her from behind, and even as her squeal of alarm broke from her lips her bodice had been ripped wide, spilling her breasts out of her chemise. They were taken in hand, each plump globe squeezed hard as she was marched quickly to the bed and thrown down across it. She lay shaking but passive as her skirts were thrown up and her splitters pulled apart. With her bottom bare she lifted it, to have an already rock-hard cock immediately forced in up her soft buttery anus and jammed to the hilt in her rectum.

As he began to bugger her she was regretting the amount of time she would need to spend with needle and thread to repair her torn bodice, but the movement of his erection up her bottom had quickly pushed away all such mundane thoughts. For a moment she took it, panting out her feelings as her breasts swung wildly and her body shuddered to the hard deep thrusts, but knew there was no point in hiding her true feelings, not with Leopold. She reached back, rubbing at her pad to press the firm bulk against her quim.

He was already grunting, and she knew he'd have been nursing his erection for an hour or more in anticipation of her arrival. Sure enough, a few more hard pumps and he'd come, holding his cock deep in up her bottom with his massive hands locked tight to her hips as he filled her rectum with sperm. She was still rubbing, as hard as she could, and just managed it, her anus going into spasm on his cock shaft just as he began to pull out, so that as her climax tore through her she had a mixture of come and butter bubbling out of her gaping bottom hole and down over her fingers.

By the time she was properly finished, Leopold was already busily eating his dinner, and he gave her a toothy smile as she rolled over, content as always after he had sodomised her. Lucy returned the smile and sat up, waiting until he was finished before she retrieved the tray, taking care to unlock and relock each door in turn as she went. In Richard's room she paused to blow her breath out. As always her buggering had been sudden, fierce and not altogether satisfying.

Richard was better, slow and thoroughly rude, and for a while she allowed herself to daydream. He certainly enjoyed her body, while she knew the family secret, which removed a whole host of difficulties certain to arise with anybody else. Perhaps, just possibly, he might choose to flout the demands of his social status and marry her, but no, it was hardly likely. Better was the possibility that Ned Annaferd might begin to show interest, and as she nipped upstairs to play with herself for a second time it was him she was thinking of, and how it would feel to be first whipped in front of him, then sent to him to be sodomised as an addition to the punishment.

Victoria moved stealthily across the scullery floor and out into the stable yard. Behind her, the house was absolutely quiet, even Leopold was asleep. Outside, a gibbous moon painted the landscape gunmetal and black, a place vague and amorphous, as if, she thought, Matthew Widdery had run out of coloured paints.

It took a little courage to move out across the yard, but she reminded herself of who she was and never once hesitated as she made her way down to the gate. Thoughts of Billy Sugden were very much in her head, and her hand was locked tight on the handle of the French bayonet her grandfather had brought back from the Napoleonic wars. In the shadows of the wall the blackness was absolute, but she felt her way forwards with her fingers trailing on the wall.

Reaching the path to the village seemed to take forever, but at last she found herself clear of the woods. Her night fears were replaced with worry that somebody might see her, and she hurried forwards, the tension inside her growing ever greater as she neared Constable Apcott's cottage. It stood alone in its little garden, the scent of flowers strong in the still, warm air as Victoria scampered up to the front door and pushed her carefully prepared message through the letter box.

She retreated hastily, knowing that with the message delivered her guilt would be plain, not in the eyes of Constable Apcott and the law, but in those of her family. Her father had made it very plain that the convict and the police were to be left to their own devices, and she had directly disobeyed him, leaving her biting her lip as she hurried back towards Driscoll's.

The woods she had left so recently now formed a black and unwelcoming tunnel, but she pushed on, again feeling her way until she reached the gate. Her tension was fading as she locked it behind her, only to spring back as a shadow detached itself from some bushes.

'I am armed!' she warned, barely able to speak for fear as she flourished the bayonet.

'There's no cause for that, Miss Victoria,' a familiar voice answered her.

It was Ned Annaferd, but there was none of the usual deference in his tone, which was now sneering.

'Whatever are you doing here!?' Victoria snapped. 'Go away at once!'

'I'll go away presently,' Ned answered, 'but first, I'd like you to do for me what Lucy does for your father and brothers.'

'You want me to serve you a late supper?' Victoria asked.

'Not that, the other thing.'

'What . . .' Victoria began in annoyance, and stopped, struck dumb by sheer outrage as she realised what he was suggesting.

'Seems fair to me,' Ned went on, now with just a trace of a whine in his voice, 'when everyone but me seems to be getting plenty of what's good for them, and you should be glad of it, seem so . . .'

'Glad?' Victoria spat, finding her voice. 'Glad, me, the daughter of the house, glad to be asked to . . . to manipulate you, or whatever filthy behaviour you had in mind, you, the stable boy!? How dare you!'

'I dares,' Ned replied, 'on account of how I knows you just sneaked out the grounds, to meet with your young man, I reckon. Now he can't be quality, can he, 'cause I don't see Reverend doing anything like that at all, nor Doctor neither, and you ain't been gone long enough otherwise. So he'll be one of the lads to the village, won't he, and I'm as handsome as any of they toads, I reckon.'

Victoria had stayed quiet during his little speech, desperately trying to fight down her outrage enough to make a sensible decision. It would be disastrous if her errand was revealed, and almost as bad if Ned reported that she had been making assignations with a boy from the village, especially when there wasn't one. Unable to face the humiliation of servicing his penis for him, she decided on bribery.

'I shall give you one shilling,' she offered.

'Don't want a shilling,' he answered, 'what I want is that dainty little hand wrapped around my pego and those fine fat churcks out of that dress the meantime, and to rub myself between . . .'

'Why you little beast!' Victoria gasped, and lunged.

Ned Annaferd caught the glint of moonlight on the bayonet and hurled himself backwards into the bushes where he'd been hidden, and through them. His foot met sloping soil, then nothingness and he was tumbling backwards, to land with a splash in the lake. For a brief moment his head was underwater and he was thrashing desperately at the reeds all around him, before he'd come up again, gasping for breath. His upper body was in the water, his legs lying on the bank he'd fallen down, with the bushes an irregular mass against bright moonlight, also Victoria Truscott's head.

'Ned?' she asked.

He made to reply, but some disgusting slimy substance was in his mouth and all that came out was a sputtering noise, giving him long enough to collect his wits before she spoke again.

'Ned? Are you hurt?'

'I . . . I think you've done me a mischief, Miss Victoria,' he answered.

'Well perhaps that will teach you to treat your betters with proper respect,' she answered, but there was doubt in her voice.

'I'm sorry, Miss Victoria,' he lied. 'I'm awful sorry, but . . . but I think I've broke my leg.'

'Can you climb up?' she asked, now clearly worried.

'I think, perhaps,' he told her, pulling his body up from the muck and water. 'Oh how that hurts.'

'You really are a most dreadful nuisance!' Victoria hissed, but she had extended a hand as he crawled to the top of the bank.

Ned answered with a groan of pain, and tried to support himself on her shoulder as he stood up.

'You'll soil my dress!' Victoria snapped, moving quickly away.

Ned fell over, his cry of surprise and pain as he toppled and hit the ground not entirely false.

'Oh, Miss Victoria, have pity, please,' he groaned.

'I really don't see why I should,' she answered. 'Try to get up.'

Ned tried, hauling himself to his feet with a great deal of display and clutching his leg even when he was finally upright.

'It's not broken at all,' Victoria stated.

'It hurts awful bad, Miss.'

'I dare say it does, but you needn't expect any sympathy.'

'I'll never manage the stairs, Miss,' he said as she began to walk away.

'For goodness sake!' she answered.

Victoria hesitated as she stepped back from the chair where she'd sat Ned Annaferd in his tiny room above the stable block. The arrogant demanding boy who had accosted her by the gate now slumped limp and moaning softly from the pain in his leg, no longer a threat. Yet his knowledge was, and once the pain had gone away his gratitude was all too likely to turn to resentment. It was almost pitch black, the single window allowing only enough light to make the shadows confusing, and she allowed her hand to stray to her mouth, biting the tip of her glove.

'Miss Victoria?' Ned asked, speaking in a strained whisper.

'Yes?' she demanded.

'I'm wet, Miss Victoria,' he said, wheedlingly, 'and like to catch a chill. I need to be in my bed. Pull off my trousers, would you, please? It hurts so much to bend.'

Victoria hesitated before she replied.

'If you're being dirty with me, Ned Annaferd . . .'

'No, Miss . . . I swear it, Miss . . .'

Again Victoria hesitated, and he spoke again, his voice full of tears.

'Please, Miss . . . I'm hurting so awful bad . . .'

'Oh very well!' Victoria snapped. 'But you needn't think I've forgotten your earlier behaviour.'

It was true, his outrageous demands burned in her head as she crouched down beside his bed: to take his cock in her hand, to bare her breasts for him as she pulled at it, and no doubt more, had she given in. She tugged at his trousers, but they wouldn't come down over his hips and the motion only made him wince.

'You'll have to undo your buttons!' she hissed.

'Miss, please,' he answered, faint with pain.

Victoria bit her lip, her head full of conflicting emotions: shame and sympathy, arousal and annoyance at herself for feeling aroused. Yet he was clearly in pain, and it was not hard to tell herself that she was only being charitable as she put her hands to his buttons. His trousers were rough, and wet, but also old, and the buttons came loose easily, two at the top, the first of those holding his fly closed, the second . . . and she stopped, jerking her hands back with a fresh gasp of outrage. He had no underwear, and her gloved hand had brushed something hard, round and all too familiar.

'You beastly little pig!' she snapped. 'All this time you've been telling me you're hurt, and your . . . your thing is hard!'

'I can't help it, Miss!' Ned whined. 'You . . . you're so very beautiful, and just to smell the scent of you, and . . .'

'That's quite enough!' Victoria answered, trying to sound stern but with her voice cracking.

She couldn't see, but she knew his hard cock was now sticking up out of his fly, ready for her hand, to be squeezed between her breasts, put in her mouth . . .

'Please, Miss?' Ned asked, but he didn't say what he wanted.

Victoria's hands were shaking, her throat dry. She could smell his cock and feel her own arousal, which was rapidly overcoming her pride and resentment for who he was and his behaviour. She thought of how many times she's let her imagination go over local men, never of her own status, of who her lover was, and she had made her decision. It had to be done, after all, to keep him silent, and she would reveal nothing of her true feelings.

'Very well, Ned Annaferd,' she said evenly. 'I'm going to tug your thing, if you still want that, but it's not because I want to. You're to be silent over tonight, and I want you to know that you're a beastly wicked boy to take advantage of a woman this way.'

Even as she spoke she had reached out, and now took hold of his shaft, stiff in her hand, and hot even through her glove. She began to pull up and down, trying to do it as fast as possible and somehow convey distaste for her task instead of her rapidly rising excitement. It was not easy, her quim already swollen and urgent, her juice trickling sticky down between her bottom cheeks to wet the tiny hole between.

Ned Annaferd's only response had been a groan which might just about have been a thank you. Victoria's mouth was pursed as she continued to tug, resentment still warring with desire, but losing. She wanted to rub herself, and to lay bare her chest while she did it, the way he had demanded, and to fold them around the now straining penis in her hand, and to kiss the tip as it bobbed up and down between her breasts the way she'd been taught, and to take it properly in her mouth and suck on him until he erupted down her throat . . .

Something inside her seemed to snap. She let go of his cock, and with fumbling urgent motions unfastened the front of her dress and the chemise beneath to pop out her breasts, full and heavy in her hands as she spoke, her voice now a hoarse croak.

'There you are, you dirty beast. My breasts are bare. That's what you wanted, isn't it? To see my bare breasts, and I'm sure you want to touch them too, like the filthy little pig you are.'

Ned responded immediately, reaching out to take one plump globe in his hand and sighing as he began to explore her. Victoria swallowed hard as her nipple popped out under his thumb, and her resistance had gone completely. She leant forwards, gaping for his cock and taking it in, to suck urgently on the long hard shaft as he gave a gasp of surprise. He tasted good, and to have a cock in her mouth again felt wonderful, so wonderful she could no longer resist the dirty act he'd demanded.

Quickly undoing the last two buttons of his fly and freeing his balls, she pushed close, spreading his thighs to get her breasts around his erection. There was no gasp of pain as she pressed on his hurt leg, only an excited moan, and in the back of her mind she realised she'd been tricked. It didn't matter. He was fucking her breasts, his cock bobbing up and down between them and the rough cloth of his trousers rubbing on her stiff nipples. She began to jiggle herself on his cock, to slap them together and to kiss his cock head as it bobbed up between, all the dirty tricks she'd been taught, until she could no longer hold back from taking her own pleasure.

Her hand went down, one knee cocked up to let her burrow beneath her skirts and she had found her quim, rubbing herself and fingering her deflowered hole as she took him in once more, masturbating him into her mouth as he fondled her breasts. He came almost immediately, with an ecstatic grunt, filling her mouth with thick salty spunk just as her own orgasm had begun to rise in her head. She swallowed deliberately, delighting in the filthy act and still tugging hard on his cock, to milk jet after jet of come down her throat as her cunt begun to contract against her hand. Despite her best efforts to swallow her mouth was full of spunk, which exploded out from around her lips, all over her gloved hand and his balls, but she was coming, lost to all decency as she let his cock slip from her mouth and began to rub his mess in her own face, smearing it over her cheeks and nose and chin as shudder after shudder passed through her body.

At last her orgasm faded and she sat back, gasping for breath, spunk and saliva hanging from her chin in a sticky slippery beard, to fall in clots on her heaving naked chest. She rubbed a little into her nipples, still excited and telling herself that he couldn't see how dirty she was being anyway as her senses began to return to normal. His breath was coming in gasps too, but at last he spoke.

'I . . . I always thought you were a dirty one, Miss Victoria.'

'Well you can put that thought right out of your head, Ned Annaferd,' she replied as she began to adjust herself. 'I did that because you made me, no other reason, and you needn't think otherwise. Now, do I have your word you'll be silent?'

'I'll be silent, right enough,' hc assured her, 'but you'd do well to keep me reminded.'

Victoria knew full well what he meant, and her mouth set in chagrin as she thought of how it would be to have to bare her breasts for him and masturbate him whenever he wanted it. She knew she'd be doing it, and rubbing her quim too, yet it was still horribly shameful, as was the suspicion that he'd tricked her, which became certainty as he got up easily and opened the door for her.

As she left she was telling herself that whatever the cost might have been she had succeeded in her mission. Constable Apcott would get the note.

Six

Harland Wolfe turned at the sound of Capleton's subdued cough.

'A policeman is asking to speak with you, sir. Constable Apcott, of Bidlake.'

'Then I imagine you had better show him in,' Harland Wolfe responded, 'with Miss Stukely's permission, naturally.'

'By all means,' Miss Stukely agreed.

Capleton withdrew, to be replaced by an agitated constable, who immediately held out a roughly square piece of paper towards Wolfe.

'Good morning, Mr Wolfe sir,' the constable began. 'Hearing you were in the district, sir, I was hoping you might be kind enough to take a look at this, sir. Pushed through my door in the black hours, it was, sir.'

'I am already involved with two cases, constable,' Harland Wolfe stated, glancing at the piece of paper, 'although admittedly somewhat intertwined, but yes, with a simple problem like this I can no doubt spare you a moment.'

A number of letters had been pasted onto a square of card to form a message, stating simply – 'Sugden is in Lydford Woods'.

'I was wondering if you could make anything of it, sir,' the constable enquired.

'No doubt,' Wolfe replied, taking the note and subjecting it to a cursory glance. 'Your mysterious benefactor, constable, is a woman of good education living within your own parish. I would venture to suggest Miss Victoria Truscott.'

'That's extraordinary, Wolfe, even by your standards,' Dr Manston interjected. 'How can you possibly be so absolute?'

'Elementary, my dear Manston,' Harland Wolfe replied. 'Do I really need to explain?'

There was a general chorus of affirmation, and Harland Wolfe allowed himself a smile before he began.

'Sometimes I feel as if I should keep my methods to myself. You look on me as if I were a great conjuror, but once I have revealed myself I vouch you will all remark how simple the matter is.'

'Not at all, Mr Wolfe,' Miss Stukely assured him.

'Then I shall explain,' Harland Wolfe went on. 'You will observe that the note is made up of letters cut from a copy of the *Times*. As Dr Manston will tell you, I have made something of a study of the different typefaces used in the production of our papers, both national and local. Indeed, I have written a small monograph on the subject. The leaded bourgeois type of a *Times* article is quite distinctive. The *Times* is not read by the ill-educated. Now, Constable Apcott, you say the note was pushed through the letterbox of your cottage in the early hours, and that you are responsible for Bidlake Parish?'

'Yes, sir,' the constable answered.

'And the Driscoll Estate is also in Bidlake Parish?'

'Yes, sir.'

'Excellent. So then, note the short length of the cuts. A pair of small scissors has been used, but they are straight, rather than curved. Not nail scissors then, but, I would suggest, sewing scissors. It would be a rare man who thought to use sewing scissors for such an exercise. Thus we have a well-educated woman who lives in Bidlake Parish, for what woman would take such a note to any but the nearest police station, let alone at dead of night?'

'But why Miss Truscott?' Miss Stukely asked.

'Bidlake is tiny,' Harland Wolfe replied, 'and, while it is possible that there may be alternative candidates, the balance of probability points to Miss Truscott. Dr Manston has questioned her, and he tells me she rides over from Driscoll's to the moor. No doubt she has caught a glimpse of Billy Sugden, but as a young lady of quality she does not wish to draw attention to herself. She is also in the habit of riding across Dartmoor at a full gallop, which suggests a vivacious and romantic nature. No doubt the idea of a secret note appealed to her.'

'As you say,' Miss Stukely admitted, 'it seems so very simple when you explain.'

'I may even be wrong,' Harland Wolfe replied, 'just possibly, but in any event I suspect that the information is valid. They are an old family, the Truscotts, I believe, and a Truscott was involved in the original legend of the hound, was he not?'

'As old as anybody in these parts, sir,' Constable Apcott responded, 'and squires to the Beare Estate as well as Driscoll's. Biggest landowners in these parts aside from the Russells, they be, and they've a pretty penny besides.'

'Are you are a local man, constable?' Miss Stukely asked.

'Born and bred,' he replied, 'and been constable these twenty years, since when old John Truscott was squire, John as was in the wars with Boney, that was. But I'm running over, and . . .'

'No, no, do go on,' Harland Wolfe requested. 'You probably know the district better than any man we have yet had the opportunity to interview, and so in return for my assistance in the matter of the note, perhaps you would answer a few questions?'

'Gladly, sir,' Constable Apcott answered.

'First of all,' Harland Wolfe went on, 'what is the local opinion on the legend of the hound?'

'There's differing tales on that,' the constable responded, 'about how Black Shuck'll follow folk down along of a lane at night, and if you runs, he'll have you, but if you keeps your head he'll walk beside you, just as if he was your pet. As to Roger Stukely, well they say the hound got him when he was after a farmer's maid, but what I reckon is, he ran into her father's farm dogs coming the other way, they didn't take kindly to his doings, and that served him. You don't want to argue with a moor dog, sir, for certain sure. They do say there wasn't enough left of old Roger's head to recognise him, begging your pardon, Miss Stukely.'

'A very reasonable theory, constable,' Harland Wolfe agreed. 'Evidently you are a man of some intelligence. What of recent events, the death of Sir Robert Stukely in particular?'

'Not easy to say, sir. Sir Robert didn't have nobody against him, not to my knowledge. Used to be a lot of bad blood in these parts, sir, between Stukelys and Truscotts particular, but that all went when Sir Robert bought into the mines with his African money. You know the tale of old Henry Truscott's maid, I dare say?'

'No,' Harland Wolfe admitted. 'Do go on?'

Constable Apcott cast an uneasy glance at Miss Stukely before he continued.

'Suki, her name was, seem so, and a rare beauty by all accounts, from Africa, very dark, and . . . and with perfect smooth skin, beg pardon, Miss, but you needs to know that for the story. Squire Stukely, who was as mad as a March hare if you want my opinion on it, he had some book, witchcraft it was, I suppose, and he wanted it bound proper. Ordinary leather wasn't good enough for him, not old Lewis Stukely. Human skin, he wanted. It was Suki he chose, only she weren't big enough around to meet his need, she weren't, so old Squire Stukely, he keeps her to fatten up a trifle.'

'Great heavens!' Dr Manston interjected.

'Rightly said, sir,' the constable agreed before he went on. 'Now there's some as say Henry Truscott was more than just Master to that maid, all sorts of tales there are, but any road, he weren't too keen on having her skinned up like she was a jack rabbit or something, so he gets roaring drunk, he does, and he comes over here, with Todd Gurney, whose grandson . . . or great-grandson he might be, he works over to Driscoll's this day, he does . . . Anyroad, killed old Lewis Stukely dead, he did, Henry Truscott, right here in this house. Not that the bad blood didn't go back before, 'cause there was Spanish Stukely, the traitor, and some as say it wasn't the hound as killed Roger Stukely at all, but that old John Truscott shot him, and scat his brains all abroad, which was why his head . . .'

'Thank you, constable,' Miss Stukely said a trifle faintly.

'A remarkable tale,' Harland Wolfe added, 'but not, I suspect one that has a great deal of bearing on this case. I understand there have been no marriages between the two families?'

'Never, not back hundreds of years,' Constable Apcott confirmed.

'Which fact,' Harland Wolfe went on, 'makes Truscott unlikely to be involved in the present case, whatever may have occurred in the past. No, Miss Stukely, in my experience when murder is perpetrated on a wealthy individual one should immediately look to those who seek to gain by the death.'

'You are not accusing me, surely?' Miss Stukely asked in shock.

'Not at all,' Harland Wolfe assured her. 'To have arranged the matter from the Dakota Territories would have required extraordinary resource, both financial and in terms of organisation. Nor do I suspect the Reverend Samuel Potts, who is next in line, and is a nonagenarian clergyman resident in the Isle of Man. Your aunts, Maude and Frances, both died without issue, as did Sir Robert himself, which leaves us with something of a puzzle, a puzzle I intend to solve. But for now, I suggest, Constable Apcott, that you gather your colleagues and make a sweep of Lydford Woods. Indeed, my case here has become something of a waiting game, and with your permission I will join you, perhaps Dr Manston also.'

'Gladly, sir,' Constable Apcott replied.

Genevieve yawned as she pulled the large china pot from beneath the bed. Mrs Capleton, she suspected, was trying to feed her up, either that or the housekeeper simply produced far too much at every meal by force of habit. Sir Robert, she knew, had been a man large in every dimension, which perhaps accounted for Mrs Capleton's ideas on food, but a dish of trout followed by mutton stew with enormous dumplings and huge flowery potatoes liberally coated with butter, then a jam roly-poly pudding seemed excessive, especially at lunch time on a hot day in late spring. Even with the great detective and his assistant present half the food had gone uneaten.

The huge lunch had left her tired, and with both Harland Wolfe and Dr Manston off somewhere in Lydford Woods in search of the convict, she had decided to take an afternoon nap. She was also a little drunk, and wondering if it would be pleasant to tease herself to climax. With the servants going about whatever servants did in their wing of the house and Nanna Bloss in a state of nervous prostration she was sure she would have the time, but first she needed to relieve the tension in her bladder from the three bottles of wine they had shared over lunch.

She placed the pot carefully in the middle of the floor and lifted her skirts, rather enjoying the mildly erotic routine of baring herself. As she unbuttoned the panel of her drawers she was wondering how it would feel to do the same for a man, not some crowd of drunk roaring cattlemen and miners, and certainly not the sort of man who would pay for the privilege, but somebody young and virile, with a touch of dash about him. Dr Manston was certainly brave, but really too old, and while Harland Wolfe was physically attractive he seemed oddly cold. Richard Truscott was better, and she turned her head to watch herself in the mirror as she let the panel fall to show off her bare bottom, imagining his eyes fixed on the display she was making of herself.

It was an intriguing thought, if her behaviour was a little silly, and she was smiling gently as she placed her legs to either side of the pot and squatted down. Settling her bottom onto the warm rim, she relaxed, allowing her pee to gush out, first tinkling on the china and then splashing as her puddle grew rapidly deeper. She gave a contented sigh as the pressure within her bladder gradually reduced, and a muted giggle as she dismounted the pot and saw just how much she'd done. It was nearly half full, a deep golden pool of urine.

Having her bottom bare felt nice, and she determined to keep it that way, teasing herself until she could hold back no more. She had just decided that it might be nice to go downstairs that way when heavy footsteps sounded in the corridor. Genevieve sighed and bit her lip. But the thought of a possible spanking had sent a shiver the length of her spine, and her mouth came a little open as she looked up at Nanna Bloss, half in fear, half in anticipation. The big woman looked angry, and Genevieve's fear took over as she began to stammer.

'Should . . . should you not be resting, Nanna? You have had a terrible shock, after all.'

'You're the one who has a shock coming,' Nanna Bloss stormed, shaking something white in Genevieve's face. 'It was you who sent the mark, wasn't it, you little bitch!'

'No!' Genevieve protested. 'Not at all!'

'Liar!' Nanna Bloss yelled. 'Do you think you can fool me, you idiot little brat? I've spoken to the boy you paid to take it to Lydford, who called just now to see if there were any other errands we might like doing. Now get here!'

Genevieve tried to scrabble away, but the big woman snatched out, catching a handful of hair. Squealing pitifully, Genevieve was dragged back, but instead of being hauled across Nanna Bloss' lap, she was pressed down onto her knees. The grip in her hair tightened, and to her horror she realised her head was going to be forced into her chamber pot. She began to fight, struggling frantically against the pressure, but Nanna Bloss merely laughed and continued to move Genevieve's head nearer to the rim of the pot, deliberately slowly, and stopping to leave her victim's nose just a few inches above the deep pool of piddle. Genevieve began to babble.

'Nanna, please, no! Not this, not this!'

'It'll do you good, maybe this'll teach you a lesson?' Nanna Bloss grated as the first few locks of Genevieve's hard touched the surface of the piddle.

Her face was right over the pot, the scent of her pee strong in her nostrils as she was held in place with her feet kicking behind her and her hands slapping on the floor in pathetic remonstrance. She cried out as the hand in her hair was twisted tighter still and her head forced down another inch, then began to panic.

'No, Nanna, please, no! I beg you . . . anything, anything at all, but not this! Spank me, please spank me . . . spank my bottom and I'll be ever so kind after! I'll lick, and everything . . . anything, but not this . . . no!'

Her words broke off in a scream as her head was jammed suddenly down, abruptly cut off by a splash as her face went into her puddle. She went frantic, kicking and clawing at the carpet, but her head was held firmly in the potty, her face completely submerged, blowing bubbles in her own urine. Yet her ears were still above the surface and she could clearly hear Nanna Bloss' cruel laughter from above her.

She was jerked up, gasping, with piddle dripping yellow from her nose and mouth and hair, only to be thrust back under, and again, her face splashing in the puddle of urine as Nanna Bloss began to talk.

'You'll not do that again, do you hear me, you little wretch. He's about, somewhere, Saul Roper is, but like as not it's not my life he's after, or he'd have sent the pips already. When he comes, you little bitch biter, I aim to have him satisfied, with your money, and with your body. Is that straight?'

'Yes, Nanna, yes . . .,' Genevieve gasped, spitting piddle as she struggled for air. 'I'll be good, Nanna . . . I'll do anything you say. Now stop, please!'

Nanna Bloss merely laughed and shoved Genevieve's face back into the chamberpot, holding her under as she went on.

'You'd better be, my girl, because there are worse things than this as can be done to a girl who won't do as she's told, and which don't leave no marks, neither. Imagine how you'd feel right now if you'd done your full business?'

Genevieve began to wriggle more frantically still as the words sank in and Nanna Bloss laughed once more. Again Genevieve's face was pulled up, this time leaving her gasping for air and dribbling a mixture of snot and urine from both mouth and nose.

'Now suck some up,' Nanna Bloss demanded, 'and I want to see you swallow.'

Genevieve began to wriggle again, but her face was promptly dunked and held under again.

'Going to be difficult, are we?' Nanna Bloss demanded, and she began to hoist up Genevieve's skirts at the back.

'No, not a spanking too!' Genevieve wailed as her face was pulled up once more. 'Nanna!'

'Do as you're told then,' Nanna Bloss demanded.

'OK!' Genevieve sobbed. 'I'll do it!'

'You will,' Nanna Bloss assured her, 'and you'll get your hiney smacked and all.'

'But you said!'

'I said to take a drink of your piddle, and when I tell you to do something, you do it, smart. Now drink!'

Genevieve was sobbing as her skirts were hauled high, exposing her still bare bottom. She knew her quim was wet from her earlier dirty thoughts, and her crying grew more bitter still as her tormentor spoke out in surprise and disgust.

'Well strike me! I never thought to see the girl who'd cream her cunt over having her face dipped, I really didn't. A spanking, that's normal enough, but a dunking!'

'I didn't!' Genevieve snivelled, but Nanna Bloss just laughed at her.

'The state of your cunt says different. Now stick that hiney up and get drinking.'

A heavy swat landed across Genevieve's bottom, catching her unawares so that her face went in the piddle again. Another smack and she'd pouted out her lips, desperate to placate the big woman who had her so completely under control. She sucked up a mouthful of her urine and tried to swallow, only for it to erupt from her mouth as the next smack caught her bottom. Nanna Bloss laughed and the spanking slowed down to a hard, even rhythm that allowed Genevieve to suck up another mouthful and swallow it down.

Nanna Bloss laughed once more to see the disgust on Genevieve's face as the first swallow of piddle went down. Her anger had died, to be replaced by sheer cruel amusement as she tortured the helpless girl. It was funny, and the fact that Genevieve's cunt was creaming was funnier still, keeping her chuckling as she spanked, harder and faster now, to set Genevieve's bottom cheeks bouncing as she struggled to swallow down mouthful after mouthful of pungent urine.

For the sake of a bit of variety, Nanna Bloss began to dunk Genevieve's head once more, and to hold it under so she could enjoy watching her victim blow bubbles and wriggle pitifully in her grip, all the while spanking away at the now pink cheeks. Five times she did it, with Genevieve growing ever more frantic, before Nanna Bloss ordered her to start drinking it again. This time Genevieve obeyed without hesitation, and Nanna Bloss began to spank harder still, until the trim pink cheeks were wriggling in pain and the slender legs had begun to kick in true desperation.

Yet still Genevieve was trying to drink her piddle, now red in the face, her cheeks bulging, her beautiful hair sodden and dripping, her bottom open to show off her anus between the rapidly pinking cheeks, every detail adding to the big woman's delight, and she decided that she would have to have her victim lick her, then and there. She stopped spanking, pulled Genevieve's face out of the potty and dragged her over to the wash stand, where she ducked it in fresh water instead. With Genevieve wet and panting, her bottom red and nude, she was put on her knees and her face pressed to Nanna Bloss' naked cunt. Immediately she began to lick.

'That's my Ginny,' Nanna sighed as the little sharp tongue began to work on her sex. 'You know your place, don't you? Know what's good for you, don't you, at least once you've had your hiney warmed.'

Genevieve didn't answer, her mouth busy with Mrs Bloss' cunt, using both her lips and tongue in what was either willing depravity or a very good imitation of it.

Nanna Bloss let it happen, her eyes staring greedily down as Genevieve licked, her mind running over the sheer joy of torturing the hapless girl, until at last she came. Still she kept her grip in Genevieve's hair, only relaxing it when she had recovered herself enough to speak.

'Now you,' she ordered, releasing Genevieve.

Genevieve looked up out of red-rimmed eyes half covered by the bedraggled mess of her hair. She wore a moustache of cunt cream and there was snot running from her nose, a soiled filthy mess, yet still she managed to shake her head.

'Not ready for it yet?' Nanna Bloss chuckled. 'You will be, girl, just you wait. I've seen girls like you before, dirty little bitches every one of them, for all they puts up a fight. Best clean yourself up then, I suppose, if you haven't the courage to admit who you are.'

Richard Truscott stood below the windows of Stukely Hall, most of which were open against the heat. There had been no mistaking the noises issuing from them, those of a girl being spanked, and quite hard to judge by her squeals. Undoubtedly Genevieve was the victim, and equally undoubtedly Mrs Bloss was the one giving the spanking, a combination he found almost as delightful as if he himself had been the one to apply his hand to her delightfully formed rear.

Now that the spanking was over he had decided to wait a little, in order to allow her to compose herself, but with five minutes gone he walked forwards to rap on the door with his cane. There was a long pause before Capleton opened the door, and another while he stood in the drawing room admiring the portraits of long dead Stukelys. Finally she appeared, composed but a trifle puffy around the eyes, which provoked a touch of sympathy before the image of her blubbering across Mrs Bloss' knee pushed it aside.

'Good afternoon, Miss Stukely ... Genevieve,' he greeted her. 'A glorious day, is it not, and a shame to be shut up indoors. I was hoping you would join me for a walk, if not on the moor then perhaps in Lydford Woods?'

'I believe there is a manhunt in progress in Lydford Woods,' Genevieve replied. 'The convict, Billy Sugden, had been reported there, and both Dr Manston and Mr Wolfe have gone to join in the pursuit.'

'Ah, ha, fine sport, I dare say,' Richard responded, 'but perhaps not quite the thing for a lady. Perhaps I can tempt you to a turn on the moor then?'

Genevieve hesitated before answering.

'Mr Wolfe has advised against it, but yes, in your company no doubt I am safe enough.'

'No doubt,' Richard agreed, easing a few inches of steel free to demonstrate his sword stick. 'So the celebrated Harland Wolfe has finally put in an appearance, has he? I dare say your difficulties will be disposed of in no time then.'

'That is my most earnest hope,' Genevieve responded.

'The fellow really is extraordinary,' Richard assured her, wondering if it would be wise to speed up his intended seduction now that Harland Wolfe was about.

Genevieve accepted Richard's arm as they stepped from the Hall, wondering how best to make it clear to such a respectable English gentleman that she would look favourably on any proposition or advance he made on her. With her other plans now wrecked by the brilliance of Harland Wolfe and her own sheer bad luck, it seemed the only way possible of getting rid of Nanna Bloss.

Once married to Richard, he too would have a vested interest in avoiding scandal. No doubt he would be angry with her, but he seemed very much a man of the world, while the reputation of his ancestors was positively ferocious. Perhaps they could pay Nanna Bloss off, or even allow her to go on living at Stukely Hall, although the thought made Genevieve's teeth grind.

'You are most fortunate in this aspect,' Richard was saying as he steered her down the yew alley, 'although it can be bleak in winter.'

'There are ways to keep oneself warm, no doubt,' Genevieve replied, and gave a gentle squeeze to his arm at the same time as she held her breath a little to make herself go pink.

'Indeed there are,' Richard remarked after just the briefest pause, then chuckled. 'Do you ride?'

'Indeed I do,' Genevieve answered.

'Perhaps we might ride together, you and I?' he suggested.

'I would be delighted,' she answered, now blushing for real.

'I also,' Richard agreed, 'but do we wait for the bleak winter, when it will warm our blood, or perhaps we might allow ourselves a little latitude?'

Genevieve took a moment to reply, now thoroughly flustered.

'I confess that I would not be unwilling to allow at least some latitude, so long as I have some assurance of your good will.'

Richard chuckled but didn't reply, leaving Genevieve with her hopes soaring as she was escorted from the moor gate and along the banks of the little stream to where it met the River Lyd in a swirl of white water beside a broad clear pool. An ancient stone bridge stood to one side, but before they could reach it, Richard had swept her up in his arms, lifting her easily, and splashed across the ford to the far bank.

Once back on dry land he put her down, but did not let go, instead pressing his mouth to hers. The Hall was no longer visible, and Genevieve gave in to her feelings after no more than a second, letting her arms come around him in a lingering kiss that set her heart pounding and her head dizzy. His hand had begun to move down her back, and she let him take one cheek of her still warm bottom in hand before breaking.

'I fear we are observed, Mr Truscott . . . or rather, Richard,' she said, nodding to where she had caught a movement from the corner of her eye just as they began to kiss.

Richard glanced up toward Brat Tor, where the bearded head of the painter projected from above his easel like the stopper of a bottle.

'It's only Matthew Widdery,' he replied, 'and frankly I suspect the fellow of being so short-sighted I doubt he can see us. How else to account for his painting, after all?'

Genevieve allowed herself a smile as she once more offered her arm, but rather than accept it Richard fell to one knee in the grass and spoke again, his voice as ardent as she could have possibly hoped for.

'In fact,' he said, 'to the blazes with Widdery. I don't care if we have ten thousand witnesses. There is no shame in my passion for you, Genevieve, and I will not hide it, nor hold back from my declaration for a moment longer. I love you, and I would be honoured should you agree to be my wife.'

For all her careful calculations, Genevieve found herself close to tears, and with a lump in her throat too large to permit her to speak. She nodded instead, and as he rose once more she allowed him to gather her into his arms without thought for the watcher on the tor, nor resistance until his hands moved to cup her bottom and one breast.

'Not here,' she gasped, pulling back.

'Somewhere private then,' Richard demanded, evidently without thought of being refused. 'I need you now, Genevieve.'

'I also,' she admitted, 'but . . .'

'Don't be concerned for your maidenhead,' he

interrupted, sending the blood boiling to her cheeks. 'For that I can wait, but not for you.'

Genevieve had only been thinking of the shame of baring her recently smacked cheeks to him if he wanted to see her bottom, but he was already pulling her by the hand towards a thick stand of gorse and hawthorn. There were patches of smooth grass among the bushes, and Richard had quickly laid Genevieve down, fumbling at her clothes despite her protests.

'Richard, please! What of Mr Widdery? He has seen us!'

'Damn Widdery,' Richard growled, 'and damn these confounded fastenings!'

Genevieve gave a squeal of alarm as he gave up his attempts to open her dress and simply tore it wide from her neck to her belly, her chemise with it, to leave her chest exposed and heaving.

'Hmm, rosebuds!' he said, and buried his face between her breasts, kissing and licking until she was giggling despite herself.

Her need had been strong anyway, and it was all too easy to give in, especially with the thought of Nanna Bloss' undoubted anger to stimulate her passion. She lay back, taking hold of his head and stroking his hair as his mouth found one nipple, sucking her quickly to erection and flicking at the little taut bud with his tongue.

Even as he explored her breasts he was hauling her skirts up, and she let him, unable to do more than sigh even as her thighs were quickly tucked up and spread, baring the seat of her drawers to his eager hands. One tug, and the buttons had been ripped free, exposing her quim to the warm afternoon air. A grunt of satisfaction from Richard and he had moved lower, rolling Genevieve's thighs higher still and burying his face between them, her cry of surprise changing to a sigh as his mouth found her sex.

He began to lick, a sensation so exquisite she immediately realised why Nanna Bloss wanted it of her. She could do nothing but lie back in ecstasy, her eyes closed and her fingers entwined in his hair as he lapped and probed at the lips of her cunt and between, exploring the taut arc of her maidenhead, and higher, onto the sensitive little bud of her clitoris, where he stayed, lapping faster and faster until her back had begun to arch and her muscles to go into contraction. He was going to make her come, but stopped an instant before it was too late, to scramble quickly around beside her. She saw that his cock was free of his fly, standing hard and proud.

'Take me in your mouth,' he demanded.

'I've never . . .' she began, only to be silenced as he pressed his cock against her lips.

Her mouth came open of its own accord and Richard gave a long heartfelt sigh as eased his cock in, not deep, but holding her head to make sure she didn't pull away as she began to suck him, tentative, then clumsy, but with rising enthusiasm as the taste and feel of his erection got to her. So often she'd wondered how it would feel to take a cock inside her and, as she sucked, the need to open her thighs and let him in was rising. Her quim ached, and she kept her thighs wide, half hoping, half dreading that he would simply mount her and take her maidenhead then and there.

She was his to do with as he pleased, her feelings not only sexual, but of deep gratitude, and something more, for providing the release so urgently needed after her treatment from Nanna Bloss. Never would she be the grovelling pathetic creature that the big woman wanted, but she would do the same things for Richard, joyfully, and as he finally eased his cock free of her mouth she had spread her thighs as wide as they would go.

'By God that's a tempting target!' Richard swore as he got between her legs. 'But best not . . . not yet.'

His excitement was blatant, his cock rearing up from his belly over hers, his breath coming hard, his mouth a little wide as he looked down on her body. Genevieve looked back, meeting his eyes as she spoke.

'You may, if you wish. I am yours.'

'Thank you,' Richard answered, and pressed the head of his cock to her quim.

Genevieve gave out a whimper as she felt the meaty helmet of his cock press to her hymen, bracing herself for the sharp pain she'd been told about, but it never came. Instead he began to rub himself on her sex, sending little thrills of pleasure through her each time her bump was touched, until she was moaning and clutching at her breasts in ecstasy, her eyes closed and her thighs spread as wide as they would go to make herself completely available.

Still he rubbed, until she was creaming so heavily she could feel it trickling down between her bottom cheeks and was arching her back in an effort to press herself against him more firmly. Only when his cock pushed lower, to smear juice over her anus did she open her eyes, looking up to Richard in alarm.

'You wouldn't, Richard, please?' she managed.

He simply put his finger to his lips, quietening her as he continued to rub his cock against her bottom hole. Genevieve groaned, unable to make herself stop him or even resent what he was doing, but frightened of the pain as her anal ring began to grow slowly loose and open. It didn't even seem cruel, just a necessary surrender if she was to keep her maidenhead intact.

Richard's thumb found her cunt and she was being masturbated as he continued to open her anus, pushing his cock to the now mushy hole, returning to her sex to collect more cream and smearing that on in turn. A weak thank you escaped her lips for the trouble he was taking to get her bottom hole ready when he could so easily have merely rammed his cock up.

She barely even realised that his head was in, her hole so slippery and soft he could probe her easily, while the thumb on her bump was bringing her to such heights she actually wanted his cock up her bottom, mumbling broken pleas as she rubbed her nipples and teased the outlines of her breasts.

'Do it, my darling . . . put yourself in, if you must . . . and I know you must. Please, put it in . . . put it in . . .'

'Anything to oblige a lady,' Richard grunted, and he pushed.

Genevieve gasped as her bottom hole gave to the pressure, spreading wide on his helmet, and more, the neck and head of his cock now in up her bottom. She grabbed her own legs, rolling herself high in a gesture of utter abandonment and watching the glee on Richard's face as he eased himself deeper. She could feel her penetrated anal ring pulling slowly in and out on his cock shaft, and knew he could see, something so exquisitely intimate it made her buggering all the better.

She could feel him inside her as her rectum filled, his penis pushing deeper and deeper still, until she felt it was filling her right to the top of her head. Never had she imagined that having a man inside her could feel so good, least of all up her bottom, and she was groaning out loud and telling him she loved him as his balls pressed between her open cheeks.

His reply was the same sweet assurance, and he'd begun to pump himself in and out up her bottom, his thumb still working her cunt and his balls slapping between her cheeks as he buggered her. Genevieve cried out as she felt her contractions start, fluid squirting from her cunt and her anal ring in spasm on Richard's cock, and as the full power of her orgasm hit her she was screaming, blind with ecstasy and writhing herself onto the cock in her rectum even as he grunted, shoved deep and she realised she'd been given a gut full of sperm at the perfect moment.

Richard didn't pull out, but came down on top of her, holding her in his arms as she shivered and gasped her way through a climax far beyond anything she had experienced before. Their mouths had opened together as well, in a kiss that lasted long after both of them had finished their orgasms.

Richard lay back on the grass, his eyes closed in bliss as he thanked God, the devil and any other being he could think of. Genevieve was everything he had hoped and rather more. Innocent yet wonderfully lewd, so sweet and yet so dirty, exactly the sort of girl he had always wanted, and what little doubt he'd had about her suitability as a mate was now gone. All that remained was to ensure his father was in no position to object.

She was snuggled against his shoulder, toying with his cock like a child with a new toy, a situation he was reluctant to bring to an end. Only when the strident note of Mrs Bloss' call rang out from the direction of the house did Genevieve finally move.

'Oh dear, Nanna wants me,' she said.

'Ignore her,' Richard advised.

'I . . . I really can't,' she said.

Richard propped himself up on one elbow, at once amused and jealous. Clearly Genevieve was afraid of a spanking if she failed to heed the big woman's call, making him wonder if he should tell her he knew that she was still under discipline, or simply keep quiet and spank her himself when the time was ripe. Given how sweetly she'd surrendered herself to a buggering, it seemed likely she'd also enjoy a smacked bottom, and yet it was still debatable whether it should be presented as a pleasurable game, necessary marital discipline, or both. A few questions were in order.

'We might be a mile into the moor, for all she knows,' he pointed out. 'If we keep to the bushes we can get well clear before we're in view, and she'll simply assume you didn't hear her.'

Genevieve looked doubtful, then giggled and nodded. Richard quickly tidied himself up, took her hand and led her away, crouched low to avoid the risk of detection. Matthew Widdery had disappeared, although his easel was as before, and Richard avoided the area, coming out from among the gorse and hawthorn beside Doe Tor Brook, with the Hall now a grey shape in the middle distance.

'I must say,' he remarked as he took her hand 'that Mrs Bloss is not altogether my idea of a lady's companion.'

'I have never known another,' Genevieve admitted.

'Old nanny was she?' Richard asked.

'Something of the kind.'

'Ah, yes, I can see that would be awkward,' Richard replied, picking his words with care. 'I mean to say, she probably still thinks of you as a little girl.'

'Not entirely,' Genevieve responded, 'although, yes, she is a most forceful woman.'

'She sees herself as your moral guardian, I expect?'

'She is concerned with my morals, certainly.'

'Are you very attached?' he queried.

Genevieve made a face and walked several paces before answering.

'Truthfully, I would prefer to be without her, but I must recognise my obligations. I thought, perhaps, she might be allowed to occupy the Hall, but I know nothing of your own arrangements.'

'The Hall?' Richard retorted. 'Good heavens, no! I dare say she has been a worthy servant, but if we're going to pension her off it would be to a cottage somewhere. There are plenty to choose from, both on my family land and your own.'

'I feel Nanna would be disappointed in a cottage.'

'Come, come, Genevieve, you mustn't let her hold the

rule over you so. She goes in a cottage, and that's that.'

Genevieve didn't answer. Content with the prospect of pensioning off Mrs Bloss, Richard turned his mind to his other difficulties and how to broach them, only to realise that claiming to have let slip family secrets to Genevieve didn't mean that he actually had to do so. That way, if his father still proved obdurate he would have given nothing away, while if he was successful she could be told in the fullness of time.

It was definitely the best course of action, and he confined himself to small talk as they followed the brook past the decaying remains of the old Wheal Frederick mine and up to where the long ridge of dry land rose towards Hare Tor. As they climbed higher the view grew ever wider, with much of western England seemingly laid out beneath them to the west and the valleys and crags of High Dartmoor to the east. Sounds were also very clear, the call of a raven so far above them it was little more than a black dot, the bark of a dog on some distant farm, and other dogs, fainter still, mingled with human shouts.

Richard stopped, peering down the long slope to where the river disappeared among the first trees that filled the valley all the way to the Tamar.

'Do you suppose they've managed to flush Sugden out?' he asked.

Before Genevieve could answer a figure burst from the woods, his ragged prison suit identifiable even at a distance. He was running, apparently with every ounce of strength in his body, and seemed to be headed for the rocks of Hare Tor not a quarter mile to Richard's side. Genevieve's grip tightened on his hand, but he stayed where he was, his voice deliberately nonchalant as he spoke.

'He's going well, I'll say that for him.'

'Should we not move further away?' Genevieve asked.

‘Not at all,’ he answered her. ‘I want to see the chase. Do you gamble at all?’

‘I . . . I have occasionally played cards with money at stake,’ she admitted.

‘Splendid,’ he answered. ‘I knew I’d chosen the right girl. A guinea says he makes it as far as Hare Tor rocks.’

‘Are you really not afraid?’ Genevieve asked.

‘Only of losing my guinea,’ Richard responded as new figures began to appear among the trees.

First was Harland Wolfe, distinctive in his tweeds, then a pair of policemen holding dogs, and others, with the somewhat stocky figure of Dr Manston close to the rear. Sugden was well ahead, but as the dog handlers reached the open moor they let slip their beasts, two great bloodhounds which immediately began to bound after the convict.

‘I suspect I shall be paying you a guinea,’ Richard said with regret, ‘although he’s certainly giving the Peelers a run for their money, dogs and all.’

Sugden was indeed moving with impressive speed, but it was clear he would be run down before long. The dogs were moving up on his flanks, sealing him into a trap in response to the whistles of their masters, but still he ran, behind a low rise of moor and out again, onto the flank of Hare Tor itself, leaping from boulder to boulder with desperate energy.

‘He’ll never make it,’ Richard breathed, even as Sugden turned at bay.

The convict wrested a chunk of granite from the grass, lifting it to use as a weapon, but the bloodhounds had stopped, still two hundred yards down the slope from him and well to either side, both sniffing the ground and ignoring the yells of their masters. Sugden dropped the rock and began to run again, but neither of the dogs followed, both snarling defiance but at no obvious enemy.

‘That’s peculiar,’ Richard remarked.

'I really think we should come away,' Genevieve urged as Sugden bounded up the slope, no longer aiming for the summit of Hare Tor, but the slope between it and where they stood.

Richard simply drew his sword stick and flourished it, shouting out as he did so. Sugden saw, and immediately changed his course, crossing the ridge a bare hundred yards in front of them.

'Fine sport on the moor this afternoon,' Richard remarked, 'and that's a guinea you owe me, my darling. But whatever is the matter with those dogs?'

The bloodhounds had begun to advance once more, but slowly, crouched low with their hackles raised and their lips drawn back to show their teeth. Harland Wolfe was not far behind them, and others, while Sugden had already disappeared over the lip of the Rattlebrook Valley.

'Should we lend a hand, do you think?' Richard enquired. 'I know the land better than most, after all. Then again, hardly a ladylike pursuit, I suppose?'

'I feel safe enough, so long as I am by your side,' Genevieve responded, 'but please do not risk a confrontation. Sugden has a most evil reputation.'

'True enough,' Richard admitted. 'We'll climb up onto Amicombe Hill then, where we can see any sport there might be without taking a risk.'

He was about to move forwards again when a voice hailed them from down the slope. Harland Wolfe was approaching, panting with exertion, but the thrill of the chase showed in his voice as he came up to then.

'Miss Stukely . . . Mr Truscott, I presume. The convict Sugden came by here, did he not?'

'Yes,' Richard replied, 'and ran on into the valley. You have him trapped, unless he chooses to risk the mire or run through Rattlebrook Works.'

Harland Wolfe touched his heavy oak stick to his hat and made to run on, only to stop dead as a frightful scream rang out from somewhere ahead of them, abruptly silenced. The detective ran forwards and Richard followed more cautiously, stopping where a cluster of rock overhung the steep slope that ended in the brook below. Harland Wolfe was already down there, standing over the prone body of Billy Sugden. The convict was dead, and where his throat should have been was an ugly red hole.

'You're all fools!' Mrs Bloss raved. 'You men with your reason and your scientific evidence, and you can't see what's before your very eyes!'

'Pray calm yourself, Mrs Bloss,' Harland Wolfe urged, 'there is no evidence to suggest that whatever creature tore out Billy Sugden's throat was of supernatural origin. To the contrary . . .'

'No evidence?' she broke in. 'So how come nobody saw the creature, and how does it feed? It's this Black Shuck creature, I'm telling you.'

'If that proves to be the case,' Harland Wolfe responded, 'there is little I can do about the matter. However, for the present I intend to accept Dr Robinson's report that the injury inflicted on the unfortunate Sugden was caused by a dog of exceptional size. Yes, we might have expected to see the creature, but the fact that we did not proves nothing.'

Mrs Bloss gave a snort of contempt but stayed silent. Harland Wolfe looked around the room, considering the people assembled in the drawing room of Stukely Hall: Mrs Bloss, Dr Manston, various policemen, Miss Stukely, Richard Truscott, Dr Robinson, Widdery the painter and Greville the lawyer, Capleton the butler. All had seen the corpse of Billy Sugden, a sight so horrible it had sent the normally stolid Mrs Capleton into a fit of hysterics.

One of them knew more than he would admit about the death of Sir Robert Stukely and subsequent occurrences, and with the events of the afternoon the net had begun to close. Indeed, aside from the necessity of protecting Miss Stukely, his principal difficulty lay not in apprehending the villain, but in ensuring that he also unearthed sufficient evidence for the matter to be brought to a successful conclusion before a court of law. Unfortunately what seemed the easiest solution was not entirely compatible with his primary concern.

'For the present,' he stated, 'we must take advantage of the fact that this new development forces the local constabulary to take the matter seriously. Is that not so, Inspector?'

'You will have our full co-operation, sir, Miss Stukely,' Inspector Allard assured them. 'I'll have armed men making a sweep of the moor tomorrow, and if there's anything to be found, we'll find it.'

'Ah, yes,' Harland Wolfe replied. 'I will need to speak to you about that in a while, if I may, but for the time being, I trust you will be able to spare a constable to keep an eye on Miss Stukely?'

'Constable Apcott has already volunteered for this duty, sir,' the inspector replied.

'Which,' Harland Wolfe stated, 'along with Dr Manston and myself, should afford adequate protection. Despite the events of this afternoon I feel that there is little risk to others . . .'

'Like the convict, I suppose you mean?' Mrs Bloss interrupted.

'Yes, I've been thinking that too,' Dr Manston added. 'It's been months since Sir Robert died and not a sign of this beast, then it makes a vicious attack on Sugden. Why Sugden?'

'A very good question, my dear Manston,' Harland Wolfe replied. 'Why Sugden indeed?'

'And what's it supposed to feed on, I asked?' Mrs Bloss added. 'You never answered me that.'

Harland Wolfe allowed himself a slight smile before answering.

'As to how the beast feeds without depredation upon livestock, I have my theories.'

Seven

'The convict is dead?' Victoria Truscott declared in delight. 'Oh how wonderful! I can ride where I wish once more.'

'Oh no you can't, young lady,' her mother replied. 'Not with some rogue dog loose on the moor.'

'Mama!' Victoria protested.

'I wouldn't worry too much, Vicky,' Richard put in as he speared a piece of sausage. 'The police are making a sweep of the moor today, and are sure to turn up whatever killed Sugden.'

'Richard, please,' Nell chided gently. 'This is no sort of conversation for the breakfast table.'

'I don't see why not?' Charles Truscott retorted. 'I'm only sorry I missed all the excitement. Shame about Lucy, though I'm surprised she's taking it so badly. Tough little thing, usually.'

'Who's going to take Leopold his breakfast then?' Richard chuckled. 'Care for a go, Vicky?'

Victoria stuck her tongue out, earning a sharp admonition from her mother.

'Victoria, really! Anybody would think you were still in the nursery, and you too, Richard.'

'Eliza then,' Richard suggested.

'Certainly not,' Nell responded. 'Eliza is the only person who understands my hair, and I will not have her indisposed.'

'I suggest Ned Annaferd,' Victoria put in.

'Do not be vulgar, Vicky,' Nell retorted. 'Really, you are quite impossible this morning. You must do it yourself, Richard.'

'If I must, I suppose,' Richard answered.

Victoria hid a snigger behind a mouthful of kedgeree and turned her mind to other things. Despite her cleverness in leading the police to Billy Sugden without giving herself away, the moor was still out of bounds to her, and if what Richard said was true her lover might be in danger. She had to be there, without delay, but that meant finding an excuse for her absence and evading the vigilance of Luke Gurney, which was not easy. Yet even if she did escape it was hard to see what she could do, while the police might very well already be out on the moor.

Quickly finishing her breakfast, and earning herself yet another admonition from her mother for bad manners, she ran up to the top floor, peering from the window with the best view across the moor. Sure enough, a line of men was visible, no more than tiny black dots against the verdant green and pale greys and browns, but unmistakable. Even if she left immediately, and rode Cloud as fast as was possible, they were going to reach the Tavy long before she did, and what then?

To make matters worse, thunderheads had begun to build up over the moors, leaving the air thick and sticky and casting a weird light across the scenery. She hesitated, thinking how much easier it would be to simply stay indoors, perhaps curled up in the library, but set her jaw and started downstairs, determined to at least make the attempt.

Richard knocked gently on the door.

'Leopold?'

There was no answer.

'Leopold, I have your breakfast.'

'Where's my Lucy?'

Richard jumped back in shock, despite having known more or less what to expect. His brother's deep gravelly voice had come from directly on the opposite side of the door, and without warning.

'Um, would you mind standing back, old chap?' he tried. 'I want to come in . . . with your breakfast.'

'Where's my Lucy?'

'She's not here this morning, I'm afraid,' Richard lied.

'I want my Lucy.'

'I know just how you feel, believe me, Leopold, but she's not here. Now be a good chap and stand back from the door.'

'Where's my Lucy?'

'She's . . . she's gone up to . . . to the moors,' Richard tried, desperately searching for an explanation his brother would accept. 'To see her aunt.'

The answer was a bass growl. Silence followed, and after a while Richard turned his key in the lock and pushed the door gently open, letting himself into the musky darkness of Leopold's room.

'I'll just put the tray down,' he said. 'It's bacon and eggs . . . you like bacon and eggs, and there's a sausage too.'

Leopold gave a satisfied grunt and Richard relaxed a little, and caught his brother's fist in the side of his jaw.

Victoria crossed the stable yard with feigned nonchalance, hoping there would be nobody to see that she was in her riding habit rather than her proper day dress. Her father was reading the *Times* in the morning room, her mother giving instructions to the cook, Richard feeding Leopold. Luke Gurney, she hoped, would be in the carriage house, readying the trap for cook's visit to the market, which left only one person she might encounter.

She entered the stables block, and to her annoyance found him standing outside a stall, whittling a stick –

Ned Annaferd. The gaze he turned to her was far more familiar than she would have liked.

'Saddle Cloud for me,' she ordered imperiously.

'Your father said you're not to go out,' Ned replied, his tone frankly insolent.

'I am to give Cloud exercise, that is all,' Victoria answered him, 'now look sharp, unless you wish me to have to speak to Mr Gurney.'

'And what if I were to speak to your father?' Ned mocked. 'Whatever would he say, to know his little darling meets with one of the village boys for a bit of kiss and cuddle, though after the way you were the other night, I suspect he gets a sight more, don't he?'

'Mind your manners, Ned Annaferd!' Victoria snapped. 'What happened was . . . was a singular event. I was not myself, and you gave me your word to hold it a secret.'

'So I did,' he answered, 'and so I will, so long as you let me see those pretty churcks now and again, and perhaps give me a chew of my pego.'

'I shall do no such thing!' Victoria hissed, and hesitated, her tone very different when she spoke again. 'At the least, Ned, do not use just awful words. I am not a heifer, I am a woman. My bosoms would be a more polite description of my figure, and one simply does not mention the . . . ah, necessity of affectionate acts.'

'How d'you know what to do then?' Ned asked. 'I means, if I can't ask you for a chew of my pego, how'd you know I want him chewed?'

'One . . . one simply indicates one's desire,' Victoria explained, blushing pink. 'Now, please . . .'

'What if it's dark?' Ned objected. 'Or would you rather I just stuck him in your mouth, unexpected like?'

'No I would not!' Victoria snapped. 'You are a dirty little pig, Ned Annaferd, and I believe you are doing this on purpose to make me blush. Now look, it so happens I need to go up to the moor today . . .'

'What, with some dirty great dog on the loose?'

'I shall be on Cloud, and besides, the police are taking care of the dog at this very instant . . . if there is a dog at all.'

'So what's your business? Your young man work to Rattlebrook peat cut, do he? Word'll get about, you know, if . . .'

'Never you mind my business,' Victoria cut him off. 'I am in a hurry, that is all you need to know, and if you let me out of the lane gate and keep quiet, then perhaps I'll . . . I'll do what you want when I come back, but not . . . not like before.'

'How d'you mean then?' Ned demanded. 'I don't get to go in your mouth?'

'No you do not!' Victoria answered, blushing dark once more. 'I . . . I will do it with my hand.'

'And churcks on parade?' he demanded, his voice more mocking than ever. 'Oh, sorry, Milady, I mean to say, with your bosoms bare.'

'You really are the vilest beast!' Victoria exclaimed. 'But very well, I'll do it bare.'

'What, all bare.'

'No, with . . . with my bosoms bare.'

'And I want it when you leave, elseways you might not feel so generous when you gets back.'

'I have given you my promise.'

'When you leave, Miss.'

'Oh . . . oh very well, beast!'

Ned Annaferd grinned as he started towards Cloud's stall.

Ned sighed as he fed his cock into Victoria's mouth. She was squatted down in front of him, in among a clump of laurel by the lane gate to Driscoll's Estate, her riding habit open to show off her plump pink breasts, of which he'd already had a good fondle. It had been particular fun to tweak her nipples erect and hear her involuntary little sighs as the buds stiffened in his fingers, and his cock had been half hard when he'd got it out on her. The furious glance she'd shot him as she took hold and began to tug him had been good too, as was the look of consternation on her pretty face as she sucked cock.

She looked a fine picture, with her little black top hat still on and her immaculate riding habit dishevelled, her face at once so innocent and so haughty, but with his erect penis stuck in her mouth. It would have been very easy indeed to come, either down her throat or to soil her face, perhaps even all over her hat, but he was determined to hold off until she began to get dirty, as he was sure she would. Maybe then she would let him fuck in her cleavage, or even show him her bottom and the little virgin cunt nestling between her thighs. It was an enticing thought, and he wondered how it would be to just take her, right there on the ground with her skirts thrown up and her sweet pink bottom nude for fucking, her tight hole stretching to his prick, her cry of pain as her maidenhead burst . . .

At least he had to see.

'How's about a peek at that bum?' he sighed. 'I bet you've a darling bum.'

Victoria didn't answer, but her sucking immediately became more insistent. Ned closed his eyes in bliss, imagining taking her virginity, only to open them again as she pulled off his cock and spoke.

'Anything to make you quicker!'

She was doing her best to look angry as she stood up, but the effect was ruined by her flushed skin and a strand of spittle hanging from her chin. He just grinned.

Victoria turned, shame and desire warring in her head as she began to lift her skirts behind. Ned had taken his cock in his hand, nursing his erection as he watched her come bare, first her stocking-clad legs, then the seat of her drawers. She was forced to push her bottom out so that her skirts would stay up on her back, with her cheeks pressed firmly to the thin cotton of her panel-backs as she began to undo them. Ned looked fit to burst, his eyes popping from his head and his mouth wide, and as the first button of her drawers came loose he had begun to tug himself in earnest.

Suppressing a smile for how easy it was to control him once she had his cock out, she continued to undo her buttons, working from the top down, each one revealing a little more creamy bottom flesh. Ned's wanking became more and more frenzied, and as the final button came loose under her fingers and the panel fell to expose the full glory of her bottom he had begun to grunt. Victoria stuck it out, deliberately teasing him.

It did feel good, there was no denying it, with her breasts hanging free and her bottom bare as he worked himself to ecstasy over the sight of her. Her quim felt ready, and yet the loss of her virginity was not a secret she was prepared to give up, and as he stepped closer a thrill of fear and excitement ran up her spine at the prospect of simply being taken as she was, bent down and fucked rudely from behind, her hips gripped hard and his cock pumping in her cunt, just like her lover . . . and probably left pregnant.

'Between my bosoms,' she gasped. 'You like my bosoms.'

Ned nodded, unresisting as she squatted down once more, this time to squeeze his towering cock between her breasts. She began to jiggle them and to bounce them up and down, inviting him to fuck in her cleavage, and after just a few firm pushes and a bit of grunting she was rewarded with a fountain of come, erupting from his cock to splash in her face and over the smooth creamy surfaces of her breasts.

'You dirty beast,' she managed, but there was no venom in it, and she was giggling as she pulled her handkerchief from her sleeve to wipe up his mess.

'Now that was fine,' he sighed. 'I swear you've the best pair of udders . . . 'cept perhaps for your mother.'

'Why you . . .' she began, and broke off at a whinny of alarm from Cloud where they had left him tethered in the lane. 'See what that is, Ned.'

He quickly put his cock away and disappeared among the laurels, leaving Victoria to mop up his come from her breasts and face, hastily now, and stopping at a cry of fear followed by a dull thud and another whinny from Cloud. She covered herself as quickly as she could, not even bothering to fasten the panel of her drawers, crawled in among the bushes and peered cautiously out at the lane.

Ned Annaferd lay prone on the ground, apparently insensible. Beyond him, Cloud was pawing fretfully at the dirt and tugging on his bridle, and beyond the pony, the gate stood open.

'I have important news, Nanna,' Genevieve stated cautiously.

'Oh, and what's that?' Nanna Bloss demanded.

'I am engaged to be married to Mr Richard Truscott.'

Nanna Bloss' face immediately began to grow dark. Genevieve stepped quickly back.

'Oh you are, are you?' Nanna Bloss replied. 'And how is that then, without my permission?'

'Your permission, Nanna?' Genevieve queried as the big woman drew closer still. 'But Nanna . . .'

'My permission,' Nanna cut her off, her fists now on her massive hips as she pushed her face close to Genevieve's, 'which is what you need before you so much as dab the piddle off your cunt. Don't you ever learn?'

'But Nanna . . .'

'Hush your mouth and listen, you stupid little trollop. How do you think it'll be when you're married to your fine Mr Truscott? What place'll there be for me, and what fun will I get out of you? Answer me that?'

'I . . . we . . . Mr Truscott has kindly offered to provide you a pension and a cottage on his land, free of rent,' Genevieve stammered. 'It is a most generous offer!'

'So you're planning to put me out to grass, are you?' Nanna Bloss grated. 'Why, you ungrateful little bitch, after all I've done for you. Didn't I take you in when you were no more than a child? Didn't I keep you fed and a roof over your head?'

'You made a thief out of me!' Genevieve protested.

'How else were you to pay your way?' Nanna Bloss demanded, red-faced with rage. 'Did I make a whore of you? Did I?'

'You aimed to!' Genevieve gasped, stung by her words and at the sheer gross injustice of the question.

'And maybe I will yet,' Nanna Bloss snarled, 'but for now I aim to teach you a lesson you'll never forget, and maybe smack some sense into that stupid head of yours.'

'No more cruel punishments, please, Nanna!?' Genevieve begged. 'Spank me, if you must, and use me for your pleasure, but . . .'

'Oh there'll be cruel punishments,' Nanna Bloss assured her. 'There'll be cruel punishments each and every day from here on, until you learn to do as you're told, and I . . . but no, maybe not. If it's a spanking you reckon you deserve, then a spanking you shall have. Come here.'

Nanna Bloss' powerful grip had closed on Genevieve's arm, and she found herself being dragged from the room.

'Where . . . where are we going, Nanna?' she asked in rising alarm as she was hauled towards the head of the stairs. 'Downstairs? But Nanna, the constable is at the door . . . Nanna!'

The cruelty on Nanna Bloss' face had brought the truth home to Genevieve, and she began to struggle frantically, but to no avail.

'Don't like it, do you?' Nanna Bloss laughed. 'Not in front of other people, do you?'

'You cannot!' Genevieve cried. 'Not in front of the constable. He will not let you, Nanna, he will not!'

'We'll see, shall we?' Nanna Bloss replied. 'I know men, you see, know them well, and my bet is he'd like nothing better than to watch an uppity little brat like you get it on your bare arse. And why shouldn't he? Nothing wrong in it, is there, watching a brat get what she deserves?'

'But . . . but Nanna, I am the lady of the house!' Genevieve wailed.

Nanna Bloss merely laughed. They had reached the landing halfway up the stairs, despite Genevieve's best efforts to cling onto the banisters, and she found the blood rushing hot to her face as she realised that Constable Apcott had come in from the gathering thunderclouds and was not outside the door, but inside, looking up at her in puzzlement.

'Is all well there?' he queried.

'Just a little matter of domestic discipline,' Nanna Bloss assured him, 'but perhaps you'd be good enough to hold her down while I give out her punishment.'

'No!' Genevieve screamed, but the constable's face had filled with doubt.

'I'm not sure that would be right, Madam,' he said scratching one ear. 'I mean to say, what with myself not being family . . .'

'Oh I'll do it myself then, really!' Nanna Bloss complained as she jerked Genevieve down the last couple of steps.

Constable Apcott stepped back against the front door, red-faced and looking highly uncomfortable, but making no move to intervene as Genevieve was dragged to where a straight-backed chair stood beneath a portrait of some long-dead ancestor. She was fighting furiously, determined not to let it be done, for all that Mr Greville and the butler had already seen her get the same humiliating treatment.

As before, her struggles only served to make Nanna Bloss more determined. Genevieve was hauled into place across the big woman's lap, her skirts and bustle turned up to show off her drawers and her drawers opened to show off her bottom. With her rear cheeks pouting out from the open panel her struggles redoubled in fury, but she was held firmly in place and the spanking began, hard swats laid full across her cheeks. As the pain blended with her agonising humiliation she burst into tears, bawling her eyes out and thumping her fists on the big woman's legs and the floor, begging for mercy and gasping to each and every smack, kicking her legs to add the display of her rear cunt lips and her anus to her disgrace.

She wasn't even sure if the constable was there any more, but it was all too easy to imagine his little piggy eyes fixed on her bare bottom, inspecting every crease and tuck with deep interest as he watched her cheeks flatten and bounce. It wasn't fair, it wasn't fair at all, not when she was engaged to a wealthy man, not to spank her naked bottom in front of a country constable who was sure to tell everybody he knew about what he'd seen. He'd seen everything too, her virgin cunt and her recently fucked bottom hole, and Genevieve knew she was still loose after playing with a candle in bed that morning as she remembered how good Richard Truscott's cock had felt up her bottom. Yet the spanking hurt so much she couldn't stop herself from kicking her legs and bucking her bottom, both movements making her cheeks come apart to show off the rude little hole she'd taken so much pleasure in, but which now brought her the most agonising shame.

The spanking stopped, as suddenly as it had begun, but Genevieve was not released. Instead, Nanna Bloss took one hot cheek in each hand and with a sudden motion, spread them wide. Genevieve screamed as her anus was put on open deliberate display, and began to fight with renewed fury. Nanna Bloss merely tightened her grip around Genevieve's waist and hooked one tree-trunk leg around a calf, adding the exposure of Genevieve's embarrassingly moist cunt to the display as she spoke.

'What's this? Been playing tickle Miss Brown-Eye, have we, or don't tell me, you haven't let that Mr Truscott pop it up your hiney, have you?'

Genevieve's scream of humiliation rang out over Nanna Bloss' words, and with a desperate convulsive jerk she threw herself to the side. The chair went over, Nanna Bloss tumbling backwards in a spray of lacy petticoats, and Genevieve was free. Barely noticing that the constable had gone back outside, Genevieve ran, through the back of the house and out along the yew alley, heedless of everything but her burning shame.

Dr Manston stood on the ridge beside Hare Tor, looking out across the Tavy Head Mires. High above, bruise-coloured clouds were building, and the air had a boiled taste to it as the storm gathered. There was a constable to either side of him, each a hundred yards away, and more beyond, stretching in a line well over a mile long. Every tenth man held a bloodhound on a chain leash. Ahead and behind was empty moor, or apparently empty moor, and the doctor had one hand locked on the grip of the revolver in his pocket as he walked. As he skirted an outlying clump of grey granite boulders his heart jumped at the sudden appearance of a figure, but it was Harland Wolfe, a stout ash stick clasped in one hand.

'Close, is it not?' Harland Wolfe remarked.

'Decidedly,' Dr Manston agreed, 'and I do wish you wouldn't jump out like that.'

Harland Wolfe chuckled.

'Stealth, my dear Manston, is an important element of my craft. You have your service revolver, I trust?'

Dr Manston displayed his weapon.

'Good,' Harland Wolfe went on, 'not that I expect you to need it, but it is best to be prepared.'

'I would have thought I might very well need it,' Dr Manston responded.

'Not at all,' Harland Wolfe replied. 'The hound, and it is a beast of flesh and blood, make no mistake, must be chained, otherwise it would have taken sheep. No, it is kept chained until needed, and I know where.'

'Let us go there then!'

'To the contrary, it is not the beast we seek, after all, but its master. Indeed, it is my intention not to find the beast, but to flush whoever controls it from cover. He is a clever man, Manston, an adversary worthy of our steel. So far, he has managed to elude me, which as I think I can say without false modesty is no easy task, but today I hope for better.'

They had passed the last of Hare Tor rocks, and stood at the lip of the valley, looking down across the green expanse of Tavy Head Mires, with Fur Tor rising beyond as a ghostly form in the storm light.

'Keep your eyes peeled for any man not in the line,' Harland Wolfe advised. 'It is within the next mile or so I expect to find our quarry.'

'We must break up a little to skirt the mire,' Dr Manston pointed out, 'but what of this fellow here?'

There was a man below them, tall, with dark skin and a bold hawk-like face, standing barefoot in Rattlebrook stream.

Genevieve came to a stop halfway up the slope of Brat Tor, biting her lip in uncertainty. She had no desire whatsoever to explain herself to the policemen who were searching the moor above her, nor to risk meeting the beast they were searching for. On the other hand, Nanna Bloss was clearly not finished with her, and she dared not go back for fear of a further spanking and no doubt some yet more humiliating punishment.

At length she sat down on a rock, only to rise again at the tenderness of her bottom, which had been thoroughly smacked twice already that day, once in front of Constable Apcott. Nanna Bloss was grown bolder, and it seemed that nobody else particularly cared that she was still under discipline. Certainly the Capletons didn't, rather they seemed to regard regular spankings for her with complete indifference, and while the constable had at least had the decency to withdraw, he had all too obviously considered it none of his business.

She burned with indignation for their attitude, and frustration for her helplessness. Nanna Bloss still thought Saul Roper was around, but now seemed determined to stay put, and use Genevieve's favours to bribe him, fuelling her indignation still further. Richard Truscott, Dr Manston, perhaps even Harland Wolfe, would come to her aid, she was sure, but the embarrassment of admitting to them that she was still spanked would be unendurable, while she was not at all sure it would make any difference, especially once the detectives had left, when she would be at Nanna Bloss' mercy until she got married, which was another problem. Unless she broke off her engagement she risked exposure and undoubted disgrace. Richard Truscott would hardly marry a woman known to have been a child thief, to say nothing of the more serious matter.

Gingerly, she sat down once more, this time on a tuft of grass and, placing her chin in her hands, she began to sulk, only to look up as a single oily raindrop splashed onto her dress. She glanced back to Stukely Hall, but her bottom cheeks tightened in anticipation of the thrashing she would undoubtedly get if she returned before Dr Manston and Harland Wolfe. The viaduct where the railway crossed the edge of her land was closer, and would provide shelter without getting her bottom smacked or her face put to Nanna Bloss' cunt.

As the heavy drops began to patter on the dry ground, she started down the slope.

'I'm afraid we're going to get most fearfully wet,' Dr Manston remarked.

'Come, come, Manston, a little rain never stopped us,' Harland Wolfe replied, 'and here is Allard, perhaps with some news.'

The Inspector was approaching, but his expression was far from sanguine.

'Not a sign,' he said. 'You've had no luck either, I take it?'

'All we've found so far is Dr Robinson's cook,' Harland Wolfe supplied, 'who explains that he was searching for frogs.'

'Frogs?' Inspector Allard queried.

'They eat them, you know,' Dr Manston explained, 'the French.'

Inspector Allard returned him a look of disgust but no great surprise. Harland Wolfe spoke again.

'And that, I fear, is that. I suggest you order your men to turn back.'

'Turn back?' Allard queried. 'But we're no more than halfway across the moor.'

'Closer to a third,' Harland Wolfe replied, 'but nevertheless we appear to have drawn a blank.'

'I don't understand you, Mr Wolfe,' Allard admitted.

'Nor I,' Dr Manston put in.

'We have failed to draw our quarry, it is as simple as that,' Harland Wolfe responded, 'although I do not doubt that we are watched, and were it not for this rain, I might still hope for success.'

'I know my duty, sir,' Allard went on, 'and that's to search the moor from west to east.'

'Then I suggest you continue,' Harland Wolfe responded, 'but you will find nothing.'

The Inspector cast a doubtful glance at the scenery, now dim as the rain began to patter down, with Fur Tor no more than a dark shape and the ridge behind them invisible.

'Come, Manston,' Harland Wolfe suggested. 'We must start back, or we risk straying into the mires. I wish you good luck, Inspector Allard.'

The Inspector gave them a half-hearted salute and blew his whistle, starting the line forwards once more. Dr Manston started after Harland Wolfe. He was already beginning to get wet, and the storm was evidently going to be a heavy one, leaving him thinking regretfully of the hearty lunch Mrs Capleton would no doubt be putting together at Stukely Hall.

Genevieve sat beneath the towering arch of the viaduct, watching the rain lash down to either side of her. She herself was at least moderately dry, having found a patch of grass in the lee of the wall and sheltered by bushes on three sides, creating a little world of green plants, grey granite and grey rain, in which she felt entirely alone. Nobody could see her, and she was sure nobody would come across her unexpectedly, allowing her thoughts to turn gradually towards her bodily need.

Her quim was wet and felt urgent, a shameful condition when it was a consequence of being spanked, but not an easy one to ignore. With nothing better to do and so very alone, the temptation to play with herself had grown steadily since she had taken shelter. Twice already she had raised her knees and allowed them a little apart, only for her pride to get the better of her. Now she was telling herself that just because it was the spanking which had made her excited didn't mean she had to think about it while she touched herself.

It would be much better to think about Richard Truscott, the way he had kissed her, so tender yet so forceful, and caressed her body, how he'd torn her clothes in his excitement, and fed from her breasts, how he'd put his mouth to her quim and taken her right to the edge of ecstasy, how he'd made her accept his cock in her mouth, but best of all, how he'd eased it up her bottom and buggered her.

She had closed her eyes as she ran through her memories, and at the thought of being buggered her back had begun to arch, pushing out her breasts and sex in wanton abandonment. No longer wishing to hold back, she began to tease herself, first stroking her nipples through her bodice, then allowing her thighs to come up and open to spread her sex wide beneath her clothes.

Very gradually, and still with her eyes closed, she began to disrobe, loosening her dress until she could push it down around her waist, unlacing the front of her chemise and peeling the sides apart to bare her breasts, and all the while imagining she was doing it for him. She was smiling as she began to toy with her nipples once more, now bare, her mouth set in a sleepy happy smile. Both little buds were already hard, and almost painfully sensitive to the touch of her fingers, while she was sure her breasts had grown a little fuller since her arrival at Stukely Hall.

Her quim needed touching too, but she held off until the urge had become a physical ache before rolling up her legs into the same lewd posture in which she had held herself as Richard had taken her up her bottom. Slipping one hand beneath herself, she quickly tugged her still unfastened drawers loose from under her cheeks and held the panel up, deliberately showing off her quim and her bottom hole too. She could smell her own scent, and was imagining how it would feel on her wedding night, when Richard finally took her virginity, as he had promised to do.

She would roll herself up, her beautiful white dress spread out around her like a flower, her stockinged thighs at the centre, and her drawers, open to show off the turn of her bottom cheeks, the tiny moist hole between, and her quim, nude and virgin, her maidenhead stretched wide, ready for his cock to be plunged through it and inside her body. A strong shiver passed through her at the thought, and her hand went to her quim. She began to touch, just gently, teasing her bump and stroking the tight arc of flesh that held her inviolate until she chose to surrender herself to her chosen man.

'Richard . . .,' she sighed, as her thumb began to circle her clitoris, 'oh, Richard, I wish you were here . . . You could take me now, I wouldn't mind . . . I wouldn't mind at all.'

Thrusting her sex out, she begun to rub harder on her clitoris, now eager to bring herself to ecstasy. Her thighs came wider still, spreading her quim to the warm moist air as she masturbated, her back already arched tight, her mouth open in ecstasy, then in a scream as a heavy weight settled on her, powerful hands gripped her waist, and a long thick cock was rammed deep in up her open cunt, bursting her hymen and spattering her inner thighs with her virgin blood.

Her eyes sprang open, to find a great bearded face staring down into hers, the eyes the only visible feature in a mane of ginger hair. Again she screamed, shock, pain and fear filling her head, but there was nothing she could do, trapped beneath his weight as his cock pumped into her helpless body, fast and furious, forcing moans from her throat for all her horror. He seemed to be all hair, his hips and legs were pushed to her bare skin as well as the tangle against her cunt, and that was rubbing on her already engorged clitoris with every thrust of his body. She came, utterly helpless to stop herself, her mouth wide in a long scream of mingled despair and ecstasy, her body in violent contraction beneath his, fluid squirting from her penetrated cunt all over his belly and her own, and again as his pumping rose to a manic crescendo, forcing the breath from her body and ending with a barely human cry as he came deep inside her.

Genevieve felt the spunk explode from her cunt and her helpless orgasm hit a third peak, stronger even than before, and accompanied by another scream as much for her ruined virginity as the ecstatic reaction she could do nothing to prevent. His cock was still in her, driven deep, and there it stayed even as her contractions gradually subsided. Only when she was finally lay still did he pull loose with a final bestial grunt, to shamble off among the bushes, a great hairy creature, more ape than man.

'That was a woman's scream!' Dr Manston exclaimed, but Harland Wolfe was already running through the downpour towards where the dreadful sound had rung out.

'By God, Miss Stukely!' he swore and followed.

Another scream followed, and a third, faint but clear enough, and he was running down the slope of Arm's Tor, heedless of the danger as his boots slipped in the rapidly thickening mud and stumbled over rocks. His hat went, and his stick, but he clutched the revolver in his pocket and ran all the faster for his mounting fear of what might lie ahead.

'There!' Harland Wolfe yelled from ahead.

Dr Manston looked up, to catch a glimpse of something through the sheeting rain, a figure coming towards them, but as it became distinct he stopped in his tracks, frozen in fear and astonishment. What was coming towards them was no man, but some huge ape-like creature, well above six foot in height, naked and covered in reddish hair from its toes to the top of its head, save for two glaring eyes, a double line of teeth, and a large heavy penis, wet with rain and streaked red with blood.

'What in God's name is that!?' he gasped.

'Never mind what it is, shoot it, damn you!' Harland Wolfe yelled back as he turned to flee the advancing creature.

Dr Manston snatched out his revolver, struggling to quell the shaking in his hands as he lifted it, but the creature seemed to have divined his intent, hurling itself to one side even as the shot rang out. A spurt of gorse flowers showed where the bullet had gone and he fired again, but too late. The creature had vanished among the rocks and bushes, to leave Harland Wolfe prone on the muddy ground but untouched, and as Dr Manston lowered his gun he saw that a bedraggled half-naked girl had come out from beneath the nearby railway viaduct: Miss Stukely.

Eight

'What in God's name do we do now?' Charles Truscott demanded.

'Lucy must go to him,' Nell suggested. 'She alone can calm his poor soul.'

She was red-eyed and sobbing, and Richard saw his father take a deep breath before he continued.

'Lucy is still in a state over that wretched cousin of hers, while we have no idea where Leopold is in any event.'

'Still on the moor, no doubt,' Richard supplied.

'And hunted!' Nell added.

'Yes, quite,' Charles agreed. 'Clearly we must act with despatch.'

'I'll ride over and volunteer to join the hunt,' Richard suggested. 'With luck I can find him first, or at least draw the search off.'

'Do so,' Charles instructed him, 'and take Luke Gurney with you.'

Richard rose from the table, only to stop short. Leopold stood in the doorway, his great body caked with mud, his face set in a forlorn scowl. Nell immediately ran to him, taking her son in her arms, a hug Leopold returned rather too forcefully, obliging Richard to intervene before his brother could grow amorous.

'There, there, old chap,' Richard said, gingerly

attempting to detach Leopold's hand from his mother's left buttock. 'Lucy's upstairs, you know.'

As he led Leopold gently from the room his mind was racing. A great deal needed to be done, and fast, to protect his brother and the family honour, and to somehow quash the wild rumours spreading around the district. Yet first and foremost he wanted to see Genevieve.

'So this is our beast,' Dr Manston declared, settling himself into the armchair he had made his own in the drawing room of Stukely Hall, 'no hound, but some unknown ape, doubtless trained by whoever seeks to kill Miss Stukely, and he himself must be no less a monster!'

'No, no,' Harland Wolfe responded with a dismissive gesture, 'you have it quite wrong. Whatever we saw yesterday, it was not the beast.'

'But surely . . .'

'Consider the facts,' Harland Wolfe interrupted. 'The legend mentions a hound, not an ape, and it was the footprint of a hound found where Sir Robert died. Dr Robinson is adamant that whatever tore out Billy Sugden's throat had a canine dentition, not an anthropoid one. Furthermore, the creature did not kill Miss Stukely, although it had every opportunity to do so.'

'Do you mean to say there are two beasts out there?' Dr Manston demanded.

'So it would seem,' Harland Wolfe admitted, 'and yet can it be coincidence that one appears on the very same day we are hunting for the other? I suspect not. There are tangled threads here, Manston.'

'It is beyond me, certainly,' Dr Manston admitted.

'But not, I trust, beyond me,' Harland Wolfe responded. 'Indeed, the case has parallels. You will recall the giant rat of Sumatra, no doubt?'

'All too vividly,' Dr Manston confirmed.

'The situation here is similar,' Harland Wolfe went on. 'There are many threads, so there are many avenues of exploration. For instance, as with the rat, the ape is of evident maturity, which makes me wonder where it grew to that maturity. There are no travelling circuses in the vicinity, nor zoological gardens, while both Dr Robinson and yourself attest that it is of no known species. Thus, the creature must have derived from one of the world's few remaining great areas of wilderness, and to have brought it back, for whatever purpose, would require considerable means and a well-equipped expedition. Or . . .'

Harland Wolfe fell to brooding.

'This is all very well, Wolfe,' Dr Manston put in, 'but should we not be out on the moor?'

'The hunt may be left to the police and their bloodhounds,' Harland Wolfe responded. 'There is an intellectual side to this problem as well as a physical, and it is that on which I intend to concentrate. This might, I suspect, be a three-pipe problem, but first a word with Constable Apcott might prove worthwhile.'

Dr Manston fetched the constable from his post at the front door and once more made himself comfortable.

'Constable Apcott,' Harland Wolfe began, 'you have heard, no doubt that yesterday Miss Stukely was attacked by some form of ape?'

'Yes, sir,' Constable Apcott replied doubtfully.

'Now,' Harland Wolfe continued. 'You have lived here all your life, and know both the area and the local families well. Do you recall any expeditions by wealthy men, to Africa perhaps, or the Canadian provinces?'

'There was Sir Robert Stukely, sir,' Constable Apcott stated. 'Made his fortune in Africa, he did, and he came back wealthy, to take up his estate here when his uncle died.'

'That I already know,' Harland Wolfe answered. 'Are there any others?'

'Squire Truscott,' the constable supplied, 'he was years in Hungary, where his wife's from, he was, but that was more than thirty years back now, after poor Nell Truscott lost the baby. Still . . .'

Constable Apcott had gone silent, and appeared distinctly uncomfortable.

'Do go on,' Harland Wolfe urged.

'Well, sir, I don't rightly like to say, sir,' Constable Apcott muttered, 'and maybe it's nothing but a parcel of old crams, but . . .'

Again the constable stopped.

'Any detail, no matter how trivial, may be of interest,' Harland Wolfe told him, 'unless of course your hesitancy comes from a no doubt commendable sense of loyalty, in which case perhaps you would prefer to wait until Inspector Allard is present?'

'Oh no, sir,' Constable Apcott assured him, 'it's only that there's rumours, sir, about goings on at Driscoll's, and sometimes, on a still night, you hears noises, the wind, like as not.'

'The Truscotts are a wealthy family, I believe,' Harland Wolfe continued, 'and also well connected. Do they entertain a great deal?'

'Oh no, sir,' the constable replied, evidently relieved at the change of subject. 'Old John, he used to have an annual ball, and all sorts of capers, but Charles, he's a quiet man, and Nell likewise. Keep themselves to themselves, they do. Built a great wall right around the estate, he did. Never got over the loss of that baby, I don't suppose. Not that he doesn't make a good squire, mind you, you won't find a man more popular in his village, and he's generous with his wages, and his terms. Never dismissed a servant, has Squire Truscott, and proud of it.'

'A remarkable man, it seems,' Harland Wolfe answered. 'This wall, when was it built?'

'Twenty-five, thirty years gone, sir, not long after he and his wife got back from foreign parts.'

'I see,' Harland Wolfe stated. 'Perhaps it is not time for a pipe after all, Manston. I think we may safely leave the good constable on guard here, if you would care to accompany me to the Driscoll Estate.'

Genevieve Stukely lay propped up on the pillows of her bed. Although she knew she should have been in hysterics, and had every right to be, she felt oddly detached, as if the terrifying event of the day before had been only a particularly vivid nightmare. She knew it was not, the sting of her ruptured maidenhead giving ample reminder of what had happened to her, and yet she found it hard to resent even that.

She had heard Harland Wolfe and Dr Manston leave, and was now worried, only not so much for the possible reappearance of the massive ape but because she was once more at the mercy of Nanna Bloss. The ape, she felt, might even have been preferable, and at the all too familiar creak of the big woman's tread on the stair her stomach had begun to flutter.

'So how's my little actress?' Nanna Bloss sneered as she appeared in the doorway, now dressed in a vast pale-blue gown and mop cap which made Genevieve think of a grotesque pantomime version of Little Bo Peep.

'Actress?' she queried. 'How do you mean, Nanna?'

'You know full well what I mean,' Nanna Bloss laughed. 'Think I'm stupid, do you? This is some new nonsense you've cooked up with Dr Manston and his fine detective friend, isn't it, just so I'll keep away from you?'

'No,' Genevieve protested. 'Every word I have said is true, while I have said nothing of how you treat me to either Dr Manston or Mr Wolfe.'

'A likely story!' Nanna scoffed. 'Show me your cunt.'

'Nanna!' Genevieve protested, but the big woman was already advancing on her with obvious ill intent. 'OK, there is no need to be beastly to me. I will show you I am not a liar.'

Nanna Bloss gave a grim chuckle and folded her massive arms across her chest as Genevieve reluctantly pushed down the bedcovers. Her nightie had ridden up, and most of her legs were already on show, so that only a small adjustment was necessary to bare her pubic mound. Throwing a wounded look at Nanna Bloss, she opened her thighs.

'There,' she said, 'are you satisfied?'

The big woman grunted and leant close, poking two fat fingers at Genevieve's sex to spread the lips and show off the deflowered hole between. Now pouting badly, Genevieve nevertheless allowed the inspection, even as a single finger was slid in up her hole.

'Oh yes, you've been had, right enough,' Nanna Bloss stated as she eased her finger from Genevieve's quim, 'but whom by, that's the question?'

'I told you all!' Genevieve answered indignantly as she covered herself. 'It was some great hairy apeman, and both Dr Manston and Mr Wolfe saw it too!'

'Most convenient, I'm sure,' Nanna Bloss retorted, 'but only an out and out fool would believe you, whoever claims to have seen this apeman. Where's it live then? And why has nobody seen it before?'

'I . . . I don't know!' Genevieve protested. 'But I am telling the truth.'

'And I'm auntie to President Harrison,' Nanna Bloss scoffed. 'What I reckon is you let yourself go a bit with that Dr Manston . . .'

'Certainly not! Dr Manston is a gentleman, and besides, I am betrothed to . . .'

'You're a whore, that's what you are, and always were. If it weren't for your lucky chance I'd have you walloping the mattress back in Deadwood by now, and enjoying it too. It was that Dr Manston had you, wasn't it? He's sweet enough on you, that's for certain, or did you let 'em share you, you dirty little trollop? One up the cunt, one up the hiney, I'll be bound, eh?'

'I did not,' Genevieve said weakly, but Nanna Bloss merely snorted and went on.

'And what was it I said about disobeying me, the last time I tried to smack some sense into you, what was it? I said I'd punish you, didn't I?'

Genevieve's response was a sulky silence.

Richard flicked his whip to the haunch of his horse, setting his sulky bouncing across the rutted surface of the track, only to be forced to draw on the reins as another vehicle appeared coming towards him. Drawing into a convenient field gate, he waited, eager to move on until he recognised the trap as one belonging to the Stukelys, and then the occupants as Harland Wolfe and Dr Manston. As they drew close he raised his hat, praying that they were not on their way to Driscoll's.

'Good morning,' he greeted them. 'Have you run your mysterious hound to earth yet?'

'I fear not,' Harland Wolfe replied, 'but this is a happy meeting. Dr Manston and I were just driving over to Driscoll's in the hope that your father and yourself might be able to provide us with a little background.'

'As you know,' Richard responded, 'we are always delighted to be of assistance, but I fear we have already told you all we know. Indeed, to us country folk the entire matter is wholly mysterious.'

'My questions are more in connection with the events of yesterday afternoon,' Harland Wolfe went on. 'You have heard, no doubt?'

'Yes, it is quite terrible,' Richard said quickly. 'In fact, I was just driving over to enquire after Miss Stukely's wellbeing.'

'She is a strong young woman, and shows remarkable fortitude,' Harland Wolfe assured him, 'but you must not let us detain you.'

Richard hesitated, glancing towards the moor, then back to where Burley Down rose above the fields. There was no help for it, the family had to come first.

'Perhaps it would be better if I allowed Miss Stukely to rest,' he said, 'while I fear my father is apt to be abrupt with strangers.'

He gave a last regretful glance in the direction of Stukely Hall and began to wheel the sulky about.

Lucy rubbed the soap vigorously into the mud-caked hair of Leopold's belly. Being a conscientious girl, and not wishing to put the household to unnecessary expense, she had removed all her clothes except her drawers and the cunt pad which kept her virginity safe. It had clearly been a sensible choice, for Leopold's cock had already begun to stiffen, and he was no longer feeling sorry for himself.

'Not until I'm done with you, Master Leopold!' she urged for the third time as one hairy hand moved to her breasts.

Unfortunately the way they wobbled as she scrubbed at his dirty body seemed to fascinate him, and the moment she had detached his hand he put it back, grinning now as he fondled her, with the tip of his cock head already starting to protrude from the meaty hood of his foreskin.

'If you must then,' she sighed, 'but mind you let me get you properly clean.'

He answered with a grunt and Lucy continued to wash, her eyes flicking occasionally to his penis as it grew swollen and stiff. She knew it would be going up her, because there was no other way of getting him calm enough to ensure he would go back into his room, and she had been careful to butter her bottom before starting. Now, with the bathroom door safely locked and no chance of being disturbed, she found she was really quite keen to let her tensions out with a good buggering, especially when she had such a perfect excuse.

'Just your back parts now, Master Leopold,' she instructed, 'if you'd roll over for me, please.'

She made a motion with her hands as she spoke and he responded, splashing around to wet her breasts with water and soap bubbles as he got on all fours. Lucy began to soap his back and buttocks, marvelling as always at how hard his muscles were beneath the shaggy red hair that covered his body, and before long her hand had slipped down between his legs, to massage soap into his scrotum and tug gently on his cock as she told herself that his dirty bits needed to be washed just like the rest of him.

Genevieve lay face down on her bed, stark naked, her arms tied behind her back with a strip torn from her nightie, her ankles lashed tight with another, her mouth plugged with more of the same, her bottom pink from spanking. Nanna Bloss had dealt with her hard, making her strip off her own nightie to go nude and delivering a blistering over-the-knee spanking which had left Genevieve tear-stained and gasping with a burning bottom and, inevitably, a shamefully moist quim. She'd had her thighs spread for inspection as soon as the spanking was over, and when Nanna Bloss had seen the state Genevieve was in she had laughed. After a few extra swats to her quivering bottom cheeks, Genevieve had been tossed on the bed, tied up and gagged with the torn remains of her pretty new nightie. Now, she could only wriggle feebly as she awaited her fate, listening to the sound of the big woman's footsteps on the stairs.

Nanna Bloss appeared in the doorway and Genevieve's eyes came wide in alarm. In each of the big woman's hands was a young marrow, long and fat and green, the smaller of the two perhaps twice the size of Richard Truscott's not unimpressive cock. She didn't need to be told where they were going, and began to squirm frantically on the bed and mumble entreaties through her gag, but her efforts only made the cruel glitter in Nanna Bloss' eyes all the more intense.

'Whatever is the matter, Ginny?' Nanna asked in mock surprise. 'You're so keen on cock, I'd have thought you'd enjoy something a little bigger, and I've made sure they go in nice and smooth.'

As she spoke, the big woman had held up the smaller of the two marrows, and Genevieve saw that a large glistening blob of goose grease was balanced on the top, with runnels of fat already trickling down the sides. She began to panic, writhing in her bonds in an attempt to get off the bed, despite knowing there was no way of escape. Nanna Bloss simply caught her, pulling her back to the middle of the bed and rolling her face-down once more.

'The more you struggle, the worse it'll hurt,' Nanna Bloss pointed out. 'Now get this under you.'

She was holding the marrows in one hand, but still made quick work of inserting the bolster under Genevieve's stomach, to leave her with her bottom pushed up and a little open, quim and anus available for penetration.

'Quiet your wriggling,' Nanna Bloss ordered, and applied another hard slap to Genevieve's bottom.

Genevieve couldn't, too panic-stricken to do as she was told no matter what the consequences. Another barrage of hard slaps was delivered to her bottom but still she writhed and sobbed, then went into a frantic jerking motion as she felt the head of a marrow press between her cheeks. Nanna Bloss merely laughed and changed her position, leaning across Genevieve's body. Now trapped completely, Genevieve still kicked and squirmed as the marrow was rubbed between her cheeks, smearing goose grease the length of her slit and over her anus.

'Will you stop it?' Nanna warned. 'Or shall I put the big one up your hiney hole?'

The marrow had been removed from between Genevieve's cheeks as Nanna Bloss spoke, but still she wriggled, with the goose grease melting slowly in her anus and trickling down into the open hole of her cunt.

'Determined little bitch, ain't you?' Nanna Bloss said. 'But I'll break you, see if I don't.'

Again Genevieve felt pressure between her cheeks, and again she began to jerk and writhe. Nanna Bloss' grip tightened, the marrow was forced deeper, squashing against Genevieve's anus, which immediately began to spread to the pressure. Genevieve's eyes popped and her cheeks bulged as she felt her anus start to gape, wider and wider until she was sure she would split, and yet still Nanna Bloss pushed, until suddenly it was in, jammed up her back passage with a thick squelch.

'There we are. I said it would go,' Nanna chuckled. 'Now for your cunt.'

Genevieve's eyes were watering for the bloated sensation in her rectum, but she was buggered, and her struggles had died to a feeble wriggling as the second marrow was pressed to her quim, and up, sliding into the sopping hole with embarrassing ease. Now doubly penetrated, she collapsed over the bolster, sobbing through her gag as Nanna Bloss began to pump the thick loads in and out. As she was fucked she found it impossible not to grunt and pant, just as she had grunted and panted with the apeman's cock inside her, the sensation of being so full simply too much to allow her to hold back.

At Driscoll's, Lucy was in a similar state, knelt in the bath with her wet pink bottom sticking out of her open drawers and Leopold's erection thrust to the balls up her soapy buttered bottom hole. The soap stung, making her eyes water, and he was being even rougher than usual, jamming himself in and out of her gaping anus as she clung to the bath with her dangling breasts slapping on the enamel to every thrust. Her cunt pad had come a little adrift too, and she was praying that he'd finish off up her bottom without deciding to ruin her, because there was nothing she could do to stop it happening if he did. He was too strong, too determined, and so she simply clung on, grunting her way through her buggering and hoping against hope that she'd still be a virgin when he was done with her.

Her prayers were answered sooner than she'd expected. Leopold's grip tightened in the flesh of her hips, he jammed his cock as deep as it would go and gave a long satisfied grunt as he spunked up in her rectum. Lucy let her breath out slowly as he held himself in with the soft contractions of her anus milking the sperm up her bottom. He was done, and once she'd cleaned up and got him into his room, so would she be, lying on her bed as she masturbated to the thought of what had been done to her.

She winced as he pulled free, leaving her bottom hole to close with a soft fart that blew out a puff of bubbles between her cheeks, making Leopold laugh. Blushing slightly, Lucy quickly washed herself and climbed out, removing her soggy drawers before taking a towel for herself and wrapping another around Leopold. Getting him dry was always a task, and she began to rub vigorously at his hairy body, unsure whether or not she was going to like it if his cock grew stiff again before she was finished.

'You'll appreciate the necessity of protection,' Richard extemporised frantically as Harland Wolfe glanced up at the newly sharpened spikes topping the wall of

Driscoll's. 'As you no doubt know, we employ a great many miners, and discontent is always something one needs to take into consideration, then of course there's the Cornish, just over the border.'

He attempted a light laugh, but it came out as a gurgle.

'I was given to understand that your family were among the best of employers?' Harland Wolfe asked quietly.

'We, er . . . we do out best,' Richard responded, 'but there's always the possibility of, um . . . agitators, that sort of thing. There was a book published last year, you may know, by this fellow called Marx[9], and father has rather taken it to heart. He wants blood running down the lanes, that sort of thing, er . . . Marx, that is, not father . . .'

Richard trailed off. They had reached the main gates, and he was obliged to dismount in order to get both the trap and his own sulky through before locking them behind him. Harland Wolfe said nothing, but watched everything, with the faintly supercilious expression Richard was beginning to dislike intensely. Now he was leading his horse on foot in a desperate effort to play for time, all the while praying Lucy had managed to render Leopold docile or better still get him to sleep. As they approached the house he was dreading the joyous but distinctly unnerving howl Leopold was apt to emit when he came, but Driscoll's seemed unusually peaceful.

'Do come around to the stable yard,' he offered. 'My groom, Gurney, will see to your horse.'

Luke Gurney himself had appeared, and took the horses, leaving Richard to conduct his visitors indoors. His father was still in the morning room, reading the paper as was his habit, and Richard made a hurried introduction.

'Father, may I introduce you to Mr Harland Wolfe, the celebrated detective, and his friend, Dr Manston. Mr Wolfe, Dr Manston, my father, Charles Truscott.'

For a moment Charles looked both astonished and horrified before he managed to collect his wits and rise from his chair, extending a hand towards Harland Wolfe as he spoke.

'Ah, yes, I have heard so much of your exploits, Mr Wolfe. There was that episode with the racehorse, Silver Star, of course, and many another. But it is you who are Mr Wolfe's amanuensis, is it not, Dr Manston?'

'I have occasionally been permitted to put our less delicate cases on public record, yes,' Dr Manston admitted.

'Generally in the most sensational form,' Harland Wolfe added, 'but it is for his courage and tenacity I admire Dr Manston, rather than his literary ability.'

'Ah ha,' Charles replied noncommittally. 'But what can we do for you, Mr Wolfe? I trust that you do not suspect us of harbouring this monstrous hound?'

'Not at all,' Harland Wolfe responded. 'I merely wish to clarify one or two small matters in connection with the case, and specifically, the unfortunate events of yesterday afternoon.'

'If you'll excuse me a moment,' Richard remarked, and walked from the room with as much nonchalance as he could muster.

The moment he was out of view he darted up the stairs, climbing to the second floor with long silent strides. Reaching the bathroom, he poked his head around the door, but there was nobody there, merely some water on the floor and a mingled tang of soap and sex in the air.

'He's finished with her, thank God for that,' he muttered as he withdrew, moving down the corridor to his own room.

Leopold was standing by the bed, stark naked, his great hairy body towering over Lucy as she sat sucking on his cock with her eyes closed in bliss. Richard came to a halt, feeling somewhat awkward, but Leopold merely grinned and began to show off, fucking Lucy's mouth and rubbing his cock in her face.

'My Lucy,' Leopold said happily.

'Er . . . yes, quite, very nice too,' Richard replied, 'but, um . . . I'll show you a new trick. That would be fun, wouldn't it? Lie on the bed, there's a good chap. Lucy, climb on top of him and sit on his face while you suck, and for the sake of us all keep your fanny on his mouth when he comes.'

'But my pad!' Lucy protested.

'Never mind your damn pad!' Richard hissed, and quickly changed his tone at a warning growl from Leopold. 'That detective fellow, Wolfe, is downstairs, and if Leo starts howling the house down . . .'

Lucy nodded and scrambled around to where Leopold had already laid himself on the bed. Richard watched as she quickly pulled her drawers and cunt pad down and off, then mounted up, stark naked as she lowered her bottom into Leopold's face. Leopold licked eagerly and Lucy shivered in pleasure even as a rich blush spread across her face. Her hand closed on the big cock sticking up from among the thickness of Leopold's hair, she leant forwards a little and she was sucking, his helmet between her lips as she masturbated him into her mouth.

'Good girl,' Richard stated. 'I'll make sure there's another half-crown in your wages this week. Now once you're done, get Leo into his room and stay there yourself. Get out the toy soldiers or something, but keep him occupied.'

Lucy nodded around her mouthful of cock and Richard slipped from the room.

Genevieve lay on her back, her twin holes still straining to the marrows pushed well up into each, her hands and feet still tied. Only her gag had been removed, and she was earnestly wishing it hadn't as Nanna Bloss began to pull up the skirts of her enormous dress.

'Yes,' Nanna Bloss was saying, 'that's what I'll do. I drop a curtsey on your face, the way we used to do to girls as wouldn't do their share, and you can lick me that way while I gives you a good fucking.'

'Nanna, must you?' Genevieve implored. 'I will do as I am told, I will! I will be a good girl, and . . . and . . . oh, Nanna, please not like that!'

The bed creaked as Nanna Bloss climbed on, her monstrous bottom towards Genevieve's head, with the huge buttocks covered only by a pair of fantastically trimmed drawers, on which even the buttons were covered in pale pink silk and topped with tiny roses of the same fabric. Genevieve was still babbling entreaties as the big woman bunched her skirts and swung one tree-trunk leg across. With her tormentor now sat now directly over her face, Genevieve began to panic, writhing in her bonds and wide-eyed in horror. One of the fancy buttons burst, unequal to the strain of holding in Nanna's vast bulging buttocks. A big hand came back and another button was tweaked open, a second, a third, and the panel fell away, baring the broad pasty expanse of Nanna Bloss' bottom, right in Genevieve's face, the twin cheeks fat and round and heavy, the crease between a dark slit clogged with hairs save where a large moist anus showed among the tangles.

'And you can clean my arsehole too, while you're about it,' Nanna Bloss remarked, and sat down.

Genevieve's pathetic begging was cut off as her face was smothered in reeking bottom fat. She'd turned her head, but that only meant her cheek was pressed to Nanna's cunt and her ear against the wet anal hole, while her mouth was half covered by heavy pink flesh.

'Better do as you're told,' Nanna warned, and Genevieve's legs had been taken and lifted by the strip of material binding her ankles. 'Come on with you, lick while I gives you a good pumping, you'll enjoy it.'

Genevieve blurted out an immediate urgent denial, barely coherent from her squashed mouth, but her legs had already been rolled up, and her body twisted to one side, leaving the marrows in her holes sticking out. Nanna took hold of the one in Genevieve's cunt and began to pump it in an out. Two firm pushes in her straining hole and Genevieve was gasping at the foetid air, unable to stop herself. Nanna Bloss gave a wiggle, rubbing her bottom onto Genevieve's head.

'Come along with you, Ginny my girl,' Nanna growled, 'you know where you want to put that tongue.'

A mewl of protest escaped Genevieve's lips, but she was already telling herself it would be best to get it over with, and as the pumping in her cunt grew faster and deeper she was twisting her head. Her nose slipped into the musky bottom slit, her lips pressed to Nanna's anus, and with a last miserable shame-filled sob she had given in, poking out her tongue into the slippery acrid hole.

'That's my Ginny,' Nanna Bloss laughed as Genevieve began to lick her bottom, 'now you get your tongue well in there and clean me out nice, then I'll treat you to a mouthful of cunt.'

Nanna Bloss gave another wiggle, settling her bottom in Genevieve's face as she continued to pump the marrow in and out. Lost to the feelings of her body, confused to the point of hysterics, Genevieve licked at the big woman's anus, her tongue now well up the soft wet hole and her mouth full of the taste of bottom.

'Good,' Nanna sighed. 'I always knew you'd be a dirty one, from the day you came to me. Now my cunt.'

Genevieve gulped in a mouthful of air as Nanna moved, before her mouth was filled with hot slippery flesh. She began to lick at the big blubbery cunt lips, her nose now up Nanna's spit-wet bottom hole, and still the marrow worked in her cunt. Nanna began to grunt and rub her bottom in Genevieve's face, pressing down harder still. Genevieve could no longer breathe, her mouth full of pungent slimy cunt juice, her face plastered with spit, the marrow now slopping in her hole, but Nanna was coming, her weird grunting noises rising to a thunderous crescendo like a dozen sows giving birth at once as the orgasm hit her.

Unable to breath, unable to see, unable to control her jerking limbs, Genevieve could only keep licking until Nanna had finished. At last the motion of the marrow in her cunt stopped and Nanna lifted a little, allowing Genevieve to gasp in air that seemed the sweetest she had ever known for all its musky reek. She lay back, panting in exhaustion as the big bottom lifted from her face.

'Now you,' Nanna puffed, 'and you can lick my hiney hole while I does you.'

'Nanna, no, I . . .' Genevieve managed before her face was once more smothered between the vast bottom cheeks.

She began to wriggle again, but Nanna Bloss merely settled herself down more comfortably, her sloppy open anus now pressed to Genevieve's cheek once more. Utterly helpless, Genevieve could only squirm pitifully in her tormentor's grip as her legs were pulled higher still, allowing Nanna to get at both marrows. A feeble moan escaped her lips as the two fat vegetables began to move, pulling in and out of both cunt and anus, faster, and faster still as a thumb found Genevieve's bump.

'Go on, lick my arse,' Nanna urged. 'It's what you need, and we both know that.'

Genevieve shook her head, but the marrows working in her holes and the thumb running on her cunt were making her want to do it, and with a final despairing sob she had twisted her head around and stuck her tongue back in up Nanna's bottom, only no longer for her tormentor's pleasure, but for her own.

'That's my Ginny!' Nanna laughed. 'Go on, lick it, you dirty little whore, lick it well!'

Genevieve no longer needed to be told. Her tongue was pushed in up Nanna's bottom hole as deep as it would go, licking the open slippery cavity and trying to probe deeper still. Her cunt and anus felt impossibly bloated, her bump on fire, and every muscle in her body had begun to jerk as she went into a set of spasms at once so agonising and so ecstatic that before the orgasm was over she had been brought to the very edge of losing her senses.

'There are all sorts of tales in these parts,' Charles Truscott remarked as his wife filled Dr Manston's glass with Malmsey. 'Take Cutty Dyer[10] for instance, a bloodthirsty ogre who lives in the moor streams and drags unwary travellers down under the water.'

'In this case both Dr Manston and myself saw the creature quite clearly,' Harland Wolfe stated. 'Although it was raining hard at the time there can be no doubt that it was real, while Miss Stukely's account is equally persuasive.'

'Perhaps it was a man in an ape suit?' Charles Truscott suggested.

'This possibility has already occurred to me,' Harland Wolfe answered, 'and the beast did indeed seem sufficiently intelligent to be aware that Dr Manston intended to fire at it.'

'Remarkable,' Charles admitted, 'but I fail to see how I can help you.'

'No?' Harland Wolfe queried. 'We were hoping you might be able to shed some light on the matter.'

'I fear not,' Charles told him.

'I am afraid we can't help you at all, Mr Wolfe,' Nell Truscott supplied, 'although I very much wish we could.'

'Any detail might be of importance,' Harland Wolfe insisted. 'For instance, has a similar creature ever been seen in these parts before?'

'No, no, absolutely not,' Charles answered as Richard returned to the room. 'Richard, there you are. Can you think of anything that might assist Mr Wolfe with his investigation?'

'Nothing whatever,' Richard stated, 'save perhaps that some great ape has escaped from a circus or a private menagerie, although I know of none in these parts.'

'I was suggesting it might be a man dressed up in a suit,' Charles put in.

'Ah, yes . . . very likely,' Richard agreed. 'Perhaps he is somebody known to Miss Stukely and wished to molest her without risking recognition?'

'An ape suit, merely to avoid recognition?' Dr Manston queried. 'Would not a mask suffice?'

Richard shrugged.

'Perhaps he wished to horrify her? Perhaps this is the same person who has the dog? There are a dozen possibilities, but it is you, after all, who are the detective, Mr Wolfe.'

'Just so,' Harland Wolfe responded.

'I expect you'll be needing your potty now?' Nanna Bloss chuckled as she eased the marrow free from Genevieve's bottom hole.

'Yes,' Genevieve admitted sulkily. 'Please could you untie me?'

'Yes, why not?' Nanna Bloss agreed. 'I like to see you kick and wiggle about the way you do during a punishment.'

'But, I have been punished, Nanna,' Genevieve protested.

'Punished?' Nanna Bloss demanded. 'That was no punishment, Ginny, that was just a little fun, between friends as it were. For your punishment, your face is going in your pot, once you've filled it that is.'

Genevieve's mouth had come open in horror-stricken disbelief, but she knew she was helpless and after a moment hung her head in meek submission. Nanna Bloss chuckled and came close, quickly tugging Genevieve's bonds loose.

'Now the pot,' Nanna ordered.

No words could encompass Genevieve's feelings, and she knew that a protest would only fuel the big woman's cruelty in any event. With her face set in misery but also submission she squatted down over the pot, her bottom lowered carefully onto the hard china rim and her thighs well apart. Nanna Bloss watched, gloating, as Genevieve squeezed the contents of her bowels out into the pot. Her bladder gave way too, adding a thick stream of urine to the filth beneath her.

'Finished?' Nanna Bloss demanded as a last plop sounded from the pot beneath Genevieve's bottom.

Genevieve gave a small miserable nod and stood up, to glance from the window as she wished with all her heart that she was anywhere but in her bedroom with the big woman who was about to dunk her face in the contents of her potty. Two men were visible on the slopes of the moor, Matthew Widdery and Dr Robinson, the one seated at his easel, the other walking across the flank of Doe Tor. Without further thought, Genevieve snatched up the chamber pot, hurled it at Nanna Bloss and ran, leaving the room to the sound of an unpleasantly sticky splash followed by a bellow of rage.

Terrified, she fled down the stairs and out into the garden, ignoring Mrs Capleton's horrified expression at the sight of her naked body. Only in the garden did she hesitate, not wishing to run out onto the moor in the nude but not wishing to return indoors either. A flash of white caught her eye and she realised that Mrs Capleton had been pegging out washing in the servants' yard, but Nanna Bloss had already appeared in the door she had just left, roaring with rage, her huge extravagant dress wet and filthy, her face the colour of beetroot.

Genevieve darted for the servants' yard as Nanna Bloss started forwards. There were only sheets on the lines, but she snatched one and kept running, out of the back gate and onto the moor, pausing only when she was sure she was well enough clear of her pursuer to wrap the sheet around her body. Nanna Bloss was some way behind, and shook a fist as she saw Genevieve had stopped, then called out.

'Better you get back here, Ginny, or the hound'll get you!'

'I'd rather him have me than you, you wicked old woman!' Genevieve stormed. 'And besides, Dr Robinson is up on the moors. I shall go to him, and I shall tell him how you treat me, and I do not care what you say about me. I do not care!'

Nanna Bloss made to reply, then abruptly darted forwards, but Genevieve was already running, indifferent to the coarse grass and the pricks of baby gorse on her bare feet. The moor rose ahead, and to her horror it was empty, Matthew Widdery's easel standing abandoned and Dr Robinson vanished. Yet he had to be close, and she ran on, alongside the brook where she had walked with Richard Truscott and beyond, with Nanna Bloss stumping behind.

'They seem the most respectable of people,' Dr Manston remarked as their trap drew out of sight of the gates of Driscoll's. 'A trifle insular, perhaps, but that is perhaps to be expected in so remote a part of the country.'

'Did you really notice nothing amiss?' Harland Wolfe queried.

'No, I can't say I did,' Dr Manston admitted. 'They guard themselves well, it is true, but Richard Truscott has explained their reason, and he seems a most amiable young man, his father also, while Mrs Truscott I thought charming.'

'What of the shuttered windows?' Harland Wolfe enquired.

'Shuttered windows?'

'Surely you observed that the last two windows to the right on the second storey were shuttered and closed while most of the others were open?'

'No, I can't say I did, but how could that be of importance?'

'It might not be, but it is a warm day, and somewhat close. Why have the shutters closed save to conceal what lies within? Also, of one thing we may be absolutely certain. Mrs Truscott is not Hungarian. Her accent is London, with a veneer of the West Country. Did you observe the contents of their sideboard?'

'Whatever has that to do with anything?'

'We were offered Malmsey. A Hungarian lady would serve Tokaji. Then there is the matter of the servants' wages, which, as Constable Apcott pointed out to us, are known to be unusually high. This suggests to me a desire for loyalty. Yes, Manston, it is at Driscoll's we shall find the answer to the mystery of the giant ape, and as to whether it relates to the hound, we shall see. For now then, a brief visit to Bidlake Church and then back to Stukely Hall.'

Genevieve came to a panting halt on the ridge beside Hare Tor. Beyond, the heart of the moor stretched away into the distance, as bleak and empty of human life as the wild hills of her childhood. Yet she had seen Dr Robinson cross the same ridge on which she stood, while Matthew Widdery also had to be somewhere not too far away. Even a peat cutter or a shepherd would have done, because Nanna Bloss was still coming behind her, slow but determined.

Ahead, the hillside fell steeply away, levelling out to an area of brilliant green dotted and broken only by the occasional cluster of granite rocks with weatherbeaten thorn trees growing among them. Her feet were scratched and aching, and the soft grass offered respite and a chance to get yet further ahead of her pursuer. Staggering forwards with the sheet clutched tight around her body she began to make her way down the slope.

It was hard going, rocks mixed with patches of bog and reed, every surface hard or wet, forcing her to pick her way slowly down. Long before she had reached the bottom she heard Nanna Bloss' yell from behind and above, demanding she come back. Genevieve only hurried the more, finally letting herself down onto the broad carpet of verdant green as Nanna appeared at the top of the slope behind her.

Immediately she realised that the ground was unstable, her foot sinking into the moss, which shivered as she pulled it free. She remembered Dr Robinson's advice about the treacherous bogs, and how they could swallow a man and his horse without trace, but another furious bellow from behind her forced her on, leaping from tussock to tussock with desperate energy. Again and again she slipped, again and again her feet sank into muck and water so that she had to hurl herself forwards to break free. Her sheet was lost, torn away on a bristle of reeds, to leave her nude and sobbing with fear as she ran, and behind her Nanna Bloss yelled out one more time, only for the sound to be cut off by a ghastly sucking noise.

Genevieve screamed and threw herself forwards, towards where a clump of rocks protruded from the mire like so many broken teeth. Twice she dared to glance back; all that remained of Nanna Bloss was a lacy mop cap lying forlorn on a carpet of mud and moss. Sick with fear, Genevieve ran on, but as she reached the sanctuary of the island her screams rang out again, more piercing than before. Squatted down among the rocks, its blood-shot eyes glaring full into her own, was a monstrous black hound.

Nine

'Good God, it's Miss Stukely!' Dr Manston exclaimed.

Harland Wolfe swore under his breath as he jumped down from the trap. Miss Stukely was approaching the gate to the yew alley, her pale body naked, scratched and spattered with mud, her beautiful hair in wild disarray, her face slack with exhaustion. Both men ran to her, and as she saw them she collapsed, Dr Manston quickly taking her in his arms as she began to babble.

'The hound . . . it is out there . . . among the rocks in the mire . . . the hound, and Nanna . . . Mrs Bloss, she is gone . . . dead!'

'Taken by the hound!?' Dr Manston swore.

'No,' Genevieve gasped, 'by the mire . . . she was sucked down by the mire.'

Genevieve went limp, fainting into Dr Manston's arms.

'We must get her indoors,' he declared. 'Mrs Capleton! Mrs Capleton!'

The housekeeper emerged, took one horror-stricken look at Genevieve and rallied round, helping as they took her inside and laid her down on her bed. Dr Manston began to check her vital signs and look for injuries, but was relieved to discover she had nothing worse than scratches, while she had soon sunk into a troubled sleep. Leaving her to the care of Mrs Capleton, he returned downstairs.

'The poor girl is asleep,' he told Harland Wolfe as he entered the drawing room. 'What an escape she must have had!'

'From the mires, no doubt,' Harland Wolfe replied calmly, 'from the hound, probably not.'

'Whatever are you talking about, Wolfe?' Dr Manston demanded. 'She says she saw it. Do you doubt her word?'

'Not at all,' Harland Wolfe stated, 'but the hound is chained up.'

'How can you know that?'

'Do not the facts speak for themselves?' Harland Wolfe enquired. 'The lack of sightings, the absence of depredation? Furthermore, I have visited the creature.'

Genevieve opened one cautious eye. Nobody was about, and she allowed herself a long heartfelt sigh. It was over, all the years she had been in thrall to Nanna Bloss had finally come to an end, and in a way in which no possible blame could attach to herself. She felt exhausted, her body bruised and scratched, her quim and anus sore and loose, with an urge to scream constantly bubbling up at the back of her mind, and yet as she propped herself up on the bolster over which she had so recently been spanked and abused her mouth had spread into a soft contented smile.

'Well, really, Wolfe, this is a bit much,' Dr Manston declared. 'I do think you might at least have told me!'

'Calm yourself, my dear Manston,' Harland Wolfe urged. 'As I have mentioned before, the mere capture of the hound and identification of the malefactor is inadequate in this case. We must have a case to be put before the courts, and furthermore, I, personally, will not be satisfied until I know the motive behind such dramatic criminality.'

'And how do you propose to do that?' Dr Manston demanded.

'My intention,' Harland Wolfe stated, 'again as I have mentioned, was to play a waiting game, but events with Mrs Bloss and the apeman have somewhat complicated matters. For a satisfactory conclusion we need the co-operation of Miss Stukely.'

'Miss Stukely?'

'Indeed. How better to flush out both hound and master than to present them with the target of their maleficence?'

'You intend to use Miss Stukely as bait?' Dr Manston demanded. 'I forbid it, Wolfe, absolutely forbid it, both on medical grounds and –'

'And as somebody who has conceived an affection for her?' Harland Wolfe queried.

'However did –'

'Come, come, my dear Manston. It hardly requires a detective to notice such things, never mind a detective of my calibre.'

'In that case,' a voice remarked from the door, 'I feel it only proper that I should tell you I am engaged to be married to Miss Stukely.'

Dr Manston turned in surprise, to find that Richard Truscott had entered the room.

'My apologies for arriving unannounced,' Richard stated, 'but as Constable Apcott was standing in the open doorway, and this is my fiancée's house, I felt it not inappropriate. Do I understand that there has been some further development?'

Genevieve's smile had disappeared, to be replaced by a thoughtful grimace. Struggling to keep the horror at the back of her mind, she forced herself to address the problems she still faced. How much of what had happened between her and whatever she had met beneath the arch of the viaduct had become public knowledge, she was not sure. Several people had seen both the creature and the state she was in, so it seemed all too likely that if Richard Truscott did not know already, he soon would. She could not hide it from him.

On the other hand, only three people knew her maidenhead was lost: Mrs Capleton, who never seemed to say anything to anybody, Nanna Bloss, who was dead, and Dr Manston, who had inspected her quim, a process more embarrassing than being fucked, if hardly so frightening. As a doctor, he would presumably be discreet or, at least, it seemed a reasonable hope.

Briefly she toyed with the idea of pretending she was still intact, sure that a gentleman of Richard's standing would not probe too deeply with his questions. Unfortunately he was certain to want to probe just as deeply as he possible could with his cock, on their wedding night if not before, and if the creature's penis hadn't made completely sure her maidenhead was destroyed, then the marrow Nanna had inserted would definitely have finished the job. Nor could she concoct some story about having accidentally deflowered herself, not when Richard had seen her open, virgin quim just days before.

She shook her head, trying to rid herself of the confused sensations building up inside her. Every time her train of thought crossed something rude the horror of recent events threatened to bubble up once more, but a little ecstatic shiver also ran down her spine, the combination of two things that should have been so completely at odds with one another making her wonder if she was going mad.

Clenching her fists in determination, she pushed the thought aside. She would remain sane, just as she had remained sane through everything else, even if the worst came to the worst and by some ill twist of fate she was carrying the beast's child.

'I see,' Richard remarked, thoughtfully steepling his fingers as Harland Wolfe reached the end of his explanation. 'A difficult situation, to be sure. What are Miss Stukely's thoughts on the matter?'

'We have yet to consult Miss Stukely,' Dr Manston answered, somewhat stiffly.

'Then I shall do so,' Richard offered. 'After all, the final choice must be hers.'

He sat back, trying desperately to think. Both in order to get around his father's objections and for the sake of practicality, he had to admit to Genevieve that the creature who'd caught her, and presumably had his way with her, was not some wild beast but his brother. It was hardly an easy admission to make.

Then there was the matter of the hound, which clearly needed to be resolved, and as Harland Wolfe had explained, merely shooting the thing was no good at all. Whoever controlled it would merely come back, no doubt with some less elaborate but equally murderous scheme. Harland Wolfe was also right in suggesting that the best way of catching the man was to use Genevieve as bait, however distasteful the idea. That meant persuading her to do it, hardly an easy task at the best of times, never mind when she was in hysterics.

Asking her to act as bait for the hound and telling her the crazed apeman was his brother was clearly a bit much for one occasion. It would have to be the hound first not only because it presented a more serious threat, but because once the case was solved she would be able to get rid of Harland Wolfe, who knew far too much, was far too clever, and was no doubt charging a substantial fee.

'I shall go to her now,' he announced.

Now biting her lip with tension, Genevieve continued to consider her options. If she had been made pregnant by the beast and Richard discovered, that would without doubt mean the end of her hopes, and utter disgrace. It was no good waiting until her wedding night, perhaps months away. She had to persuade him to have her as soon as possible, preferably now, otherwise her pregnancy might seem suspiciously short. There was no choice, and as she heard him calling to her from the stairs she quickly adjusted her position, lying back on the bed in apparent exhaustion with her nightie disarranged to leave one small breast peeping out from among the frills of her bodice. A few last adjustments to make her hair look at once as dramatic and as beautiful as possible and she called out in a weak voice.

'I am here, my darling.'

'Ah, yes, so I see,' Richard responded somewhat awkwardly as he entered the room. 'How are you? I mean . . . if that isn't an entirely foolish question?'

'Hold me, my darling,' Genevieve sighed. 'I need your arms around me.'

'Oh, um . . . happy to oblige, of course,' Richard responded, stepping close.

'It would, I think, be wise if you were to lock the door,' Genevieve pointed out.

'Ah, yes, absolutely,' Richard responded, and did so, then came to sit on Genevieve's bed, taking her hand in his, although he was having difficulty keeping his eyes off her naked breast.

'I need to be held, my darling,' Genevieve told him, 'held tight. I never want you to let me go again.'

She'd put her arms out as she spoke, gathering Richard in. He responded, holding her with genuine feeling, but making no attempt at any further intimacy. Genevieve kissed him and he kissed back, but still his hands remained behind her back. Genevieve began to stroke his hair and nibble at his neck, but he continued to soothe her. Genevieve put a hand to his crotch, squeezing his cock and balls through his trousers. He was already hard.

'I fear you excite me beyond reason,' he explained, 'but if you wish, I might . . .'

Genevieve cut him off by pressing her mouth back to his as her fingers began to fumble open the buttons of his fly. There was no more resistance. His cock sprang free, hot and hard in her hand. As they kissed she began to masturbate him, and he had quickly tugged down the front of her nightie to fully expose her breasts, fondling each in turn. She kicked the bedclothes to one side, allowing her thighs to come up and open, her nightie dropping away to expose her quim. Richard was no longer hesitant. Climbing onto her, he began to move down, intent on licking her, but Genevieve pulled hard, trying to make him simply mount her as she spoke.

'I am ready now, my darling. Take me.'

'I should really get you ready, you know,' Richard said as he slipped a hand between her cheeks to tickle her anus.

Genevieve shook her head.

'Take me as man and wife, Richard, take me now.'

'But Genevieve darling . . .'

'Take me!' she demanded, reaching down to guide his cock to her quim.

Richard Truscott hesitated, but only for a moment. She already had his cock head to her hole, and he could feel how wet and open she was, confirming his fears. Leopold had fucked her, and there was only one thing for it, to do the same and pretend he hadn't noticed. After that, she would have no choice but to marry him. Not that he could stop himself anyway, with her trying to feed his cock in up her cunt, and he pushed, taking her tight in his arms as his cock filled her hole and pressing his mouth to hers as they began to fuck.

It felt glorious, far too good to stop, too good even to worry that his brother had been there first. They clung together, kissing with ever increasing passion as his cock worked faster and faster inside her, completely lost in the pleasure each was giving the other, until he could hold himself no more and came deep up inside her.

They clung together for a long time after he had finished, his cock still inside her as he slowly deflated, and when they finally pulled apart it was to lie limp in the bed, their fingers entangled, neither speaking, but each lost in their own joyous, if somewhat ambivalent, thoughts until Richard finally decided what to say.

'Never have I been so happy, my darling,' he declared.

'Nor I,' Genevieve sighed.

'And more than happy,' he went on. 'Never could I have hoped to ask for a better mate, Genevieve, for you are not only beautiful and of the most perfect character, but you have a strength and courage no man could not but admire.'

Her response was to squeeze his hand, and after a pause he went on.

'Yet I fear there is one more travail we must overcome before we can realise true happiness. As you know only too well, there is a great hound tethered among the rock of Tavy Head Mires, a hound trained to follow your scent and to kill – if I use words of horror, Genevieve, I am sure you appreciate that I do so from necessity – and we will never have peace until we are rid of this ghastly creature and its master too. Mr Harland Wolfe has made a suggestion, which is that tomorrow you should go out onto the moors, and so lure whoever this man is into releasing his hound.'

'To chase me down?' Genevieve interjected in sudden alarm.

'No,' Richard responded, 'well, yes, in a sense, although Mr Wolfe, Dr Manston, and others, myself included, will be lying in wait for the beast among Hare Tor rocks, so that we may shoot it long before it gets to you.'

'And should you miss?' Genevieve demanded.

'I will do as you ask, Mr Wolfe,' Miss Stukely stated, 'but I want my own gun, a Colt by preference.'

'Come, come, my dear,' Dr Manston began, only to be silenced by a hard look.

'I assure you I am quite capable of using one,' Miss Stukely said.

'Somehow I don't doubt that,' Harland Wolfe put in, 'and indeed, it seems an eminently sensible precaution.'

'Excellent,' Richard Truscott added. 'Then we are agreed.'

'We are indeed,' Harland Wolfe confirmed. 'However, in an association of this kind I feel it is important that each person trusts and understands the other explicitly. Miss Stukely, Mr Truscott, is there anything you might want to say?'

'No, no, nothing in particular,' Richard Truscott answered hastily.

'Nor I,' Miss Stukely added, taking Richard Truscott's hand.

'So be it,' Harland Wolfe responded. 'Mr Truscott, as you will appreciate, this is not something we can propose to the police. Certainly Inspector Allard would never permit it, while no doubt it would also be against regulations. Would you be able to provide any trustworthy men?'

'Certainly,' Richard Truscott agreed. 'My father perhaps, and Luke Gurney, our groom, for certain. He is a steady man, and there is the boy, Ned Annaferd, if needs be, while I could have a hundred miners here, if you so wish.'

'That, I feel, would be excessive,' Harland Wolfe replied, 'but your father and the grooms will be useful. Also, I would be grateful if you would let it be known that I consider the hound mere fiction and have decided to return to London on the morning train.'

'I had better return to Driscoll's then,' Richard stated, glancing from the window, 'but I shall be back first thing in the morning, in company, and armed. Genevieve, my dear, if I might have a brief word?'

Richard Truscott and Miss Stukely withdrew, allowing Dr Manston to pose a question as soon as they were safely out of earshot.

'I don't like this, Wolfe. Can we be sure the Truscotts are safe?'

'In the matter of the hound? Yes,' Harland Wolfe assured him. 'Given that Richard Truscott is betrothed to Miss Stukely, he has nothing to gain from her murder and a great deal to lose.'

'That is true, I suppose,' Dr Manston admitted regretfully.

Richard Truscott's sulky had disappeared down the drive before Miss Stukely returned, looking somewhat flushed, but also careworn. Offering them sherry, she took a large glass herself and went to sit down.

'I shall be heartily thankful when all this is over, Mr Wolfe,' she stated, 'as, God willing, it will be by this hour tomorrow.'

'God willing,' Dr Manston agreed.

'I personally,' Harland Wolfe stated, 'prefer not to rely on supernatural agencies, or blind chance. It is careful planning by which we will take our man tomorrow, and I have every confidence in our success. However, when I work, I greatly prefer to be in possession of the full facts, and so I must ask you once again, Miss Stukely, if you are prepared to reveal the full history of your association with Mrs Bloss, omitting nothing?'

'Wolfe, really,' Dr Manston interjected, but Miss Stukely had raised a hand.

'Very well, Mr Wolfe,' she said quietly. 'With Nanna gone, I confess I would prefer that all of my shameful secret should come out, if only to salve my conscience, but first I must ask on your word of honour that it goes no further than this room.'

'You have my word, absolutely,' Harland Wolfe assured her.

'Mine also,' Dr Manston added.

'Then I shall explain,' Miss Stukely promised and, after a draught of sherry, began. 'For you to fully understand, I must start with the death of my father in the year eighteen eighty-one. My mother had died when I was very young, and I had been brought up with only my father's tales for an education and little knowledge of what men deem right and wrong. With father gone, I was sent to Savannah to live with an aunt, the woman I came to call Nanna, Mrs Bloss. She was not a good woman, as I now understand, but I knew nothing of such things.

'She lived, and worked, in a gambling house near the docks, helping to make the customers drunk and encouraging them to part with their money. I also was put to work, rifling the pockets of gentlemen who had . . . had "gone upstairs" as I was taught to say, and any other piece of thievery to which I could turn my hand. Please do not judge me harshly, because to me it was simply a game, although I confess that I took pleasure in my work.'

Genevieve paused, expecting condemnation, but while Dr Manston looked shocked, Harland Wolfe's lean features showed only interest. It was as if a great weight was lifting from her soul as she went on.

'The owner of our house was a man named Saul Roper, who even from the first frightened me almost out of my wits. He was a terrible man, perhaps six and a half feet in height, and strong as an ox, always in a rage, and ready to strike anybody who crossed him, man or woman. Only as the years passed did I come to understand the full depths of his viciousness. Nanna had always been strict with me, but otherwise kind enough, but that was to change when I came of age. Saul Roper made it a point to be . . . to be the first with every girl, and I was sent for on my birthday, still in the pretty frock Nanna had bought me, pink and white, with bows, and ever so much lace . . . I now realise it was bought only to make me pleasing to Saul Roper.'

Genevieve took another swallow of sherry, fighting back tears as she continued.

'I knew what was to happen to me, and believe me when I say that next to Saul Roper, the creature I met on the moors was as an angel of mercy. He was full of cruel tricks, of which the use of a dog quirt on his victims was the least, and others of which I cannot bring myself to speak. When Nanna said I must go I tried to pretend I was ill, and when she would not believe me I tried to fight, but she was always too strong for me, and . . . and after chastising me she carried me bodily upstairs, with a great many men and not a few women looking on, and laughing for my fate.

'Saul Roper lived at the top of the building. Nanna pushed me in at the door, telling me how I must behave, but I could not. I could barely move my limbs, indeed, and Saul Roper thought I had been given laudanum, which sent him into a rage, because he liked the girls to feel all of what he did to them. He was drunk himself, and cursing and swearing he would whip both Nanna and me in the main salon, charging a dollar to watch and ten to take a turn.

'I ran, thinking he would do that and more, maybe kill me, and when Nanna saw the condition he was in she came after, fleeing that awful place together. For days we hid in the house of a client, but were soon forced to flee again, because Saul Roper was determined to find us both, and to make a terrible example of us. We went west, first to St Louis, then to Deadwood, where Nanna took employment managing the girls in a saloon, and I as a dancer. Always we were in fear of Saul Roper, and Nanna was determined to earn enough money to allow us to live far away, and in comfort, or at the least, her comfort. To this end she wished to . . . to make a harlot of me, a demand I was still resisting when Mr Greville came upon us.'

'And so you sought to make Mrs Bloss believe that Saul Roper had caught up with you in Devon?' Harland Wolfe asked.

'Yes,' Genevieve admitted, 'and I confess I sought to use you in this, Mr Wolfe. On our journey across the Atlantic Mr Greville explained the legend of the hound, and also spoke of your genius, and how you could construct the details of a crime from the tiniest of clues. I saw my opportunity. It has always been my gift to charm, and I thought that were I to lay out clues you would follow these and believe me, which with luck would be enough to make Nanna leave. Sadly, she proved too stubborn and you too clever.'

'Far from it, Miss Stukely,' Harland Wolfe replied. 'Had I not watched you lay out your clues so carefully from among Doe Tor rocks I might well have been taken in, at least temporarily. Indeed, I must commend you on your thoroughness, which certainly fooled Dr Manston here.'

'There was a Mr Pierson on the ship with us,' Genevieve explained, 'an amiable man of exceptional height and with a taste for cigars. He never troubled to lock his cabin, and it was a simple matter to take a pair of his old boots and a few Savannah cigars with the intention of leaving appropriate clues, which as you now know, I did.'

'And the significance of the five orange pips?' Harland Wolfe enquired. 'I take it that it was you who sent them, and they clearly represent some sort of threat, of vengeance perhaps?'

'Yes, a mark,' Genevieve explained. 'Whenever one of Saul Roper's company disobeyed him, or even displeased him, they would be sent one or more orange pips. To have five meant a man should flee, or die, and again I hoped this would be enough to make Nanna leave, but by ill luck she found me out.'

'Were you not concerned that this man Roper might not follow you in actuality?' Dr Manston demanded.

Genevieve hesitated, then spoke again with a sudden burst of defiance.

'Saul Roper is dead, but Mrs Bloss did not know that.'

'Dead?' Harland Wolfe enquired. 'May we ask how this came about?'

'Yes,' Genevieve answered after another, longer pause, 'you may as well have it all. One night, at a lodging house on the Missouri River I had, foolishly, taken a walk as the sun began to go down. It was among a grove of cottonwood trees that he found me, Saul Roper. He knocked me down, telling me what he intended to do with me, and if I live to be a hundred I will remember how his face looked as he stood over me and began to unfasten his clothes. He had on a gun belt, as men often do in those parts, and he had dropped it to the ground, thinking, I suppose, that I was too terrified to resist him. I was not. I shot him.'

Genevieve hung her head, her emotions spent as she waited for the two men to pronounce judgement. Neither spoke, and at last she looked up.

'What will you do with me?' she asked, her voice little more than a whisper.

'Nothing whatever,' Harland Wolfe replied immediately. 'Indeed, I commend you on your actions.'

'Well, I am not sure if commend is quite the word . . .' Dr Manston began, only to be cut off by a gesture of his companion's hand.

'I do not represent the authorities, Miss Stukely,' Harland Wolfe went on, 'and, unlike the authorities, I am not obliged to follow the precise letter of the law. Besides, even were the full details of the case laid out I suspect it would be hard to bring a prosecution. What did you do, save seek to evade a murderer and a blackmailer? You are in no way responsible for Mrs Bloss' death, after all, and in the case of Saul Roper, you could very well plead self-defence, while from a moral perspective your decision was unimpeachable. Besides, Dr Manston and myself have both given our word on secrecy in this matter, while it is plain to me that your story has no bearing on the case of the hound of the Stukelys or Sir Robert's death. So rest easy, and tomorrow we shall, with luck, lay the last of your difficulties to rest.'

Ten

Richard Truscott took a swallow from his flask, made to take a second then thought better of it and returned the brandy regretfully to his coat pocket. The sun was now above the horizon, but it was little consolation. It was still cold among Hare Tor rocks, while the grass was wet with dew and the mist still clung to the low ground, creating oddly shaped tongues in the valleys and a dead white blanket across the flat ground of Tavy Head Mires.

Nobody else was visible, each of his companions well hidden in his allotted place, and each armed. Dr Manston was on the far side of Hare Tor, Harland Wolfe himself among the tumbled boulders covering the slope above the old Wheal Frederick Mine, Luke Gurney on Doe Tor and his father right across the valley among Brat Tor rocks. In theory the line covered every possible angle from which the hound might approach Stukely Hall from the mires, but he was painfully aware that the gaps between the hunters were uncomfortably wide.

If the hound came, it would be seen, of that he felt certain, and the same was true of its master. Whether they could hit it was an entirely different matter, and he was extremely glad that Genevieve had her own gun and that Ned Annaferd would be among the trees where the estate bordered Lydford Woods.

* * *

Victoria Truscott swallowed her mouthful of sperm and pushed Ned Annaferd away. Her own sex needed attention, but there was no time to indulge herself. He had been in a hurry too, although not enough of a hurry to prevent him demanding the pleasure of his cock in her mouth, and was still attempting to do up the last of his fly buttons as he pushed a foot into the stirrup of his horse.

'Now you be careful, Miss Victoria,' he instructed, 'and keep well clear of our part of the moor, although why you'd want to go there at all with a thing like that on the loose is beyond me. Mazed, I call it.'

'Do not be impudent,' Victoria answered, although it felt rather foolish with the taste of his cock still in her mouth.

He waited as she climbed astride Cloud, then carefully locked the gates behind them and immediately set off at a smart canter towards Stukely Hall. Victoria followed at a trot, then increased her pace, only to ignore the turning for Sourton she had promised to take and continue on the Lydford Road instead.

'Cunt in face, Lucy,' Leopold demanded as Lucy set the tray down.

'If you must,' Lucy replied, trying to hide her eagerness despite knowing that it would make no difference to him whatsoever.

He was already on the bed, his eyes aglow with excitement, his fingers stroking his balls as he watched her. Lucy smiled and began to undress, quickly slipping her uniform dress from her shoulders, then opening her chemise to free her breasts. Leopold's eyes flicked from detail to detail, his cock growing gradually in his hand. Now in just her underthings, Lucy crawled onto the bed and took over, kissing his cock before sticking her tongue out to trace a long wet line down the length of his shaft.

Leopold gave a soft growl and extended a hand to Lucy's bottom, kneading her cheeks through her drawers. She reached back to split them, giving him her bare flesh, which he had begun to explore as she quickly undid one of the strings fastening her cunt pad, allowing it to slip down her leg and so leave her ready to be licked. Taking his cock in her mouth, she cocked her leg across his body and settled her bottom into his face.

He began to lick immediately, and Leopold's tongue was not only exceptionally long, but also muscular. She was soon sighing with pleasure and sucking eagerly on his rapidly growing erection as he lapped and probed, his tongue tip bringing her sensations far too sweet to resist as it wriggled in among the fleshy folds of her quim. His hands had gone to her bottom cheeks, holding them spread, and he had no compunction whatsoever about licking her anus as well as her cunt, setting her sobbing with guilty ecstasy around her mouthful of now hard penis.

Richard Truscott yawned and cursed the impossibility of getting into hiding at any time after first light. He had been awake since shortly after four in the morning, and even the coarse grass growing among the rocks was starting to feel comfortable, inviting a nap. Yet the sun was now well up, and people were beginning to stir.

Matthew Widdery had already set up his easel in his favourite spot on the slope of Brat Tor, while yet further away Dr Robinson had just emerged from his house, black medical bag in hand. As Richard watched he glimpsed a grey pony move along the lane behind the doctor's house, the rider wearing a blue habit that looked suspiciously like one of Victoria's, although she had specifically been banned from coming anywhere near the moor until both hound and master were safely under lock and key, or dead.

The second option struck him as entirely preferable, although in the case of the master it might prove awkward. When the hunters had met that morning in the dimly lit drawing room of Stukely Hall, Harland Wolfe had been adamant that the beast's master should be taken alive, but it struck Richard that the detective was primarily concerned with discovering the background to the case. Harland Wolfe, it seemed, had an inexhaustible thirst for knowledge, while Richard had no more than a minimal interest in why the malefactor had, presumably, murdered Sir Robert and attempted to murder Genevieve. Far more important was ensuring that he was unable to do so in the future.

Yes, he decided, should it come about that he had a fair shot at master and beast simultaneously, he knew where he would be aiming first.

Lucy grunted and puffed to the motion of Leopold's cock in her rectum. Her head was swimming with pleasure, her body sensitive to every sensation, not only her buggering, but the thick male taste of him in her mouth, the tickling of her breasts as they swung to the motion of his thrusts, the soft wet noises of his cock in her bottom hole. She had reached orgasm twice as he licked her, to leave her in a state of abandoned bliss, completely given over to pleasure.

Despite a licking that had left her loose and accessible behind, she had buttered her bottom with a pat from the breakfast tray, giggling as it melted in her hole and dribbled down over her virgin cunt with Leopold watching all the while. She had done it on all fours, the way he liked her best, and the way she still was now that he had eased his cock in up her buttery back passage, so deep his balls were pressing to her over-excited cunt with every push.

She was even wondering if she was going to come again, just from the overwhelming feeling of her buggering and the squashy tickling sensation as his massive hairy scrotum pressed to her sex. It seemed very likely, but she was equally eager to be spunked up before presenting herself for another long slow licking.

Richard Truscott swore out loud. This time there was no doubt. The pony just entering Tavy Cleave was Cloud and the rider Victoria, and if they were following the Tavy, there was no question at all as to where they would come out, at Tavy Head Mires.

'Headstrong little brat,' he muttered, and glanced back towards Stukely Hall.

Nearly an hour remained before Genevieve was due to leave the Hall, while if he kept below the ridge he could surely remain unnoticed, and so head Victoria off and still return to his post in time. Yet to do so meant risking exposure, and he glanced a second time towards the distant mouth of Tavy Cleave. Victoria had disappeared among the rocks and gorse, but another figure was visible, considerably further back but heading in the same direction, a man, dressed in white.

'That's Dr Robinson's cook,' he muttered to himself. 'Out after frogs, d'you suppose? Or could he . . .'

He bit his lip, silently cursing Harland Wolfe and thinking what he might have done with a hundred miners. As it was, any active man could go around their flanks with no great difficulty, and presumably lead the hound back the same way. Without further hesitation he began to move off through the rocks, presently reaching Dr Manston's position on the far side of Hare Tor.

'Look, Manston,' he hissed, and then wondered why he was whispering. 'Do you know who we're after?'

'I fear not, Mr Truscott,' Dr Manston answered. 'Mr Wolfe has a strong sense of the dramatic, and prefers to keep these things to himself.'

'Damn,' Richard swore, 'because I've just seen Dr

Robinson's cook making towards Tavy Cleave. Look, you can still see him, there.'

Dr Manston peered in the direction Richard was indicating, where the cook was visible as a tiny white figurine as he passed among clumps of gorse.

'Do you think it could be him?' Richard queried. 'Does Dr Robinson know we're out today?'

'I er . . . I believe not,' Dr Manston responded.

Richard shook his head in despair and quickly moved off among the rocks. A glance at his watch showed that forty minutes still remained before Genevieve was due to set out, and he hurried on, ducked low as he ran. At the lip of the valley he was forced to slow, picking his way carefully among the great grey boulders that littered the slope. Mist still clung to the valley floor, and he had quickly been enveloped, plunging him in a world of damp white cloud in which it was impossible to see more than a few yards.

Cursing bitterly, he made his way to where a rough path ran beside the Tavy. A cold fear quickly began to well up inside him, and his anger for his sister's behaviour with it, while the deadening white of the mist seemed to press on him with a physical force. Even the sound of the river seemed oddly muted, and he found himself straining his ears and starting at the caw of a raven, while his hand was on the butt of the revolver in his pocket.

Unsure if Victoria might have passed him, he forced himself to walk upriver, scanning the ground for the marks of horseshoes among those of the hooves of the moor ponies. None were apparent, and he had soon reached the edge of the mires, where the Rattlebrook joined the Tavy in a maze of channels and tiny boggy islands.

The click of metal on rock behind him drew his attention and he moved back the way he had come, to find Victoria, already dismounted and in the act of tethering Cloud to a thorn tree. She started when she saw him, her faced flushed with guilt and surprise, then growing abruptly stubborn.

'Where in hell's name do you think you're going?' Richard demanded.

'Across the mires,' Victoria answered, lifting her nose a trifle.

'Across the mires?' Richard stormed. 'Have you lost your senses!?'

'It's perfectly easy to cross the mires,' Victoria stated. 'You just need to know where you're treading. Cotton grass only grows over water, and tormentil only grows on proper soil, so you can tread wherever you see yellow flowers.'

'Never mind the bloody flowers!' Richard swore. 'What about the damn great dog that's out there somewhere? I suppose you're going to offer it a bone?'

'Something of the sort,' Victoria admitted, 'and really, there's no call to be rude, it's only a dog.'

'Only a dog!' Richard exclaimed. 'For goodness sake, Vicky, it tore Billy Sugden's throat out! Hold on, do you mean you to say you've been to see the damn thing before?'

Victoria hesitated before she replied.

'No, of course not, don't be foolish, but a dog is dog. Billy Sugden probably trod on his paw or something.'

'Heaven preserve me from little sisters!' Richard declared, looking up. 'So what are you doing here? If you came to gawk, you're in the wrong . . . hold on, I know that face. You're meeting a lover, aren't you?'

'No,' Victoria answered, but she had begun to blush, and he had known the expression she put on when she was feeling guilty since they'd been in the nursery.

'Yes, you are,' he stated, 'and I know who it is. It's that damn cook, isn't it?'

Victoria shook her head urgently, her face now crimson with embarrassment.

'Dr Robinson's cook!' Richard exclaimed. 'You've taken Dr Robinson's cook for a lover!? Are you mad? Think of the scandal! Think of the disgrace! Almighty God!'

'You have Lucy,' Victoria mumbled.

'Yes,' Richard admitted, 'but she is our maid. Every young gentleman enjoys the housemaids, but I don't go about making assignations with other people's maids, do I? Well, not often . . . and besides, you're a woman, a lady . . . Good God, you do have the sense to take him up your bottom and not in your cunt, don't you?'

Victoria had hung her head, her face sulkier than Richard had seen it in years, her blush the colour of plum. Something inside him snapped. He grabbed her arm, drawing a squeal of protest as she realised what was about to happen to her.

'No, Richard, you can't . . . you can't . . . you can't!' she gabbled as he hauled her after him to where a conveniently rounded boulder rose from the grasses and sedge.

'Oh yes I can,' he grated, twisting her arm into the small of her back even as he sat down, 'and I fully intend to!'

'No!' Victoria wailed as her skirts started to come up. 'No! You cannot spank me! Richard, you cannot!'

He didn't even bother to answer, but hauled her pretty blue riding habit and the petticoat beneath it high onto her back, exposing the drawers beneath. She began to fight in earnest, kicking and hitting out at him with her one free arm, but he simply tightened his grip and began to work on the buttons of her drawers.

'Not bare!' she howled as she realised he was not merely going to spank her but strip her bottom first. 'No! No, you beast! You utter beast!'

Her words broke to a squeal of pain as he twisted her arm yet tighter, but she was thrashing more desperately than ever as the panel of her drawers was slowly but surely unfastened, also pleading, threatening, and doing every single thing in her power to prevent her bottom being stripped.

'No, Richard, please! Don't bare me . . . don't!'

One button had come undone, leaving a small triangle of soft pale bottom flesh on show.

'Richard! Stop it this moment! I shall tell Mama!'

A second button had come undone, and the top of Victoria's bottom crease had been exposed.

'I won't tell, Mama, I promise! I . . . I'll be ever so kind, always . . . Richard!'

A third button had come undone and the swell of both her cheeks was bare.

'Richard! That's enough . . . spank me like this if you must, but don't bare me!'

A fourth button had come undone, leaving the tuck of one chubby bottom cheek nude to the moist air.

'No, Richard! Please . . . please . . . I beg you, not fully bare . . . spank me like this . . . aren't I showing enough . . . use my riding whip if you must, but not bare . . . not bare . . . not bare!'

The fifth and last button came open and her words ended in a scream of despair as the panel of her drawers fell away and the full plump ball of her bottom was exposed. She hung her head, sobbing brokenly for the inevitable discovery of her torn maidenhead, but Richard simply cocked one leg up to get her bottom a little higher and began to spank. It was hard, firm, purposeful swats delivered full across her bare cheeks, to make her gasp and kick and squirm her bottom about, but even with the stinging pain hot in her head and the awful humiliation of taking a bare bottom spanking over her brother's knee her worst fear was still that he would see between her legs.

'If you don't like being spanked, Victoria,' Richard grated, 'you should learn to behave like a lady!'

'Pig!' she retorted, the word a gasp between two hard smacks.

'Me a pig?' Richard answered her. 'Who's squealing? Who's showing her bottom? You're the pig, Victoria, a little fat spanky pig.'

'You beast!' she screamed. 'You utter beast! You promised you wouldn't call me that . . . you promised, after . . . after . . .'

Her words gave way to a howl of misery and self-pity as she burst into tears, but the spanking continued, slap after slap laid across her bouncing bottom, Richard now laughing and chanting out her nickname as he punished her.

'Spanky pig, spanky pig!' Richard chorused, punctuating the words with firm slaps to his sister's wriggling bottom.

His fear and tension had gone, taken out on Victoria's bare cheeks, at first in anger, then as an entirely fair punishment, now for fun, but as he saw that she was crying he began to soften. Her bottom was an even, blushing pink, much the same colour as her face, and her cheeks had started to come apart to show off the dark crease between. He stopped, intending to haul them apart and make the display of her anus a final humiliation to complete her punishment, but as he let go of her wrist she gave a squeak of surprise and tumbled off his lap.

'Whoops!' Richard chuckled as she sprawled on her back, legs akimbo and bare cunt spread to the world, bare, open moist with arousal from having her bottom smacked and without the familiar red arc of her maidenhead.

'Good God!' Richard exclaimed. 'You've been had!'

'It . . . it was on Cloud,' Victoria stammered, blushing furiously as she covered herself.

'Cloud!?' Richard demanded. 'You let Cloud –'

'No!' Victoria yelled. 'Not that! Not . . . how could you, Richard? I was riding . . .'

'. . . astride Cloud,' Richard finished for her. 'For goodness sake, Vicky, have you no sense at all? Why do you think young ladies are supposed to ride side-saddle, you little idiot? It's not for the good of your health, you know, and what, once you'd ruined yourself, I suppose you allowed this damn cook to have you? By God, if he's got a child on you I'll thrash the bastard to within an inch of his life, I swear it! And as for you, you demented little harlot, I've a mind to take your riding whip to your backside, here and now . . .'

Even as he spoke he was snatching for where the long supple whip hung on Cloud's saddle, but he'd barely managed to roll her face down by her foot and get in a couple of good strikes across her writhing bottom before her words gave him pause.

'The cook is not my lover! I swear it, Richard, on my very life! No man has had me, I swear it!'

Richard stopped, the whip poised above his sister's bottom, which was now decorated with two bright red lines against the even pink flush. She was telling the truth, he was almost certain, but he kept his grip on her ankle as he spoke again.

'Very well, so if you're not meeting the cook, what are you doing here? The truth mind, unless you want a thrashing.'

'I . . . I came to let the dog go,' she said weakly.

Lucy settled herself down on the floor, cross-legged in front of the checkers board Leopold had set out. She was still in her underthings, and in the course of their passion she had torn one of the strings loose from her cunt pad, but it made little difference. He had come three times, twice up her bottom and once in her mouth, which had rendered him as placid as he ever was, while after the five orgasms he had given her she was in no mood to go about her duties, nor to sew up her pad.

Playing checkers with Leopold was a predictable and not very exciting experience as, while he was quite capable of moving the pieces and understood how to take her, he had never been able to appreciate the concept of turns, nor understand that he could only move in certain ways. He would therefore win on either the first or second go, depending on who started, but nevertheless loved to play and would frequently do so for an hour or more before growing bored or amorous.

'Shall we try to play properly this time?' Lucy suggested, although she knew it was hopeless. 'I'll show you how, shall I?'

Leopold merely grunted and began to move a piece, placing it on top of one of Lucy's, then another, until he was holding all twelve in one great hairy hand.

'You win again,' Lucy sighed. 'Shall we play soldiers instead, Leopold?'

He shook his head.

'Quoits?' she suggested.

'Skittles,' he said.

'No, not skittles,' she said firmly as her bottom hole tightened for the memory of the last time she'd tried to play the game. 'How about marbles? You like marbles.'

Leopold nodded.

'I think they're in the chest in Miss Victoria's room,' Lucy said, rising. 'I'll just run and get them, shall I?'

He had begun to make towers out of the checkers pieces as she left the room, and with him so placid and nobody about she didn't trouble to lock the door. She was even wondering if it might be fun to leave the outer door unlocked later, in the hope that Richard might find out and maybe birch her again.

The marbles were not in the big toy chest kept under Victoria's bed since she'd begun to lose interest, nor in the old nursery. Somewhat puzzled, Lucy tried to remember if they'd been given away to any of the family's younger cousins, only to recall Victoria rolling them for a family of kittens in the stable block. Slipping a loose gown and a pair of slippers on, she went outside. The bag was still there, set on a shelf among pieces of harness, and she quickly retrieved them, running back to Leopold's room, only to discover that he was no longer there.

Harland Wolfe's mouth curved into a grim smile as he saw Miss Stukely step from the yew alley and open the moor gate. She was dressed entirely in white, her dress, her bonnet, her gloves, even the parasol in which the revolver Richard Truscott had secured for her was concealed. Against the greens and greys of the moor she made a brilliant shape, easily discernible from any of the tors amongst which his companions were concealed, and to the man he was sure would be watching.

His own grey tweeds made an absolute contrast, allowing him to blend in with the granite rock so completely that a man might have passed within fifty yards and not noticed. He was also well down among the rocks, scanning the moor through a horizontal crack where one great boulder had sheared from another.

Miss Stukely had left the small enclosure of her own land behind the gardens, and was walking slowly towards Doe Tor, pausing occasionally to admire the view or pick one of the tiny flowers that grew among the short grasses. Harland Wolfe frowned, wondering if it would be obvious to the malefactor that she was not simply taking the air, but as he glanced towards Brat Tor he saw that Matthew Widdery's easel stood unattended, while the painter himself was walking swiftly along the slope towards the high moor.

'Now I have you, my fine fellow,' Harland Wolfe chuckled, and he eased his revolver from his pocket.

* * *

'And damn well stay home, or I swear I'll leave you so you can't sit for a week!' Richard Truscott stormed.

Victoria opened her mouth to speak, thought better of it and pulled herself up onto Cloud's saddle in silence. Richard stood as he was, struggling to control his breathing for his anger at his sister's behaviour and wishing he'd spent a bit longer applying her riding whip to her bottom. Not that there had been enough time for such indulgences, and there certainly wasn't now.

As pony and rider faded into the mist he glanced at his watch, then cursed. Genevieve would have already left the Hall, yet if Dr Robinson and his cook were the culprits it made more sense to remain where he was than to climb back to Hare Tor. The cook might even be nearby, and unless Victoria had been lying and the two of them really did have an assignation it seemed very likely that she had come to release the hound. Possibly the wretched man had even seduced Victoria into doing it for him, an unbearable thought, but then again, both his sister and the cook had entered Tavy Cleave long before Genevieve would have left the house, and therefore could not possibly have known that it was time to release the hound. He put his hands to his head, cursing Victoria, the cook, Harland Wolfe and God simultaneously in his confusion.

Victoria had at least gone home, he told himself, as surely she would not dare disobey again after getting her bottom warmed? Hopefully she would soon be out of danger, while Dr Manston would hopefully be capable of dealing with anything on Hare Tor. Meanwhile, if the cook was coming to release the hound he was already in the perfect place to intercept him. Nodding grimly to himself, he took his revolver from his pocket once more and settled down to wait among the rocks.

'Mrs Truscott, ma'am?' Lucy said quietly.

'What is it, my dear?' Nell Truscott asked, as kindly

as ever as she put down the embroidery she had been working on.

'Mr Leopold, ma'am,' Lucy answered. 'He's not in his room. I . . . went to fetch something, and when I came back he was gone. I had left the door unlocked, ma'am, because . . .'

'You silly goose!' Nell responded in sudden alarm. 'Well you must find him then, quickly, and when you do, you are to calm him as best you may.'

'He was calm, ma'am,' Lucy responded, 'as calm as he ever is, but I can't find him at all! Maybe he's only playing hide and seek, but I thought it best to tell you.'

'Certainly it was best to tell me,' Nell assured her, with something close to panic in her voice, 'although you needn't think that will save you from having your silly bottom smacked later today. For the present, I shall lock myself and Eliza into the kitchen with cook, and you must search until you find him. When the poor dear is safely locked in his room you will come to fetch us. Oh dear, why today of all days!?'

'Yes, ma'am,' Lucy responded, quickly bobbing a curtsey before she withdrew, leaving Nell Truscott calling for her maid.

Victoria reined Cloud in, listening intently. The humiliation of the spanking from her brother and his discovery of her deflowered sex still burned in her head, just as her bottom burned in her drawers. The two cuts from her own riding whip were particularly bad, smarting constantly, while even at a walk the motion of her cheeks on the saddle was distinctly painful. It was also frustrating, which in turn increased the agony of her humiliation, because despite the awful shame of the way she'd been handled her quim was wet and urgent.

Despite everything, she wanted her lover, and she knew he was out there in the mist, but also that if she tried to go to him Richard would catch her, and in all probability take the riding whip to her bottom again, only harder and longer. Reluctantly, she moved on, wincing as her tender cheeks began to move against the saddle and trying desperately not to think of how it would feel to be mounted by her lover, with his cock deep in up her sopping cunt and his lean hard belly slapping against her reddened bottom.

It was impossible, the need in her sex too great. Her nipples were stiff and the cotton of her drawers sodden where they pressed to her quim. She needed fucking, and soon, or at the very least to bring herself to ecstasy beneath her fingers as she thought of how good it had been before. Again she stopped, glancing back into the swirling mist. There was nothing to see, although above her the sky was now beginning to show blue through the white, and sounds were no longer as indistinct as before.

She told herself it would only take moments to diddle herself, but she knew that was not what she wanted. Besides, the poor dog was likely to have been shot by the time she finished, and she knew she would feel awful if she had been playing with her quim when it met its end under the guns. Still hesitant, she wondered if it would be possible to urge Cloud up the opposite side of the Cleave and decided against it, choosing to tether him instead and go on foot. If Richard was waiting in the mist she could easily avoid him and so come down to the mire from another direction, while if he was on the hill she might well see him and could then drop back into the mist.

Nodding to herself, she dismounted, and quickly tethered Cloud where he would be able to graze on the lush riverside grass while she was gone. She took the crowbar she had brought from her saddlebag, and was hefting it thoughtfully in her hand as a tall white-clad figure stepped from the fog.

* * *

Harland Wolfe moved cautiouslys forwards through the mist of the Rattlebrook Valley. Somewhere ahead of him was Matthew Widdery, maybe already too far, and his mouth set in grim determination as he hurried forwards, revolver in hand. Twice he had watched Widdery cross the mire to feed his creature, making careful note of the path until he was able to follow it himself and visit the clump of granite boulders among which the beast was chained. Both times had been early on sunlit mornings, but now, with the mist still clinging to the ground, he knew that the path across the bog would be more dangerous by far.

Reaching the edge of the bog, he began to skirt it, watching for the subtle markers he had placed to ensure that he did not lose the way. At last he found them, and even as he ducked in among the rocks to await his prey a low growl sounded from somewhere out in the mist, followed by a cry of pain. Harland Wolfe darted forwards, only to have his leg sink to the knee in the sucking bog.

Quickly withdrawing, he squatted down, his revolver at the ready, and in just moments a figure emerged from the whiteness: Matthew Widdery, his bearded face set in shock and pain, a blood-stained pair of ladies' drawers wrapped tight around one arm. Harland Wolfe allowed himself a grin as he waited for his adversary to draw close, then rose to his full height, extending his revolver in clear view as the expression on Widdery's face changed to horror.

'The game is up,' Harland Wolfe announced. 'Please do not think to run, Mr Widdery. I am an excellent shot and will have no compunction whatsoever about pulling my trigger, while there is bog to either side of you. Now where is your hound?'

'It . . . it turned on me,' Widdery stammered, raising his damaged arm.

'Is it loose?' Harland Wolfe demanded.

Widdery nodded.

'Then,' said Harland Wolfe, 'you had better pray my colleagues find it before it finds Miss Stukely, for the sake of your own rotten soul.'

Genevieve paused to pick yet another flower. She now had a substantial posy and was beginning to feel slightly silly carrying it when just as many of the little moorland blooms grew within a few yards of her own garden. It was hard even to feel afraid, with the bright sunlit moor stretching in every direction save where the occasional pool of mist lingered in hollows or above the streams. Six armed men were protecting her, yet she could see none of them, and in such a peaceful place it was hard to imagine herself stalked by a murderer.

Yet the cottonwood grove in which she had shot Saul Roper had been every bit as beautiful and every bit as peaceful, and she forced herself to pay attention as she walked on. Already she had passed Dr Robinson, presumably on his way to a patient, but possibly with a more sinister purpose, while she had also noticed that Matthew Widdery had abandoned his easel. Neither one was now in sight, leaving her seeming entirely alone on the great open sweep of moorland.

Again she paused, wondering if it would look suspicious if she were to sit down on a rock for a little while, only for her blood to seem to freeze to her very marrow as from somewhere off across the hills came a long drawn-out howl.

Her lover's cock pumped in Victoria's cunt. She was on her hands and knees in the grass, terrified of discovery and yet in such ecstasy she would not have stopped it had she been able. Her habit and petticoat were up on her back, her drawers open and her bottom sticking out through the open panel, the same lewd position she had adopted in order to tempt him to mount her.

Yet she wanted more, not just the swift hard fucking she was getting, but time to be just as dirty as she could, and to bring herself to orgasm not once, but repeatedly. More importantly, she wanted it somewhere she would be completely safe, for all that the urge to be mounted and fucked had come so swiftly when she had first seen him.

'Not so quickly,' she urged, 'let me move a little.'

He didn't respond, but kept up the same firm pumping motion inside her, the thickness of his cock working in her cunt hole, so fast she found it hard to speak, or even think, for her ecstasy. Yet she forced herself to wriggle out from under him, and he let her, her cunt closing with a fart as his huge cock slid free.

She was giggling at her own dirtiness as she moved quickly away, scrambling in among the bracken, where she quickly found an altogether better place, shielded on all sides and by the mist above. Now content that she could do as she pleased without the slightest risk, she once more adopted her lewd kneeling position, her bottom stuck well up as she waited to be mounted, only to think better of it and roll on her side.

'Let me put you in my mouth,' she sighed as he reached her.

He pushed his cock at her and she opened up, savouring the moment before she took him in and her mouth filled with thick meaty penis and the strong male taste. As she sucked so he began to fuck into her mouth, with short hard thrusts, pushing his cock into her throat to make her feel dirtier still. His heavy dangling scrotum began to slap in her face as he thrust into her, making her want to suck it, and she quickly pulled back from his cock to take it in, gaping wide to let her mouth fill with pungent black flesh, an act so utterly filthy the shivers were running down her spine as she rolled his balls over her tongue. Taking his cock in hand, she began to masturbate him as she sucked on his balls.

She needed to come, and threw her legs up, spilling her habit and petticoat out onto the ground to leave her stocking-clad thighs wide and her bare cunt covered only by the open panel of her drawers, which she quickly pulled away. Her fingers found the wet fleshy folds of her quim and she began to masturbate, alternately dipping her fingers into the sopping hole he had just been in and rubbing at her aching bump.

Pulling harder on the thick cock in her hand, she took as much of his scrotum into her mouth as would go, feeding on his balls as she masturbated, with her orgasm already rising in her head. What she was doing felt deliciously, impossibly naughty, and yet she wanted more, far more, everything he could give her all at once: his cock and balls in her mouth at the same time, yet also in her hand, between her breasts, against her face, and bloating out her juicy swollen cunt, which was just where it was going for her second orgasm, a thought that brought her to her first.

Victoria's body locked tight in ecstasy as she sucked on her lover's balls, her back arched and her fingers rubbing furiously hard on her bump, her hand pumping at his cock, half hoping he would give her a faceful of spunk as she came, half praying he wouldn't so that she could carry on. It didn't happen, and even as her pleasure faded and she let his scrotum slip from her mouth she was smiling in anticipation of more.

Dr Manston half rose from his hiding place among the rocks, listening for more of the peculiar noises issuing from the mist below him. Something was happening, but Harland Wolfe's instruction to remain in line had been clear, and he hesitated to go against it. Now there was silence, but his revolver was cocked, and as a man's head lifted above the heather of the ridge, he raised it to aim, only to lower it again as he saw it was only Matthew Widdery. Then he gave an oath of surprise as he saw Harland Wolfe appear in turn, a revolver aimed at the painter's back.

'Good God, Wolfe, do you mean to say . . .' he called as the two men approached.

'This is our man, yes,' Harland Wolfe responded, his tone as urgent as it ever was, 'but the hound is loose, somewhere down in the valley. Guard this fine fellow for me, and warn Miss Stukely too, but I must go back.'

'No, Wolfe,' Dr Manston answered immediately, 'without you, the full detail of the case can never be brought to light. This evil man must be brought to justice! I shall go down after the hound.'

Matthew Widdery responded with an animal snarl, ignored by both men as Harland Wolfe replied.

'You are right, of course, Manston, my dear fellow. I have allowed emotion to cloud my judgement. You go, and God speed.'

Dr Manston gave a single stern nod and without further comment started down the slope towards the mires and Tavy Cleave.

Victoria squatted in her rude mounting position, bottom up and ready for entry. One little wiggle of encouragement and he was on her back, his lovely cock probing for her hole, and inside, pushing deep to make her moan in ecstasy, and again as he began to pump in her cunt once more.

She was in a private heaven, lost to everything but the pleasure of her body and of his, now nude with her full breasts swinging beneath her chest as he fucked her, every stitch of her clothing laid to one side as she had stripped down for her second mounting. He had been wonderfully patient, watching from one eye and nursing his erection as she peeled off her clothes, but eager enough to mount her as soon as she was ready.

His hair was tickling between her bottom cheeks, his balls slapping on her cunt with every thrust, his arms tight around her and rubbing the sides of her breasts as they swung, all wonderful sensations to keep her constantly in mind of how unspeakably naughty she was being as she was fucked. Already she wanted to come, and it was growing harder to put off the exquisite moment with every push of his big cock up her hole and every smack of his heavy balls on her flesh, until at last her resistance broke.

'Harder,' she breathed, 'do it harder . . . oh I do so love you . . . fuck me well, darling.'

She had reached back to touch herself and to feel the junction between his shaft and her own well-filled hole. Just the proof that he was in her was almost enough to tip her over the edge, but as she felt the thick slippery cock slide in and out of her hole she remembered her brother's words. He had told her to take it up her bottom, and so up her bottom it would go.

With her face set in a smile of mingled bliss and mischief, she gently took hold of the big cock and tried to ease it free. He resisted, for a moment, but as she began to tug on his shaft it slipped out. She held him tight, marvelling at her own filthy behaviour as she began to use his cock head to paint her bottom hole with her own juices.

'You . . . you can put him up by bottom,' she sighed. 'That would be nice, wouldn't it? Right up my bottom . . . sodomise me, my darling . . .'

She trailed off, her mouth coming slowly wide. The tip of his cock had slipped into her now slimy bottom hole, and he had begun to push. Her fingers clutched tight in the grass as she felt her anus begin to spread. She was gasping for air, her toes wiggling urgently, pop-eyed with astonishment for the overwhelming sensation of accepting him up her bottom, so good and at once so dirty.

'Right in, my darling,' she begged, 'fill me . . . fill my naughty bottom up . . .'

Again her words broke, this time to an ecstatic gasp as her bottom hole gave and the first couple of inches of his cock were shoved abruptly into her rectum. The rest followed, pushed in inch by inch, Victoria whimpering with pleasure as she was sodomised, and finishing with a little delighted cry as the last inch of cock was forced in up her bottom and his body pressed between her open buttocks.

He began to bugger her, short firm pushes that made her straining anal ring pull in and out on his shaft and set his balls slapping on her empty cunt. Her breasts began to swing again, and as he got faster her hand had gone back to touch herself, rubbing at her bump, easing a finger into her empty sloppy cunt hole, touching the junction of his cock and her anus to feel her ring work, rubbing her bump again, and all the while with the same exquisite filthy thought running through her head: he was on her back with his cock up her bottom . . . on her back with his cock up her bottom . . . on her back with his cock up her bottom . . .

Victoria screamed as the orgasm hit her, a wave of ecstasy far beyond her control, her cunt in violent contraction, her anus in spasm on his cock as he pumped into her with furious speed. He began to grunt and growl and she realised his spunk was pumping into her rectum to the contractions of her anus, another filthy detail that brought her to a second screaming shuddering peak, and a third.

Nothing else mattered, only the exquisite sensations of body and mind, and even as he finished off and eased himself from her gaping well-buggered anus she was still rubbing herself, her body jerking to the helpless contractions of her muscles, until at last her control went completely and she collapsed onto the grass, her hand still between her legs as she cuddled up to him with a long contented sigh.

* * *

'Good God!' Dr Manston swore as the awful screams echoed and re-echoed among the rocks of Tavy Cleave.

He ran forwards, tripped in an unseen hole among the heather and sprawled full length on the ground, but was up again immediately. Below him in the Cleave the last wisps of mist were dissipating, creating a confusing scene of green and grey and white. The screams had stopped, and he was mumbling prayers for whatever poor person had fallen victim to the hound, for their life, or for their soul. It had been a woman too, he was certain, making his pity and determination for revenge stronger still.

As he reached the side of the river he saw a white pony tethered a little way off, and immediately recognised it as Miss Truscott's. Cold fear gripped his vitals and he began to run with all his speed in the direction he felt the screams had come from. Another voice called out, male, and a moment later Richard Truscott was by his side, gasping out his words as he ran.

'That was my sister! Hell and damnation!'

Grey rock loomed out of the mist ahead of them, a boulder projecting from the slope almost to the edge of the river, indistinct, and suddenly clear as the whiteness swirled aside. Dr Manston swore, and gripped Richard Truscott's arm to bring him to a sudden stop. Standing on top of the boulder was a terrifying apparition, a black hound of monstrous proportions, its forelegs braced wide on the ground, its head lowered and shoulders hunched, its teeth bared in a terrible snarl, its red-rimmed eyes glaring into his own.

Jerking the revolver from his pocket, Dr Manston fired, but the bullet went wide. Again he aimed, and Richard Truscott too, both men drawing a careful bead on the hound even as it tensed to spring.

'Now I have you,' Dr Manston hissed between grated teeth, and his vision exploded into coloured lights as a heavy impact caught the back of his skull.

* * *

'Did you have to hit him with the damn rock?' Richard Truscott demanded.

'He was going to kill the doggie,' Victoria pointed out.

She had reached down to tickle the hound behind one ear as she spoke. It nuzzled its face into her skirts, but its eyes were on Richard and he stepped quickly back, almost tripping over Dr Manston's prone body. Victoria had squatted down, and was murmuring baby talk into the hound's ear. Richard shook his head in despair and reached down to check the doctor's pulse.

'At least you haven't killed him,' he said after a moment. 'Do you think you could stop playing with that damn dog for a moment?'

'He's not a damn dog,' Victoria retorted, still talking into the dog's ear. 'He's a lambkin, aren't you, my pet?'

'It's a hellhound,' Richard pointed out, 'which has already killed two men, and I have no desire to be the third, so would you at least mind attaching the damn thing's chain to a tree? Then you can fetch Cloud so we can get the poor man on his back.'

'I'll mind my lambkin,' Victoria answered, 'but Raoul must help you with Dr Manston.'

'Raoul? Who in hell's name is Raoul?' Richard demanded.

'At your service, sir,' a heavily accented voice spoke out as a man stepped around the edge of the boulder.

He was tall, black-skinned and dressed in a white coverall. In one hand he held a string bag full of struggling frogs. After a moment spent staring in astonishment Richard found his voice.

'You must be Dr Robinson's cook?'

'Yes, sir,' the man responded with a slight but formal bow.

'Well, be a good chap and help me with this fellow, would you? Vicky, I'll speak with you later.'

* * *

'If everybody would care to assemble in the drawing room,' Harland Wolfe stated, 'I think we may bring this case to a successful conclusion.'

He was smiling as he stepped through the door and made himself comfortable in front of the fireplace with his feet set apart and his hands clasped behind his back as he watched his audience assemble. The painter was in the custody of Constable Apcott, handcuffed but still scowling through his beard. Dr Manston was already in an armchair, his head bandaged and clearly having a little difficulty focusing, but with his usual bulldog tenacity he had refused to be put to bed. Miss Stukely was also in a chair, looking a little pale, but also relieved. Charles and Richard Truscott took high-backed chairs, their two grooms coming to stand behind them. The Capletons also remained standing, he hovering by the sideboard, she at the door. The cook, Raoul, was also present, but Miss Victoria Truscott had remained outside along with the hound, much to everybody else's relief.

'I think we may begin,' he stated. 'In terms of deductive practice, this has not been among the more demanding of my cases, although it has afforded considerable interest and I am greatly indebted to Miss Stukely for bringing it to my attention. Yes, while essentially simple, the case was certainly singular, or, to use the word Dr Manston will no doubt select for his account of it, "grotesque".

'The bones of the situation were evident to me from the first. In many of the cases I have handled there have been claims of supernatural creatures or events, but in every single one the answer, while often of complexity, has proven to be mundane. Therefore I was immediately able to exclude the supernatural. There is no Black Shuck.

'Thus, on the one hand we have Sir Robert Stukely, dead of fright after an encounter with a dog of exceptional size, and on the other we have an item of personal clothing stolen from Miss Stukely. The conclusion was inescapable, that some person or persons wished the death of Miss Stukely in turn, and intended to do so by setting this savage hound onto her. The motive for this horrible intention was also clear. Sir Robert and Miss Stukely had never met, their family being the sole connection between them.'

'But who is to benefit?' Miss Stukely asked. 'Not the Reverend Potts, surely?'

'Indeed not,' Harland Wolfe assured her. 'I eliminated the Reverend Potts at an early stage of my investigation and, as you say, no other heir could be found. However, I have always made it a maxim that whenever one has eliminated the impossible, whatever remains, however improbable, must be the truth. Therefore a potential heir had to exist, and so it proved. Mrs Capleton, if you would be good enough to fetch a razor and the necessary ancillary equipment, I have what I believe will be a fascinating introduction to make.'

The painter had immediately begun to struggle, and Harland Wolfe allowed himself a quiet smile as the burly policeman increased the power of his grip, then continued as Mrs Capleton left the room.

'These are really quite splendid portraits, don't you think? Take Sir Robert here, a fine figure of a man, although perhaps a trifle full of face for my purposes. Or the infamous Spanish Stukely . . . but no, he is too lean and his goatee beard hides the line of his chin. Ah ha, what have we here? Lewis Stukely, the skinner . . . with due apologies, of course, Miss Stukely. Or Roger Stukely. Either one will do, and as you will see, their faces are most distinctive.'

'Are you saying that Matthew Widdery is a Stukely?' Charles Truscott demanded.

'Without doubt,' Harland Wolfe replied.

'But how can you possibly know he looks like the

others?' Charles went on. 'The fellow has a beard like a quick-set hedge.'

'Deduction,' Harland Wolfe replied, 'although to be frank his efforts to escape the good constable are enough to prove my point in themselves.'

As he spoke the painter had subsided somewhat, but continued to glare from the mass of hair concealing his features. Harland Wolfe spent a moment more admiring the portraits of past Stukelys, until Mrs Capleton returned with the shaving things. Selecting the razor, he spent a moment working it on the strop before applying the brush to the pot of cream and the hot water to work up a lather.

As Harland Wolfe stepped close the painter began to struggle again, and to spit curses, but Charles and Richard Truscott moved in to assist the constable in restraining the man. Harland Wolfe was finding it hard not to chuckle as he applied the brush to the painter's face with vigorous motions, quickly covering the extensive facial hair with a thick layer of foam. Taking the razor once more, he flicked it open, only to have the man's struggles grow more desperate still.

'Now, now,' Harland Wolfe chided, 'do hold still, or you will only hurt yourself.'

Willing hands clamped the painter's head firmly into place and Harland Wolfe began his work, scraping slowly away at the densely grown hair to reveal the skin beneath. It was a slow process, but before he was halfway through he was certain his chain of reasoning was indeed correct. The painter's face so exactly resembled those of both Roger and Lewis Stukely that once the final tufts of hair had been removed and a flannel applied to clear the foam the three men might have been one and the same.

Harland Wolfe stood back, now smiling openly as every other person in the room stared with a most satisfactory astonishment. After allowing a moment for the effect to take hold, he spoke.

'Ladies and gentleman, pray allow me to introduce Mr Marmaduke Stukely.'

'Damn you, Wolfe!' the painter spat, drawing an admonition from the constable, but Harland Wolfe merely chuckled.

'But . . . but how did you know, Mr Wolfe?' Miss Stukely asked.

'It was no great matter,' Harland Wolfe admitted, 'merely a process of gathering facts and drawing certain inevitable conclusions. First, having deduced the existence of a potential heir, I sought to discover who it might be. An investigation of pictures, letters and other records in this house soon revealed the truth. Sir Robert was the eldest of the family, and therefore took the title, while he had tied his wealth to the estate, all matters of public record. As he had no direct descendants, the next in line would have been his nephew, Samuel, Miss Stukely's father. Had neither male heir produced any offspring, Miss Maude Stukely would have inherited or, failing that, the youngest of the four siblings, Miss Frances Stukely. I believe I am correct, Mr Truscott?'

'Yes, yes,' Charles Truscott confirmed, 'Robert was the eldest, then Maude, Samuel, and Frances.'

'Exactly,' Harland Wolfe went on, 'and as you so kindly informed me when I visited you at Driscoll's, Miss Maude Stukely died a spinster in 'sixty-seven, while Miss Frances Stukely took up with an improper suitor and ran away to South America?'

'That's about the size of it,' Charles Truscott agreed.

'There then is our connection,' Harland Wolfe stated. 'Miss Frances Stukely and her paramour settled in Panama, but it was not a fortuitous choice. Miss Frances bore her lover's child, but died shortly afterwards, perhaps of one of the fevers so prevalent in those parts. The child was brought up by his father, a man of most vicious habits, it seems, but he knew of his family history and was always determined to take revenge on those whom he saw as betraying his mother and also to have both estate and fortune. Thus, after making a moderate amount of capital working as a pimp both in Panama and Buenos Aires, he came to England . . .'

'This is arrant nonsense!' the painter cried out, finally breaking his silence. 'I challenge you to provide the slightest shred of proof for any of these outlandish claims!'

Harland Wolfe gave a light chuckle and went on.

'In your cottage, Mr Stukely, there is a small space under the eaves. In this space is concealed an oilskin bag, and in the bag are certain papers. Need I go on?'

'You swine!' the painter cursed. 'You broke into my house!'

'So I did,' Harland Wolfe replied, 'for while your pose as a painter provided you with an excellent opportunity both to watch Miss Stukely and to feed your hound, it also forced you to leave your rear unguarded.'

'How did you know it was him in the first place?' Richard Truscott asked.

'Again, by deduction,' Harland Wolfe responded. 'The culprit had to be close at hand, he almost certainly had to be newly arrived in the district, and he had to be able to watch Miss Stukely. Only one man fitted all three criteria. Besides, Mr Stukely is an execrable painter.'

'True enough,' Richard Truscott agreed. 'Now you point it out, it seems so simple.'

'This is always the way,' Harland Wolfe agreed, 'but I note that nobody else had managed to draw the same conclusion. In any event, this was Mr Stukely's plan, and at first it went better than he could possibly have hoped for. Having introduced himself anonymously to his uncle, he can have had little difficulty in obtaining some item of apparel with which to put the hound on the scent . . .'

'A boot did go missing, sir,' Mr Capleton put in, 'about a month before Sir Robert died.'

'As I thought,' Harland Wolfe answered, 'and even that proved unnecessary when poor Sir Robert died of fright at the mere sight of the beast, perhaps believing that Black Shuck had indeed come to claim him. Mr Stukely then planned to wait a decent period, leave the district and return some time later. His beard, of course, was his disguise, as it would have been awkward to be wandering around the district with such a distinctive face, and more awkward still to claim his inheritance. Clean shaven and bearing the documents proving himself to be the son of Miss Frances Stukely, there would have been no such difficulty. I would never have been called upon, and his plot would have succeeded, but for the perseverance of Mr Greville in finding Miss Stukely, which posed Mr Stukely with a new conundrum. This he proposed to solve with murder, and after the events of today I have no doubt whatsoever that charges can be brought, in the case of the convict, attempted murder in the case of Miss Stukely, and several others. I believe a police wagon is waiting outside the front door, constable, if you would care to remove this creature from our midst.'

Constable Apcott nodded grimly and tightened his grip and Marmaduke Stukely was led away, still spitting curses and shedding bits of beard from his clothing. Harland Wolfe waited until the wagon had pulled away, then spoke again.

'Two details remain. Firstly, the unfortunate convict, who met his death through ill luck. Am I correct, Mrs Capleton, in assuming that you provided him with some of Miss Stukely's old clothes so that he could make a warm bed for himself? He is a relative of yours, I take it, or perhaps the son of a close friend. No, do not protest, I watched you bring his food out to him on more than one occasion, but as he is dead and your actions speak more of humanity than a desire to break the law I made no mention of your actions in front of the constable. Nor will I.'

'Thank you, sir,' Mrs Capleton responded, hanging her head. 'He was my nephew.'

'Secondly,' Harland Wolfe continued, 'there is a matter I wish to discuss with Mr Truscott, if everybody would excuse us?'

Richard Truscott exchanged a worried glance with his father as they left the house. Harland Wolfe seemed altogether too clever, and too smug. Charles returned the look, but his tone was jovial as they came to stand beside the carriage which had brought them from Driscoll's that morning.

'How may we be of assistance, Mr Wolfe?'

'I was hoping you would allow me an introduction,' Harland Wolfe responded. 'It has often been said of me that I am a man who likes mysteries, whereas in fact I detest them, and never leave one unsolved if I can possibly help it. Thus, I would greatly appreciate it, Mr Truscott, if you would introduce me to your eldest son, Leopold.'

Charles began to go red, but Richard quickly intervened.

'I fear you have touched on a rather delicate subject, Mr Wolfe. My brother died in infancy.'

Harland Wolfe merely chuckled, then spoke again.

'Are you acquainted with the legend of Glamis Castle[11], Mr Truscott?'

'After a fashion,' Richard admitted.

'Might I venture to suggest,' Harland Wolfe went on, 'that the house at Driscoll's is of similar configuration?'

'How dare you!' Charles sputtered. 'What are you implying, sir?'

'Please, Mr Truscott,' Harland Wolfe said, turning to Charles. 'Given the regrettable incident concerning Miss Stukely and the supposed apeman who assaulted her beneath Beare's Lake viaduct, I think you might do better to ameliorate your tone. Indeed, while I pride myself on my discretion, I cannot allow . . .'

Harland Wolfe stopped, somewhat abruptly as the butt of Richard's revolver made contact with the back of his head.

'I realise, Mr Wolfe,' Richard Truscott stated, as he made a final adjustment to the photographic apparatus, 'that no possible apology could so much as begin to excuse our conduct, and therefore I will not insult you by offering one. Instead, I urge you to appreciate our position and understand that you have left us with no alternative course of action.'

Harland Wolfe's response was an angry mumbling made wholly incoherent by the segment of a pair of Lucy's drawers which had been forced into his mouth and tied off behind his head. Nor was that the only article of the woman's clothing about his person. He was in one of Eliza's dresses, an especially fanciful article of apple-green silk decorated with a large bow at the back, along with an expensive bustle and three layers of petticoats, in cotton, wool and taffeta respectively, each heavily trimmed with lace and the whole mass raised and pinned beneath his well-bound wrists to expose a second and equally elaborate pair of drawers. His position was no more dignified than his clothing, his body positioned across Lucy's lap as if about to receive a spanking.

Richard bent to the camera, arranging the cloth over his head and shoulders before he peered through the lens. The scenario, while no doubt effective enough, lacking a certain artistic verisimilitude. He rose once more.

'Come, come, Lucy,' he chided, 'there is no need to look so timid. You are a stern and unforgiving Mistress, well used to disciplining naughty boys. Do try to look the part.'

'Sorry, Mr Richard, sir,' Lucy answered and made an attempt to alter the naturally gentle contours of her face.

Richard frowned.

'Better, but far from ideal. Come, come now, girl, think of yourself as a Madam, perhaps the owner of the largest and grandest brothel in Plymouth, or London even. How would you like that, eh?'

'I'd not do nothing ...' Lucy began in outrage and Richard squeezed the bulb, praying that her expression would make it seem she was lecturing the unfortunate Harland Wolfe, who had also been caught unawares, so that his face was sure to be clearly recognisable in the finished photograph.

'I suspect that will be a good one,' he remarked as he began to change the plate. 'However, we need at least six before we can be sure of success, and Mr Wolfe, I suggest you co-operate, that is if you wish to retain what little dignity remains to you. There are far worse things in this world than taking a spanking from a pretty girl, believe me.'

Harland Wolfe returned a furious grimace, which Richard ignored as he continued.

'These are my terms, Mr Wolfe. You have my word that these pictures will remain entirely private, just so long as no word of this affair comes out, especially whatever you may have discovered about my brother. Where is Leopold, by the way, Lucy?'

'Out in the grounds,' Lucy admitted. 'Your mother and Eliza are locked in with cook.'

'Hmm ... best place for them, just now,' Richard answered, 'and I don't suppose Vicky needs to worry, not with that damn dog of hers, but you're to find Leopold directly we're done here. Now, perhaps if we could have one of you starting to unbutton Mr Wolfe's drawers?'

'Yes, Mr Richard, sir,' Lucy responded.

Richard waited until the second button was undone and the expression of consternation on the detective's face had reached a peak, then squeezed the bulb. Again, it seemed likely to be an excellent shot, and he was smiling to himself as he went on.

'As I was saying, Mr Wolfe, no mention whatsoever is to be made of my brother. However if you, or rather Dr Manston, wish to publish the affair of the hound, as the Deathly Dog of Dartmoor or whatever fanciful title he might come up with, you are free to do so, just so long as the names are changed, along with any other detail which might reveal the truth, perhaps the exact location of events also, but no mention whatsoever is to be made of my unfortunate brother. Nod if you agree?'

Harland Wolfe returned a single, sour nod.

'Good riddance to the wretched fellow,' Charles Truscott remarked as Luke Gurney closed the gates of Driscoll's behind Harland Wolfe. 'Now Lucy, unless you want that pretty bottom smacked you had better find Leopold and get him back into his room.'

'Yes, sir,' Lucy replied promptly.

She scampered away, doing her best to seem hurried, but slowed to a walk as soon as she was around the corner of the house. All day she had been searching for Leopold, and he was quite simply nowhere to be found. It could only be that he had somehow managed to find a key, or maybe climbed the wall in spite of the spikes, and escaped the grounds. If so she would be due a birching at the very least, but there was nothing she could do about it, and nor did she want to.

The prospect was quite appealing, if also frightening, because it was sure to be hard, but in the circumstances nobody could possibly suspect that it was exactly what she wanted. It was likely to be delivered by Richard too, and he would undoubtedly sodomise her afterwards, allowing her to thoroughly indulge her passions without risking disgrace.

Even the thought of having her bottom laid bare for the birch was giving her hot flushes, and she began to search more earnestly again, hoping that if she did find him Leopold would provide at least something of what she needed. Unfortunately he was still nowhere to be found, and wouldn't even answer when she called. She even tried the old ice house on the far side of the lake, wondering if he might have forced the door, but it was locked as usual.

Standing outside in the little copse of birch which had grown up to largely shield the stone arch of the doorway, her mind turned back to how her punishment would be. Perhaps Richard would make her pick her own birch again, a horribly embarrassing experience, but one that now provoked strongly erotic memories. Maybe, she thought, she should even make a birch now and present him with it as a gesture. Then he would be sure to take it to her bottom.

Perhaps he would even make her pick the twigs with her dress pulled up behind and no drawers on. Perhaps he would have her thrashed by Luke Gurney, or worse, horsed up on Luke Gurney's back and thrashed by Ned Annaferd, the way she'd heard it was sometimes done to girls in the village.

The thought sent a powerful shiver through her. Several times Ned had made passes at her, and while she had responded with a haughty sniff and a lift of her nose, her disdain was far from genuine, while having snubbed him would make being thrashed by him more exciting still. Yes, that would be perfect, to be horsed up on Luke Gurney's back in the stable block and thrashed by Ned as Richard looked on, then to have all three of them take turns with her, one with his cock up her bottom as she got the next ready in her mouth . . .

Lucy was blushing hot for her own filthy thoughts as she began to toy with the birch twigs dangling from the trees around her. It was tempting, very tempting, and even if she didn't give the birch to Richard she could always play with it, perhaps even apply a few strokes to her bottom, her bare bottom . . .

It was a thought she could not resist. With her heart in her mouth she moved deeper in among the birches. Her hands went up under her skirts, to tug loose the bow holding her drawers up. Off they came, leaving her feeling deliciously improper with her quim and bottom bare under her skirts. Up came her skirts and her bottom was bare behind her, a thrill more enticing still.

Her heart was hammering as she began to pick birch twigs, constantly thinking of how she must look, with her bottom bare as she prepared an instrument for her own beating. The thought made her weak at the knees, and her fingers were trembling badly as she took a ribbon from her hair and tied the twigs together to form a small but serviceable birch, just right for a girl's naughty bottom.

Just a moment to pluck up her courage and she had pushed her bottom out, reaching back with the birch, first just to tickle her cheeks, then to smack, lightly, and harder, making her skin tingle and her mouth come open in an O of pleasure. Her bottom pushed out further still and her feet came apart, deliberately showing her cunt from behind as she began to smack harder, all the while imagining how lewd she would look horsed up on Luke Gurney's back, how she'd kick in her pain, making a fine show of both cunt and bottom hole, which they would surely be unable to resist driving their cocks up . . .

'How'd you like me to do that for you, Lucy?'

She started violently at the voice, dropping the birch and spinning around, her hands clasped to her bottom in a hopeless attempt to cover what had already been seen anyway. The blood rushed to her face as Ned Annaferd himself stepped out from among the trees, and hotter still as she saw that he was holding his erect cock in one hand.

‘Don’t be shy,’ he urged. ‘Like it from Master Richard, don’t you, and Leopold and all, so how about me?’

Lucy’s mouth had begun to work, outrage and shock and fear warring in her head as she struggled to speak, but no words would come, while her face felt as if it was on fire. Ned Annaferd merely chuckled and stepped forwards, picking up Lucy’s birch and examining it with a critical eye.

‘Not bad,’ he remarked. ‘He stings I dare say. Come on then, show me that bottom and I’ll give you a cut or two, then you can suck on my pego.’

Lucy’s mouth was still working in speechless outrage, but she found herself unable to resist as he took her by the shoulder and turned her around. A sob escaped her lips as she was pushed down to force her to stick her bottom out. Ned spent a moment adjusting her skirts to make sure the full cheeky target was available to him, then began to smack her, just gently, but enough to make her tread her feet and cry out with pain and raw emotion.

She was being birched, birched on her bare bottom by a boy who’d caught her in the woods, caught her being dirty with herself, the very boy she’d been thinking of as she did it. It stung, but she deserved it, and more, to be beaten properly and in public, thrashed until she howled then sodomised in front of a dozen onlookers, and if the onlookers weren’t there, at least Ned was, with his cock at the ready.

‘Do me . . . take me . . .’ she gasped. ‘Take me, Ned.’

He had dropped the birch on the instant, coming behind her with his cock in his hand. Lucy reached back, to spread her stinging cheeks and offer him her bottom hole, still soft and buttery in anticipation of another buggering from Leopold, but as his cock head pushed to her flesh it was too low, right against the mouth of her virgin cunt.

'No!' she squeaked. 'Not there! You must marry me if you go in there, Ned . . . do it up my bottom.'

'Don't mind,' Ned grunted, and pushed.

As Lucy's cunt popped she cried out in pain and despair, but both emotions had quickly started to fade as his cock began to work in her hole and she thought of a future married to a man who would birch her regularly.

Genevieve fastened her bonnet and allowed Mr Capleton to assist her into the trap. It had been over two hours since Harland Wolfe had left with the Truscotts and their servants, without providing the slightest explanation. She waited first with curiosity and then concern, and once Raoul had left and Dr Manston retired to recover from the bump on his head sustained from an unexpected falling rock in Tavy Cleave, she had found herself alone with the Capletons. Finally she had decided to drive over to Driscoll's and find out what was amiss.

'Are you certain you wouldn't like myself or my wife to accompany you, Miss?' Mr Capleton enquired.

'Quite sure, thank you, Capleton,' Genevieve answered and gave a gentle flick of her whip to the horse's rump.

Pulling out onto the Okehampton Road, she realised she didn't know the way, but Burley Down was visible and, as Richard had pointed it out from the moor, and Driscoll's was beneath it, she reasoned that it could not be too difficult to find her route. A little later she reached Sourton village and realised she had come too far north, but as she glanced down the street she saw Harland Wolfe pass at the far end, presumably returning from Driscoll's. Turning the trap, she started down the village street, briefly wondering if she should speak to the detective first before deciding against it.

* * *

Richard Truscott glanced up at the spikes topping the main gate of Driscoll's and frowned. He had walked slowly around the entire length of the wall, but there was no sign of Leopold, nor that an attempt had been made to climb out. Yet it was hard to think where else his brother might be. Leopold had remarkable skill at concealment, fortuitously, given the various times he had escaped the confines of the grounds, but he would usually come to Lucy as soon as he grew bored of hiding and his lust kicked in once more. This time, Lucy had called for him both inside and out, but to no avail.

'Where the devil could he be, d'you think?' Charles asked as he approached from the direction of the stables.

'I have no idea,' Richard responded, 'but I had better take Lucy out in the trap, I think.'

'In a while, yes,' Charles agreed, 'but what do you make of this business with Marmaduke Stukely, eh? I said there was bad blood in the family.'

'Ah, yes,' Richard responded, and decided to take the plunge. 'I've been meaning to talk to you about that, father. The thing is, Miss Stukely and I are engaged to be married.'

'What?' Charles blustered. 'Are you mad?'

'I really have very little choice in the matter,' Richard lied. 'What happened is this. She was so distraught over what happened with Leopold that in order to comfort her I admitted that the supposed creature was in fact a man. Naturally she wanted to know how I could be sure and, well, what with one thing and other I confessed to the truth.'

'Good God!' Charles responded. 'And with that detective fellow about?'

'That would not be a concern even had we not compromised him,' Richard responded. 'Leopold, it seems, took her maidenhead, and so I was obliged to follow suit for fear she might be with child. It would be embarrassing, after all, if she were to give birth to a child who grew up with a family resemblance to us if only Leopold had had her.'

'Good God!' Charles Truscott repeated, putting his fingers to his forehead.

'So it makes sense for me to marry her,' Richard went on, pressing his advantage, 'and after all, she shows no sign of the family vices. A more gentle girl it would be hard to imagine, but she's strong willed too.'

'And how, pray, is she supposed to cope with Leopold about?' his father demanded.

'She and I can live at Stukely Hall,' Richard suggested. 'Indeed, I might even be tempted to change the name, and bear in mind that once she and I are married the only surviving Stukely will be Marmaduke, whose marital prospects are frankly poor.'

'That's true,' Charles admitted, and paused.

'Then there is the ownership of Wheal Purity to be considered,' Richard went on. 'Think how old Sir Robert would feel if he knew the stake he so carefully garnered over the years had gone straight back to our family?'

His father nodded and smiled.

'Oh very well, marry the girl, and if your children are a crew of maniacs, on your own head be it.'

'Thank you, father,' Richard responded warmly. 'I knew you would see the sense of it, but that is the Stukely trap, is it not?'

'You're not going to let her in, are you?' Charles queried as Richard started towards the gates. 'Not with Leopold loose?'

'She will have to meet him sooner or later,' Richard responded, 'and I can hardly refuse to open the gates to my fiancée.'

'I suppose not,' Charles admitted.

Richard swung the gates wide and took Genevieve in his arms as he helped her down from the trap, ignoring her questions as to where he had been, in favour of making a proper announcement of their engagement. All else was immediately forgotten and they went indoors to give the news to the rest of the family, leaving Luke Gurney to take the horse and trap.

His mother had already grown tired of hiding in the kitchen and received the news with unrestrained happiness. Victoria was more enthusiastic still, accepting a role as a bridesmaid and even abandoning her dog for a few minutes in her eagerness to discuss the new gown she would need. Richard alone was not fully relaxed, worried how he was really going to spring the news about Leopold on Genevieve. It had to be done, that much was plain, but how to go about it was a very different matter. At length he managed to draw Genevieve away from the others, and took her arm as they walked out across the lawns.

'The estate was originally owned by the Driscoll family,' he explained, 'but most of what you see is my great-grandfather's work. We were the junior branch of the family at the time, so the old home, Beare, had passed to his brother.'

'And Beare is yours once more?' Genevieve asked.

'Yes,' Richard explained. 'Grandpapa John married his cousin, Grandmama Augusta, and with no male heirs in the line Beare came to him. Quite a character, Grandpapa, and his father before him, apparently, and before that was Devil John himself, who the mothers hereabouts still use to frighten their children into behaving. Yes, we Truscotts have never lacked for er . . . character, in fact . . .'

'I like character,' Genevieve declared, pressing close to his arm, 'yours especially, and your father and mother are delightful. Miss Victoria also, she is the kindest girl.'

'Well, yes,' Richard agreed doubtfully, 'and I'm sure she'll make an excellent bridesmaid, but the thing is, you see . . .'

'It will be quite the wedding, won't it?' Genevieve interrupted. 'Is it not wonderfully romantic, to unite the two oldest families in the district?'

'Yes, undoubtedly,' Richard answered, 'quite the thing, and the end of a centuries-old quarrel as well, but . . .'

'And it must be soon,' Genevieve pointed out, 'as you were so very gallant with me on the moors the other day.'

'Yes, absolutely, rather more gallant I dare say than my . . .'

'Might we, do you think, go indoors without being seen?' Genevieve asked.

'Yes, I dare say,' Richard responded, allowing Genevieve to steer him back towards the house.

She had begun to talk about the wedding, but there was no mistaking the warmth of her attention to him, and his cock had soon begun to stir in reaction. By the time they had got round the house he had decided to postpone his admission at least until after thoroughly indulging himself with her, as then, if she never wanted to speak to him again, at least he would have had his pleasure one more time.

Coming in at the front door, they made their way quickly upstairs to his room, Genevieve struggling not to giggle and every bit as urgent as he. Richard saw that the door to Leopold's room was open, but Genevieve paid no attention, tumbling onto the bed with her arms spread wide for him.

'One moment,' Richard urged and quickly poked his head into Leopold's room.

It was empty, but the breakfast tray stood on the table, with a large pat of butter still in the dish. Smiling wickedly to himself, Richard picked it up and returned to his own room. Locking the door, he came to Genevieve, climbing onto the bed to kiss her and trail a finger across the sensitive skin of her neck. Her response was immediate, and strong, returning his kiss and pulling his head to her as her other hand slid down to squeeze the bulge in his crotch. As she freed his cock into her hand Richard was reflecting that he had made the perfect choice.

Genevieve was already in a state of bliss as she pulled at Richard's erection. She wanted him inside her, without delay, but also all the wonderful things he'd done to her before, and all the things that excited her so much, to be spanked, and licked, and sodomised, to suck his penis and have him come in her cunt.

Her legs came up and open, letting her skirts fall and inviting him to touch. He was not slow to respond, burrowing his hand in among the froth of her petticoats to find her sex, briefly rubbing the cotton of her drawers between her lips before he began to grope for the buttons holding them closed. Giggling, Genevieve rolled up her legs, making it easier for him to get at her bottom and expose her. Her hand was still on his cock, tugging gently to keep him ready, and he was kissing her and trying to get her breasts free of her dress all at the same time.

She sighed as the panel of her drawers came loose, arching her back and spreading her thighs to offer her cunt as she came naked. Richard obliged, slipping two fingers into her open hole and starting to masturbate her as his mouth once more found hers. Again she sighed, her ecstasy rising as he attended to her, and all the while squeezing and tugging at the hot erection which would soon be in her body.

Richard moved down the bed, burying his face between Genevieve's thighs to lick her, not just on her quim, but between the cheeks of her bottom too, burrowing his tongue into the tight bud of her anus.

Genevieve gave a deep urgent moan and quickly finished the job of exposing her breasts, pulling her bodice wide to take one in either hand, stroking them and pinching gently at her nipples as his tongue worked between her well-parted cheeks.

'You will, won't you?' she sighed. 'In my little hole . . . the way you did the first time?'

Richard nodded against his faceful of wet curvaceous flesh, more than happy to accept the invitation to sodomise her. A few more flicks of the tongue to her bump, one last insertion in the rosy bud of her anus, and he rose to reach for the butter dish. Genevieve giggled as she saw what he was doing, and gave a little shocked gasp as he rolled her legs high to expose her completely.

Her bottom and cunt were spread open to Richard's view, and he made quick work of unbuttoning the waistband of her drawers and pulling them off, leaving her nude from her waist to her stocking tops. Blushing with embarrassment but smiling too, she took hold of her legs beneath the knees, keeping herself completely available to him. He lifted the butter dish to show her and scooped out a large blob.

Genevieve made a little purring noise in her throat as she saw what was to be done to her and pulled her thighs up higher still, so that the full width of her bottom and all of her crease was showing. Grinning, Richard applied the butter to her already spit-wet anus, closing the tiny hole with an oily yellow plug that immediately began to melt. Taking his cock, he began to rub it around Genevieve's ring, making her sigh and shiver as she was stimulated.

She was open in no time, her buttery bottom hole giving easily to the pressure as he pushed in the head of his cock. He began to masturbate into her rectum, his eyes feeding on the taut pink ring of her buggered anus and her beautiful, ready cunt. The temptation to simply spunk up her bottom was close to unbearable, but he was determined to make her come first, and to have her in every way he could think of before reaching his climax.

He pulled his cock out, leaving Genevieve's bottom hole agape for a moment before closing with soft fart that blew out a froth of bubbles from the slippery little hole. Again she giggled, a sound so lewd and free in response to something so improper that it had him grinning maniacally and reflecting once more that she was the perfect mate as they tumbled together on the bed once more.

Genevieve cuddled close to Richard, lost to the lascivious pleasure of their game, kissing and licking as they moved together. His cock went into her mouth, tasting of butter and her own bottom as she sucked eagerly on the head. Her own fingers went into her body as she got onto her knees for penetration, probing deep into her cunt as she rubbed a thumb on her buttery bottom hole.

Richard needed no more prompting, climbing behind her to remove her hand and substitute his cock, deep up her eager cunt hole until his balls met her flesh, and again, pulling out and stabbing in, every entry making her gasp in ecstasy. Her hands were still back, and she spread her cheeks, showing off her bottom hole to him. Again, a single invitation was enough, and the next thrust was into her rectum, making her cheeks puff out at the sudden filling.

He began to bugger her in the same lewd manner he'd fucked her cunt, holding his cock and repeatedly jabbing it into her gaping hole, until she was almost out of her mind with pleasure. She began to spank herself, enjoying the thought that she thoroughly deserved it for her lewd behaviour, and as his hand moved to her cunt and his fingers began to fiddle with her she knew she was going to come.

The orgasm hit her with overwhelming force, just as his cock was stuffed back up her bottom, squeezing butter out from the gaping hole between her cheeks. He kept his cock up as she came, holding himself in to the balls as she shook and shivered her way through her climax, her anus in spasm, her empty cunt squeezing juice over his fingers and balls, her teeth clenched onto the bolster to stop herself screaming.

Richard eased himself carefully from Genevieve's bottom hole, which stayed open, oozing butter and juice down into her equally open cunt. Moving to her head, he slipped his cock into her mouth to be sucked clean, which she accepted, her eyes closed in bliss.

'Now for my turn, darling,' he breathed, 'but not in your mouth . . . inside you. Ride me, would you, my thighs ache?'

Genevieve complied, quickly pulling off her dress before mounting Richard, so that he was rewarded with the view of her bare breasts above the top of her pretty blue corset as she took his cock to guide it into her quim. She began to bounce on him, her face alive with joy as she rode, easing herself up and down on his erection as his eyes feasted on her naked body.

'I must come,' he sighed, and opened his arms to take her in.

She came down on top of him, wriggling herself onto his cock as he begun to pump into her. His hands went to her cheeks, slapping at them and spreading them as he remembered how gloriously lewd she had looked with her legs rolled up, her cunt wet and bare, her bottom hole oozing butter . . .

Richard sighed, his eyes starting to close as his orgasm began to well up, just in time to catch sight of a huge hairy figure rising from beneath the bed, directly behind Genevieve's spread bottom cheeks, erect cock pointed directly at the little buttery rosebud he'd just enjoyed.

'Leopold, no, bad Leopold!' Richard cried out, but too late.

Genevieve Stukely had gone pop-eyed as the full length of Leopold's erect penis was unexpectedly inserted into her rectum.

Notes

1 The late Victorian era must surely be regarded by all right-thinking persons as the golden age of female underwear. Drawers and chemises had evolved to extraordinary complexity: always voluminous, always trimmed with lace and often in abundance, these fantastic garments both revealed and concealed, allowing a teasing glimpse of hem or the full magnificent display of a bare bottom through the rear.

There were two principal designs for drawers, either of which might also form the lower half of a set of combinations, in which the chemise and drawers were combined to form a single garment. The original design, dating from when drawers were generally adopted earlier that century, were essentially two leg pieces sewn together at the waist, so that a split ran from belly to lower back, allowing a woman in even the heaviest skirts easy access to the intimate parts of her body, for whatever purpose. These were referred to in vulgar parlance as splitters. Notably superior were panelled drawers, in which a rear flap was held closed by buttons, a less practical garment, but one that disposed of the risk that on taking a tumble the wearer might supply any onlookers with an unintentional display of cunt.

2 The legend of Black Shuck is known to have been the basis for *The Hound of the Baskervilles*, but it

derives not from the West Country, but East Anglia, where Conan Doyle is said to have first heard it while staying in a hotel at Cromer. Black Shuck is said to follow lonely travellers at night, and only to take those who run. There are similar legends in Devon, but the ghostly dogs generally associated with Dartmoor are the Wisht Hunt, a pack of demonic hounds led by the Devil himself.

3 In *The Hound*, Dartmoor is presented as a wilderness, whereas in practice it was more settled then than today. At present, any visitor is only likely to meet with hill walkers, soldiers on exercise and perhaps the occasional author researching for a scandalous book, but in 1889 there would have been moormen looking after sheep and cattle, miners, quarrymen, reed cutters and, in the case of the Rattlebrook Works, peat cutters complete with a small railway on which to take their produce off the moor.

4 The bustle was one of the most fascinating and bizarre articles of clothing ever inflicted on the female form. Designed to simultaneously conceal and enhance the buttocks while also drawing attention to a slim waist, it developed from the crinolines of the mid-nineteenth century and evolved across the 1870s, to reach its full absurd magnificence in the 1890s, after which it diminished in size and finally vanished altogether.

The reason for the rise and fall of these extravagant skirt supports lay in the need for women of quality to keep ahead of their inferiors. When the maid purchased a bustle, panniers or a crinoline cage, milady felt obliged to purchase the new fuller style, an appetite the fashion industry of the time was eager to feed. Unfortunately there came a point when milady could no longer dress herself, or in some cases even negotiate doors or stairs, and the only choice was to return to a sleek look and then start all over again with a new style a few years later.

5 South Dakota became the 40th state of the Union on November 2, 1889.

6 The bogs of Dartmoor are not entirely undeserving of the reputation given them in *The Hound*, although it would be very unusual indeed for a man to sink without trace. The Great Grimpen Mire is said to be based on Fox Tor Mires, which the author has crossed, although admittedly not dry shod. At its centre are the spoil heaps of an abandoned tin mine, which may have provided the inspiration for a hiding place for the hound. Tavy Head is both boggy and rocky, but the mires are a convenient fiction. All other details of the moor are essentially accurate.

7 The Victorian riding habit was among the first female garments specifically designed for sporting purposes and has become one of the icons of the era. The crinolines, bustles and voluminous skirts of the middle and late nineteenth century made it almost impossible to mount a horse, much less stay on it, and in response to this a sleek elegant costume developed, allowing the female equestrian to ride with grace while retaining her modesty. There was also a touch of severity to the costume, accentuated by riding whip and silk top hat. Ladies rode side-saddle, and to do otherwise was considered scandalous.

8 In *The Hound*, Conan Doyle has Sherlock Holmes living on the moor in one of the ancient huts that had retained enough of its roof to keep out the weather. Dartmoor's hut circles, one of which this is generally supposed to have been, date from the bronze age and could not possibly have had a roof in the nineteenth century or for two thousand years before. More probably, one of the huts used by the

Dartmoor tin miners, or 'tinners', might have survived.

9 The *Manifesto of the Communist Party* first appeared in 1848, but an annotated English edition was produced by Engels in 1888, five years after Marx' death.

10 Cutty Dyer is one of the most bizarre of West Country legends, and is known across Dartmoor, but mainly associated with the River Yeo at Ashburton. He is said to be a water sprite who either catches unwary paddlers by the ankle and drags them underwater to drown, or leaps on them from the shallows and drinks their blood, as described in this charming little ditty –

'Don't ye go down river-side,
where Cutty Dyer do abide.
Cutty Dyer ain't no good.
*Cutty Dyer'll drink yer blood.'**

More bizarrely still, the name Cutty Dyer is said to derive from a contraction of Saint Christopher and 'dire', although quite how the patron saint of travellers was transformed into a vampiric ogre is unclear.

11 It is said of Glamis Castle, in north-eastern Scotland, that if the windows are counted from the outside there will always be two more than can be counted from the inside, and that this is due to the existence of a secret chamber in which a deformed scion of the family once lived, hidden from public view. Several other legends exist in relation to this, more or less macabre. The secret is also said to be known to the royal family and, although none ever admitted to it, in the nature of conspiracy theories their bare denial carries little weight.

---

*This does in fact rhyme, but only if read in a thick West Country accent.

The leading publisher of fetish and adult fiction

TELL US WHAT YOU THINK!

Readers' ideas and opinions matter to us so please take a few minutes to fill in the questionnaire below.

1. **Sex:** Are you male ☐ female ☐ a couple ☐?

2. **Age:** Under 21 ☐ 21–30 ☐ 31–40 ☐ 41–50 ☐ 51–60 ☐ over 60 ☐

3. **Where do you buy your Nexus books from?**

☐ A chain book shop. If so, which one(s)?

____

☐ An independent book shop. If so, which one(s)?

____

☐ A used book shop/charity shop

☐ Online book store. If so, which one(s)?

____

4. **How did you find out about Nexus books?**

☐ Browsing in a book shop

☐ A review in a magazine

☐ Online

☐ Recommendation

☐ Other ____________________________________

5. **In terms of settings, which do you prefer? (Tick as many as you like.)**

☐ Down to earth and as realistic as possible

☐ Historical settings. If so, which period do you prefer?

____

☐ Fantasy settings – barbarian worlds

☐ Completely escapist/surreal fantasy

☐ Institutional or secret academy

☐ Futuristic/sci fi
☐ Escapist but still believable
☐ Any settings you dislike?

____

☐ Where would you like to see an adult novel set?

____

6. In terms of storylines, would you prefer:

☐ Simple stories that concentrate on adult interests?
☐ More plot and character-driven stories with less explicit adult activity?
☐ We value your ideas, so give us your opinion of this book:

____

____

____

7. In terms of your adult interests, what do you like to read about? (Tick as many as you like.)

☐ Traditional corporal punishment (CP)
☐ Modern corporal punishment
☐ Spanking
☐ Restraint/bondage
☐ Rope bondage
☐ Latex/rubber
☐ Leather
☐ Female domination and male submission
☐ Female domination and female submission
☐ Male domination and female submission
☐ Willing captivity
☐ Uniforms
☐ Lingerie/underwear/hosiery/footwear (boots and high heels)
☐ Sex rituals
☐ Vanilla sex
☐ Swinging
☐ Cross-dressing/TV
☐ Enforced feminisation

☐ Others – tell us what you don't see enough of in adult fiction:

8. Would you prefer books with a more specialised approach to your interests, i.e. a novel specifically about uniforms? If so, which subject(s) would you like to read a Nexus novel about?

9. Would you like to read true stories in Nexus books? For instance, the true story of a submissive woman, or a male slave? Tell us which true revelations you would most like to read about:

10. What do you like best about Nexus books?

11. What do you like least about Nexus books?

12. Which are your favourite titles?

13. Who are your favourite authors?

14. Which covers do you prefer? Those featuring:
(Tick as many as you like.)

☐ Fetish outfits
☐ More nudity
☐ Two models
☐ Unusual models or settings
☐ Classic erotic photography
☐ More contemporary images and poses
☐ A blank/non-erotic cover
☐ What would your ideal cover look like?

____

15. Describe your ideal Nexus novel in the space provided:

____

____

____

____

16. Which celebrity would feature in one of your Nexus-style fantasies?
We'll post the best suggestions on our website – anonymously!

____

THANKS FOR YOUR TIME

Now simply write the title of this book in the space below and cut out the questionnaire pages. Post to: Nexus, Marketing Dept., Thames Wharf Studios, Rainville Rd, London W6 9HA

Book title: ____________________________________

NEXUS NEW BOOKS

To be published in April 2007

SINDI IN SILK
Yolanda Celbridge

After the destruction of most of the northern world in a long-forgotten war, Madagascar survives as the most powerful country on Earth. Silk stockings become the most precious currency, which only bare-breasted noblewomen and vampire girl slaves are allowed to wear. Sindi, having been a whip-wielding mistress, herself becomes enslaved, and a smuggler of illicit stockings from Zanzibar. The prince of Madagascar is victorious in the war against his twin brother, the prince of Zanzibar – but both men fall in love with her. And when it is time for the victor to choose a princess, only the girl whose legs fit the one pair of silk stockings, from the old times, will do. It is Sindi. She becomes Whip mistress of the Islands, Princesse du Fouet, and Dame des Bas Sacrés, Lady of the Sacred Stockings.

£6.99 SBN 978 0 352 34102 0

THE GIRLFLESH INSTITUTE
Adriana Arden

Probing the lowest levels of the outwardly respectable London headquarters of Shiller plc, Vanessa Buckingham stumbles into a hidden world of twenty-first century slavery. Turned into a living puppet by Shiller's enigmatic director, Vanessa is forced to record every detail of the slave-girls' lives; from intimate psychological testing at the mysterious Fellgrish Institute, through strict training and ultimate submission to the clients who hire them. In the process Vanessa must confront both her own true nature and a terrible dilemma: can there be such a thing as a willing slave? Should she expose Shiller's activities as immoral – or let herself become another commodity in its girlflesh trade?

£6.99 ISBN 978 0 352 34101 3

NEXUS CONFESSIONS: VOLUME TWO
Various

Swinging, dogging, group sex, cross-dressing, spanking, female domination, corporal punishment, and extreme fetishes . . . Nexus Confessions explores the length and breadth of erotic obsession, real experience and sexual fantasy. An encyclopaedic collection of the bizarre, the extreme, the utterly inappropriate, the daring and the shocking experiences of ordinary men and women driven by their extraordinary desires. Collected by the world's leading publisher of fetish fiction, this is the second in a series of six volumes of true stories and shameful confessions, never-before-told or published.

£6.99 ISBN 978 0 352 34103 7

If you would like more information about Nexus titles, please visit our website at www.nexus-books.co.uk, or send a large stamped addressed envelope to:

Nexus, Thames Wharf Studios,
Rainville Road, London W6 9HA

NEXUS BOOKLIST

Information is correct at time of printing. To avoid disappointment, check availability before ordering. Go to www.nexus-books.co.uk.

All books are priced at £6.99 unless another price is given.

NEXUS

☐ ABANDONED ALICE	Adriana Arden	ISBN 978 0 352 33969 0
☐ ALICE IN CHAINS	Adriana Arden	ISBN 978 0 352 33908 9
☐ AQUA DOMINATION	William Doughty	ISBN 978 0 352 34020 7
☐ THE ART OF CORRECTION	Tara Black	ISBN 978 0 352 33895 2
☐ THE ART OF SURRENDER	Madeline Bastinado	ISBN 978 0 352 34013 9
☐ BEASTLY BEHAVIOUR	Aishling Morgan	ISBN 978 0 352 34095 5
☐ BELINDA BARES UP	Yolanda Celbridge	ISBN 978 0 352 33926 3
☐ BENCH-MARKS	Tara Black	ISBN 978 0 352 33797 9
☐ BIDDING TO SIN	Rosita Varón	ISBN 978 0 352 34063 4
☐ BINDING PROMISES	G.C. Scott	ISBN 978 0 352 34014 6
☐ THE BOOK OF PUNISHMENT	Cat Scarlett	ISBN 978 0 352 33975 1
☐ BRUSH STROKES	Penny Birch	ISBN 978 0 352 34072 6
☐ CALLED TO THE WILD	Angel Blake	ISBN 978 0 352 34067 2
☐ CAPTIVES OF CHEYNER CLOSE	Adriana Arden	ISBN 978 0 352 34028 3
☐ CARNAL POSSESSION	Yvonne Strickland	ISBN 978 0 352 34062 7
☐ CITY MAID	Amelia Evangeline	ISBN 978 0 352 34096 2
☐ COLLEGE GIRLS	Cat Scarlett	ISBN 978 0 352 33942 3
☐ COMPANY OF SLAVES	Christina Shelly	ISBN 978 0 352 33887 7
☐ CONCEIT AND CONSEQUENCE	Aishling Morgan	ISBN 978 0 352 33965 2

☐ CORRECTIVE THERAPY	Jacqueline Masterson	ISBN 978 0 352 33917 1
☐ CORRUPTION	Virginia Crowley	ISBN 978 0 352 34073 3
☐ CRUEL SHADOW	Aishling Morgan	ISBN 978 0 352 33886 0
☐ DARK MISCHIEF	Lady Alice McCloud	ISBN 978 0 352 33998 0
☐ DEPTHS OF DEPRAVATION	Ray Gordon	ISBN 978 0 352 33995 9
☐ DICE WITH DOMINATION	P.S. Brett	ISBN 978 0 352 34023 8
☐ DOMINANT	Felix Baron	ISBN 978 0 352 34044 3
☐ DOMINATION DOLLS	Lindsay Gordon	ISBN 978 0 352 33891 4
☐ EXPOSÉ	Laura Bowen	ISBN 978 0 352 34035 1
☐ FORBIDDEN READING	Lisette Ashton	ISBN 978 0 352 34022 1
☐ FRESH FLESH	Wendy Swanscombe	ISBN 978 0 352 34041 2
☐ HOT PURSUIT	Lisette Ashton	ISBN 978 0 352 33878 5
☐ THE INDECENCIES OF ISABELLE	Penny Birch (writing as Cruella)	ISBN 978 0 352 33989 8
☐ THE INDISCRETIONS OF ISABELLE	Penny Birch (writing as Cruella)	ISBN 978 0 352 33882 2
☐ IN DISGRACE	Penny Birch	ISBN 978 0 352 33922 5
☐ IN HER SERVICE	Lindsay Gordon	ISBN 978 0 352 33968 3
☐ INSTRUMENTS OF PLEASURE	Nicole Dere	ISBN 978 0 352 34098 6
☐ JULIA C	Laura Bowen	ISBN 978 0 352 33852 5
☐ LACING LISBETH	Yolanda Celbridge	ISBN 978 0 352 33912 6
☐ LICKED CLEAN	Yolanda Celbridge	ISBN 978 0 352 33999 7
☐ LOVE JUICE	Donna Exeter	ISBN 978 0 352 33913 3
☐ MANSLAVE	J.D. Jensen	ISBN 978 0 352 34040 5
☐ NAUGHTY, NAUGHTY	Penny Birch	ISBN 978 0 352 33976 8
☐ NIGHTS IN WHITE COTTON	Penny Birch	ISBN 978 0 352 34008 5
☐ NO PAIN, NO GAIN	James Baron	ISBN 978 0 352 33966 9
☐ THE OLD PERVERSITY SHOP	Aishling Morgan	ISBN 978 0 352 34007 8
☐ THE PALACE OF PLEASURES	Christobel Coleridge	ISBN 978 0 352 33801 3

☐ PETTING GIRLS	Penny Birch	ISBN 978 0 352 33957 7	
☐ PET TRAINING IN THE PRIVATE HOUSE	Esme Ombreux	ISBN 978 0 352 33655 2	£5.99
☐ THE PRIESTESS	Jacqueline Bellevois	ISBN 978 0 352 33905 8	
☐ PRIZE OF PAIN	Wendy Swanscombe	ISBN 978 0 352 33890 7	
☐ PUNISHED IN PINK	Yolanda Celbridge	ISBN 978 0 352 34003 0	
☐ THE PUNISHMENT CAMP	Jacqueline Masterson	ISBN 978 0 352 33940 9	
☐ THE PUNISHMENT CLUB	Jacqueline Masterson	ISBN 978 0 352 33862 4	
☐ THE ROAD TO DEPRAVITY	Ray Gordon	ISBN 978 0 352 34092 4	
☐ SCARLET VICE	Aishling Morgan	ISBN 978 0 352 33988 1	
☐ SCHOOLED FOR SERVICE	Lady Alice McCloud	ISBN 978 0 352 33918 8	
☐ SCHOOL FOR STINGERS	Yolanda Celbridge	ISBN 978 0 352 33994 2	
☐ SEXUAL HEELING	Wendy Swanscombe	ISBN 978 0 352 33921 8	
☐ SILKEN EMBRACE	Christina Shelly	ISBN 978 0 352 34081 8	
☐ SILKEN SERVITUDE	Christina Shelly	ISBN 978 0 352 34004 7	
☐ SIN'S APPRENTICE	Aishling Morgan	ISBN 978 0 352 33909 6	
☐ SLAVE GENESIS	Jennifer Jane Pope	ISBN 978 0 352 33503 6	£5.99
☐ SLAVE OF THE SPARTANS	Yolanda Celbridge	ISBN 978 0 352 34078 8	
☐ SLIPPERY WHEN WET	Penny Birch	ISBN 978 0 352 34091 7	
☐ THE SMARTING OF SELINA	Yolanda Celbridge	ISBN 978 0 352 33872 3	
☐ STRIP GIRL	Aishling Morgan	ISBN 978 0 352 34077 1	
☐ STRIPING KAYLA	Yolanda Marshall	ISBN 978 0 352 33881 5	
☐ STRIPPED BARE	Angel Blake	ISBN 978 0 352 33971 3	
☐ TASTING CANDY	Ray Gordon	ISBN 978 0 352 33925 6	
☐ TEMPTING THE GODDESS	Aishling Morgan	ISBN 978 0 352 33972 0	
☐ THAI HONEY	Kit McCann	ISBN 978 0 352 34068 9	
☐ TICKLE TORTURE	Penny Birch	ISBN 978 0 352 33904 1	
☐ TOKYO BOUND	Sachi	ISBN 978 0 352 34019 1	
☐ TORMENT, INCORPORATED	Murilee Martin	ISBN 978 0 352 33943 0	

☐ UNEARTHLY DESIRES	Ray Gordon	ISBN 978 0 352 34036 8
☐ UNIFORM DOLL	Penny Birch	ISBN 978 0 352 33698 9
☐ WHALEBONE STRICT	Lady Alice McCloud	ISBN 978 0 352 34082 5
☐ WHAT HAPPENS TO BAD GIRLS	Penny Birch	ISBN 978 0 352 34031 3
☐ WHAT SUKI WANTS	Cat Scarlett	ISBN 978 0 352 34027 6
☐ WHEN SHE WAS BAD	Penny Birch	ISBN 978 0 352 33859 4
☐ WHIP HAND	G.C. Scott	ISBN 978 0 352 33694 1
☐ WHIPPING GIRL	Aishling Morgan	ISBN 978 0 352 33789 4
☐ WHIPPING TRIANGLE	G.C. Scott	ISBN 978 0 352 34086 3

NEXUS CLASSIC

☐ AMAZON SLAVE	Lisette Ashton	ISBN 978 0 352 33916 4
☐ ANGEL	Lindsay Gordon	ISBN 978 0 352 34009 2
☐ THE BLACK GARTER	Lisette Ashton	ISBN 978 0 352 33919 5
☐ THE BLACK MASQUE	Lisette Ashton	ISBN 978 0 352 33977 5
☐ THE BLACK ROOM	Lisette Ashton	ISBN 978 0 352 33914 0
☐ THE BLACK WIDOW	Lisette Ashton	ISBN 978 0 352 33973 7
☐ THE BOND	Lindsay Gordon	ISBN 978 0 352 33996 6
☐ THE DOMINO ENIGMA	Cyrian Amberlake	ISBN 978 0 352 34064 1
☐ THE DOMINO QUEEN	Cyrian Amberlake	ISBN 978 0 352 34074 0
☐ THE DOMINO TATTOO	Cyrian Amberlake	ISBN 978 0 352 34037 5
☐ EMMA ENSLAVED	Hilary James	ISBN 978 0 352 33883 9
☐ EMMA'S HUMILIATION	Hilary James	ISBN 978 0 352 33910 2
☐ EMMA'S SECRET DOMINATION	Hilary James	ISBN 978 0 352 34000 9
☐ EMMA'S SUBMISSION	Hilary James	ISBN 978 0 352 33906 5
☐ FAIRGROUND ATTRACTION	Lisette Ashton	ISBN 978 0 352 33927 0
☐ IN FOR A PENNY	Penny Birch	ISBN 978 0 352 34083 2
☐ THE INSTITUTE	Maria Del Rey	ISBN 978 0 352 33352 0
☐ NEW EROTICA 5	Various	ISBN 978 0 352 33956 0
☐ THE NEXUS LETTERS	Various	ISBN 978 0 352 33955 3

Title	Author	ISBN
☐ PLAYTHING	Penny Birch	ISBN 978 0 352 33967 6
☐ PLEASING THEM	William Doughty	ISBN 978 0 352 34015 3
☐ RITES OF OBEDIENCE	Lindsay Gordon	ISBN 978 0 352 34005 4
☐ SERVING TIME	Sarah Veitch	ISBN 978 0 352 33509 8
☐ THE SUBMISSION GALLERY	Lindsay Gordon	ISBN 978 0 352 34026 9
☐ TIE AND TEASE	Penny Birch	ISBN 978 0 352 33987 4
☐ TIGHT WHITE COTTON	Penny Birch	ISBN 978 0 352 33970 6

NEXUS CONFESSIONS

Title	Author	ISBN
☐ NEXUS CONFESSIONS: VOLUME ONE	Various	ISBN 978 0 352 34093 1

NEXUS ENTHUSIAST

Title	Author	ISBN
☐ BUSTY	Tom King	ISBN 978 0 352 34032 0
☐ DERRIÈRE	Julius Culdrose	ISBN 978 0 352 34024 5
☐ LEG LOVER	L.G. Denier	ISBN 978 0 352 34016 0
☐ OVER THE KNEE	Fiona Locke	ISBN 978 0 352 34079 5
☐ RUBBER GIRL	William Doughty	ISBN 978 0 352 34087 0
☐ THE SECRET SELF	Christina Shelly	ISBN 978 0 352 34069 6
☐ UNDER MY MASTER'S WINGS	Lauren Wissot	ISBN 978 0 352 34042 9
☐ WIFE SWAP	Amber Leigh	ISBN 978 0 352 34097 9

NEXUS NON FICTION

Title	Author	ISBN
☐ LESBIAN SEX SECRETS FOR MEN	Jamie Goddard and Kurt Brungard	ISBN 978 0 352 33724 5

- - - - - - ✂ -

Please send me the books I have ticked above.

Name ....

Address ....

....

....

.... Post code ....

Send to: **Virgin Books Cash Sales, Thames Wharf Studios, Rainville Road, London W6 9HA**

US customers: for prices and details of how to order books for delivery by mail, call 888-330-8477.

Please enclose a cheque or postal order, made payable to **Nexus Books Ltd**, to the value of the books you have ordered plus postage and packing costs as follows:

UK and BFPO – £1.00 for the first book, 50p for each subsequent book.

Overseas (including Republic of Ireland) – £2.00 for the first book, £1.00 for each subsequent book.

If you would prefer to pay by VISA, ACCESS/MASTERCARD, AMEX, DINERS CLUB or SWITCH, please write your card number and expiry date here:

....

Please allow up to 28 days for delivery.

Signature ....

Our privacy policy

We will not disclose information you supply us to any other parties. We will not disclose any information which identifies you personally to any person without your express consent.

From time to time we may send out information about Nexus books and special offers. Please tick here if you do *not* wish to receive Nexus information. ☐

- - - - - - ✂ -